OMEGA FORCE
THE PANDORA PARADOX

Joshua Dalzelle

©2020

First Edition

1

"So, the little bastard is causing trouble?"

"He's not a bastard!"

"Are you currently acting in a paternal or fatherly manner towards the child?"

"That's not how things are done on Restaria!" Crusher fumed. Kage had worked hard to find an angle to Crusher's story that would irritate the hulking warrior. Calling Crusher's eldest offspring a *bastard* had done the trick nicely.

"Really?" Kage asked.

"The warrior caste exists in the first place because of a strict selective breeding program," Crusher explained. "I technically have over a dozen offspring, but only three who have the correct traits to join the Legions. The eldest of the three is old enough to be given a leadership position and, apparently, it's not going well."

"What do they want you to do about it?" Jason asked. He'd sat in uncomfortable silence while Kage dug for the nerve, his thoughts on his own abandoned son. He'd been meaning to contact the boy's grandparents to check up on him, but something always came up and, recently, he felt he was putting Jacob at risk if he tried to reach out. The ConFed was coming after them all and coming hard. The intelligence reports coming from Saditava Mok's organization told them the ConFed likely already knew where to find them but was more interested in finding the financial backers of their little rebellion before they sent in their mighty war fleet to stomp them into a greasy spot.

The small insurrection had already lost one of their more powerful ships without the ConFed even firing a shot. The United Earth Navy heavy cruiser, *Eagle's Talon*, had been recaptured by a special operations team, and Captain Edgars was likely in custody on his way back to a court martial on Terranovus, Earth's colony world where most of its military operations were run from. The loss of the *Talon* was a significant blow, but it hadn't been a total loss.

Edgars had managed to get the encrypted data core Mok's smuggling network had been bouncing across the quadrant into their hands. Now, Lucky, with the help of an entire bank of specialized supercomputers they'd loaded up in one of the corvette-class ship's engineering bays, worked around the clock to break into the device. It had to be done delicately and precisely as there were undoubtedly safeguards and traps put in place by ConFed Intel.

The work was so exhaustive Jason had pulled Kage, his team's code slicer, off the whole thing when the little Veran had worked himself past exhaustion. Kage was one of the best, but the digital surgery required to break into a military-grade data vault like the one they'd secured was something best left to someone that didn't require food or rest.

"I'm not entirely sure," Crusher continued, breaking Jason's ruminations. "I assume they want me to talk to him, but I know how young male Galvetic warriors are at that age. It won't do any good. Whatever I say to him will likely just make things worse."

"How can you be sure?" Twingo asked.

"Because when my father talked to me, I stole a ship and fled Restaria," Crusher said. "That's how I ended up stuck out here with you assholes."

"How old is this kid?" Jason asked. "You weren't *that* young when we pulled you out of that box."

"I didn't say we were the same age when this happened," Crusher snapped. Lately, he'd been very sensitive about his age and had made the fatal error of letting the others know it bothered him. Now, they casually worked it into every conversation they could. The conversation droned on aimlessly, and the hum of the *Devil's* engines worked on Jason's exhausted mind, and soon, he felt his head lulling from side to side.

"Is my tale of family strife boring you?" Crusher demanded.

"Honestly? Whenever you open your mouth, I start to fall asleep," Jason said, standing up. "Goodnight, losers."

"Goodnight, Captain."

Jason clapped Crusher on the shoulder and wandered out of the galley and down the wide main corridor of the main deck. The *Devil's Fortune* was a brand-new ship, and Omega Force was her first crew since it came out of the shipyard. It smelled new and was so clean and sterile you could eat off the deck...but he still missed the *Phoenix*. The battered old gunship was small, cramped, smelly, and uncomfortable to live in, but it was a member of the family. The *Phoenix* had been their home when they needed one. She'd sacrificed herself on countless occasions when asked for the greater good. When they'd called upon her, the ship had used her awesome power to pull them out of hot zones, leaving their enemies in her wake.

The other problem with the corvette-class ship was her size. It was a welcome novelty to have so much space to stretch out in, but it presented some challenges. Omega Force's most common operational environment was on the surface or within an atmosphere. The personnel and equipment were configured heavily for planetary operations, not so much for orbital or deep space. Landing the *Devil* was technically possible but an enormous pain in the ass. The ship was just over one hundred and forty meters long and weighed close to five thousand tons. At that size, she either had to be cleared to a special heavy-capable starport or be given an exception into an unprepared landing zone and run her grav-drive the entire time to keep most of her weight off the landing pad.

This was simply unworkable for someone as impatient and impulsive as Jason.

That was why he was already making discreet inquiries along their course for anyone who might have a small combat ship available for purchase that would fit in the *Devil's* hangar bay. The *Phoenix* had been dropped off on S'Tora so his tech teams could repair the latest round of battle damage and install the upgraded components piling up in a storage unit on their base. He put up with captaining a ship class he wasn't accustomed to by telling himself that once he got his baby back, she'd be better than new. The S'Tora engineering team Twingo had put together really knew what they were doing, and he couldn't wait to see the end results.

He walked past the lift and slipped quietly into the port ladder-well, climbing up the three decks to reach the Command Deck. The lights were subdued for night hours, and the faint strains of a soothing instrumental composition drifted down the central corridor. The bulkheads were paneled in a dark gray wood veneer, and the deck was covered with a soft, dark blue carpet. There was a small but well-equipped galley and, further aft, the captain's suite where Jason now stayed. Moving forward, the corridor opened onto the ship's spacious bridge.

"All quiet?" he whispered into the ear of the only person on the bridge.

"Damnit!" Doc yelped, jumping out of the command chair. "Stop doing that!"

"I can't help it," Jason said. "The carpet makes it too easy to sneak up on everybody but Lucky."

"It's not funny," Doc grumbled, settling back down into the seat. "And yes...it's all quiet. We're another eleven hours from our first waypoint, and Lucky just reported he's successfully made it past another lock. He estimates it will be another fourteen locks on the device before he can access the data."

"So, we'll be into it well before we need to meet up with Mok and hand it over." Jason yawned. "Make sure Lucky knows I want a complete backup of the device before we give it up."

"Mok explicitly said we weren't to do that."

"So?"

"I just thought I'd point it out," Doc sighed. "You'll do whatever you want anyway."

"See? We understand each other perfectly," Jason said. "I'm hitting the rack. Kage will be up to relieve you in an hour or so."

"Is he sober?"

"Mostly."

Jason trudged back down the corridor and used the biometric scanner on the hatchway to gain entry to his quarters. He walked in and breathed a contented sigh as he looked around. Compared to the *Phoenix*'s cramped stateroom—or even his home on S'Tora, for that matter—the captain's suite aboard the *Devil's Fortune* was pure, obscene luxury. The furnishings and fixtures looked like something you'd find in the nicest of hotels and, in addition to having its own sitting room, bedroom, and head, the suite was equipped with a small galley of its own. The food synthesizer was state of the art, and he'd been able to program his preferences into it from the *Phoenix*'s database before they'd dropped the gunship off on S'Tora.

"Mok sure knows how to live right," he said, kicking off his boots and falling backwards onto the large bed. "I hope he knows he's not getting this ship back."

⸻

The chiming alert of the com panel broke into Jason's dreams. He rolled over and looked at the panel and saw an incoming slip-com call from an address he recognized. Grumbling, he stumbled over to the desk and flicked on the main terminal.

"Webb?" he croaked. "What's up, douchebag?"

"Oh, you're up," Webb said, his voice flat. "Great."

Captain Marcus Webb, former US Navy SEAL and current head of the new United Earth Navy's special warfare section, was someone he considered a friend, but it was complicated. At one point in the past, Webb had actually been ordered to hunt down and kill Jason. That had mostly been smoothed over, but the two still were guarded around one another.

"Don't sound too excited to talk to me," Jason said, rubbing the sleep out of his eyes. "It's not like you called and woke me up or anything. Is this important?"

"This could take a bit to explain, Jason," Webb said. "Do you have a few minutes, and are you sober?"

"Yes, and mostly."

"You remember how you asked me to keep an eye on Jacob for you? Well, funny story—"

"What's he done?" Jason asked. "And how does it involve you? Aren't you still on Terranovus?"

"Yeah, we're still here for now. We have a new planet that's being propped up as a military base, and this one will revert back to being a civilian colony world," Webb said. "And Jacob isn't on Earth anymore. He actually enlisted in the UEAS some years back. Thanks to his test scores and some owed political favors to you back on Earth, his name was flagged, and he was brought here to the Academy. Earned his commission and went into the Marines."

"My kid is some jarhead?" Jason griped. "Figures. But how did he get into the Academy? I guess he could have skipped some grades if he's smart, but isn't there a hard age limit?" Webb just looked at him for a minute, clearly confused.

"Jason...how old do you think Jacob is?"

"He can't be more than seventeen," Jason said, now trying to do the math in his head. "Isn't he?"

"How old do you think *you* are?" Webb asked.

"I actually have no idea anymore." Jason shrugged. Thanks to Doc's tinkering and the available longevity treatments in the quadrant, Jason looked like he was in his mid-twenties. His aging had reversed to the point he actually looked younger now than when he'd first been abducted.

"For the love of— Jacob is twenty-four years old," Webb said. "He's been a lieutenant in 3rd Scout Corps for a little over a year."

"You have him in one of your cannon fodder Scout Fleet teams?" Jason asked, his voice deadly quiet. Webb swallowed visibly.

"We didn't have much of a choice. It was the only way I could protect him."

"You'll have to help me with that one," Jason said, his voice still quiet and calm. "You're protecting him...by putting him in a forward recon unit with one of the highest mortality rates in your entire operation? I heard that Ezra Mosler was killed in the Reaches. If someone like that can be taken by surprise, how are you guaranteeing my son's safety by putting him in that sort of environment?"

"Look, Burke, I'm just doing the best with what I have. By the time I found out he was even in the military, the people on Earth looking out for him had already shuffled him into the Academy slot as a favor to you. I brought him into NAVSOC because he screwed up and took off running at full speed during an exercise in full view of God and everybody." Webb's face was flushed, and Jason could tell he was being sincere and not just trying to placate him or deflect blame.

"Wait...what do you mean *at full speed*?" he asked, a knot growing in his gut.

"Ah, you didn't know about that, did you?" Webb leaned back in his chair. "Your boy inherited some of the genetic modifications that you have—or had at the time he was conceived—and certain parties within the military's research divisions would love to take a crack at him. The only way I could keep him out of a lab or a cage was to pull him into my command before anyone knew what was happening."

"What are his enhancements?" Jason asked.

"Dramatically increased speed and strength," Webb said. "Dexterity and ability to heal are also high, but not as apparent as the first two things. I suspect he has other talents, but he's very tight-lipped about it. He was caught by a monitoring drone running through the woods at night at over twenty-five miles an hour. I had to work fast to suppress that after I found out about it."

"Damnit," Jason muttered, looking off-camera. "This isn't what I wanted for him."

"But it's the choice he made for himself," Webb said. "He volunteered for Scout Fleet duty. I assigned him to Mosler's team. He took over the mission when Mosler was murdered and brought it to a successful conclusion. He also managed to track down one of our missing cruisers so we could recover it before ConFed Intel did."

"That was him?" Jason asked. "Edgars mentioned one of your teams had arrived in the area to try and get him. He said he had a plan to deal with it."

"It apparently wasn't enough," Webb said. "Lieutenant Brown managed to subdue the ship's crew and call in the Navy strike force that was standing by to grab it."

"We just missed each other," Jason mused, his eyes tightening as he said it. "So, why bother coming clean to me now?"

"Your kid has gone rogue," Webb said. "He's figured out a way to track down Margaret Jansen—you remember her?—and he's going to try and cut the head off the snake once and for all. Jansen's One World faction has infiltrated so much of our command structure that he doesn't trust us to run the operation or to turn over the vulnerability he discovered. He's decided to write his own orders and go after her alone. Two of the battlesynths from Lot 700 are with him."

"This is giving me a headache," Jason said. "What the hell are they doing involved in this?"

"They seem to have always known who he was. Once they figured out he was in a little over his head, they deployed a support team to help him out."

"Don't you have tracking in his ship? Just go get him."

"He's not in a Navy ship. The *Corsair* was heavily damaged in the Reaches, and Jacob's team stole an old Eshquarian gunboat from some smugglers," Webb said. "We're not able to track it. We suspect it's too damaged to go on, but we're not sure if the battlesynths have access to a backup ship or if Jacob will simply buy or steal another one."

"Cut off his expense accounts," Jason said. "Easy."

"He's managed to secure independent funding," Webb said uncomfortably. "Apparently, the ship they stole had been loaded down with cash and credits. Your kid is actually quite wealthy." That jogged something in Jason's memory.

"So, he stole a load of money that was obviously being transported for laundering?" Jason asked. "Son of a bitch."

"What?"

"Saditava Mok said a human had tried to jack one of his cash loads," Jason said. "As in, Mok himself...not one of his peons."

"Mok doesn't know who he is, does he?" Webb looked suddenly concerned.

"I don't think so."

"Then we need to keep it that way. So far, we're the only ones who know where that ship came from. If Mok found out that Jacob is your son—"

"It's leverage one way or another," Jason finished. "Either to get me to do something he wants or to pressure Earth. Damn."

"So, you can see why I contacted you," Webb said. "It'd probably be better if you tracked him down than if I try to send someone and possibly have Jansen warned."

"We're not exactly available right now for the job," Jason said. The words had been torturous to utter. If his son was in trouble, the obvious thing to do would be to drop everything and rush to him. But what he was doing right now had wider ramifications and, honestly, as part of the rebellion against the ConFed, it would be dangerous for him to be too close to the people he cared about. "Given that the ConFed is actively hunting us right now, it wouldn't be smart for me to be flying to near your operations."

"Are you staying in a resort or something?" Webb asked, looking past Jason and into the room.

"Not exactly," Jason replied. "So, tell me you have a backup plan to either save him from himself or make sure he has the support he needs for a mission like this."

"My first choice was to reach out to you," Webb said. "My next best option is to try and see if I can get the rest of Lot 700 to help."

"I'm going to kick 707's ass the next time I see him."

"I would pay to watch you try. Look, I know you're pissed about this, but I thought you had the right to know whether you decide to help out or not," Webb said. "Your kid has me over a barrel right now since he's right about all the leaks within my command. It turns out my own aide was a traitor, working directly for the enemy. If I try to use my own assets to bring him in, I could end up inadvertently putting him in more danger."

"You're slipping," Jason said. "You let some jarhead lieutenant outmaneuver you and then blackmail you to get his own way."

"His tests indicate he's quite a bit smarter than you, and you were enough of a pain in the ass on your own," Webb said, smiling briefly before turning serious. "Jacob said he scanned the fleet of your little rebellion, and he didn't see a ship that matched the *Phoenix*'s profile, but it looks like you're still heavily involved. I won't pretend to tell you what to do, I just hope you recognize the risk you put us all in as a human participating in something like that."

"The...*thing*...that's in charge of the ConFed knows me personally," Jason said. "The risk is the same whether I sit it out or not."

"I don't suppose you'd care to share what you know?" Webb asked. "Our intel on the internal workings of the ConFed is beyond murky right now."

"Sure! I'll tell you what, you give me your exact location so I can come there and tell you in person," Jason said, smiling humorously. Webb picked up on the warning signs immediately.

"I...don't think so," the ex-SEAL said. "At least not until that homicidal glint in your eye fades a bit."

"But we *will* be talking about this, Marcus. I promise you that," Jason said quietly, leaning in so much that Webb actually leaned back despite the lightyears of space between them. "I can accept what you've told me on the surface, and I don't just come out and call you a liar...but the bottom line is that you tossed my boy into the meat grinder after you promised you'd keep him safe. I have some strong feelings about that."

"I can see that," Webb managed to get out. Jason had no doubts his friend remembered what happened to his spec ops team when they'd tried to come after him years ago. The first engagement ended when Jason had killed one of Webb's hitters with a single blow and threw the body back at them like a sack of potatoes. "Hopefully, we can sit and talk about it like civilized people."

"I'm all kinds of civilized, you know that," Jason said. "I'll keep my ear to the ground and see if I can let you know where Jacob is, but for right now, I'd just make things worse by trying to locate him myself."

"Understood. Webb out."

Jason flicked off the terminal and leaned back in his chair, rubbing his head. Learning that his only son had not only gone into the military but had been pulled into a special operations unit was unwelcome news. Even if Jacob had joined, Jason had assumed the kid would be pegged for some boring analyst job or maybe even put on a non-combatant starship since people were *supposed* to be looking out for him. Instead, he was a Marine in a forward recon unit. Not only that, but he had a brass pair big enough to steal ships and go rogue, calling his own shots as a lieutenant. Jason honestly wasn't sure if he was more angry or proud at this point.

"I still gotta kill Webb, though," he said, slapping his thighs and standing up. "That's a given."

Not very charitable of you.

"And where the hell have *you* been all this time?" Jason demanded of Cas, the unwelcome voice in his head.

As I've told you on multiple occasions, we're fighting a losing battle here in this implant. I had to shut down part of my own core program so I could make repairs.

"And?"

And I've bought us some time, but we need to come up with a permanent solution...soon.

Jason just grunted an acknowledgement, not wanting to get into another protracted debate with the AI program that had taken up residence in his neural implant. Cas was part of a much larger, more complex program that had been part of the operational matrix for a massive, star-killing weapon built by an ancient, long-extinct species. The program being stuck in his head was an unintended consequence of accessing a massive database file he stored in his implant called the Archive. The Archive had been entrusted to him and contained all the knowledge of that ancient race, including their weapons technology that had ultimately turned on them and wiped them from the galaxy.

The reasons Jason hadn't just purged the file from his head and had his implant replaced weren't complicated, but were profound. Since the Archive contained the last known legacy of the race he called the Ancients, he felt he was the custodian of all they were. It was a weighty responsibility he didn't take lightly. If anything happened to the Archive, the last vestiges of a mighty race of beings that had dominated the galaxy would go with it. So far his crew had not been able to guarantee that they could remove the file intact before replacing the implant, an otherwise routine procedure, since it had integrated so completely with the device.

So why even keep something as fragile and irreplaceable as that in his head to begin with? Because the terrible knowledge contained within the Archive could also be used to cause indescribable harm in the wrong hands. The weapons technology the Ancients had developed was capable of destruction and death on a scale an order of magnitude greater than anything the ConFed could build. It was these secrets that caused Jason to suffer through the headaches and the unwanted running commentary of a smartass AI. He was terrified that once the genie was out of the bottle, there would be no stuffing it back in.

"I'm going back to sleep," he said to his passenger. "So, keep it down in there."

2

"Captain, you will want to see this."

"I'm on my way," Jason said around a mouthful of pastry. He grabbed his coffee mug and walked out of the galley just as Crusher and Doc walked in, arguing loudly. For the last three days, Crusher had been soliciting parental advice from everyone on the crew, and then when they gave it, he would start a fight about how they didn't know what they were talking about.

Jason had already had his turn in the hot seat and wasn't wanting to get dragged back into it. He put his head down and sped up, looking like he had something important to do.

"Captain—"

"Busy!" Jason shouted over his shoulder as he resisted the urge to break into a run. Crusher's species had evolved from predators and, though he might be lazy and slovenly while shipboard, tended to give chase when something ran away from him no matter the reason. At least that was the theory Jason had been working on. He escaped the escalating argument just as Twingo's voice joined the fray. Jason just rolled his eyes and walked into the waiting lift.

"Deck Two."

The doors slid shut silently, and the lift dropped him down from the main deck, past Deck Three, and stopped gently at Deck Two. This was where most of the ship's storage and workshop space was located. If you walked all the way aft, you'd come out onto the hangar deck, a cavernous bay so tall it straddled decks two and three. The bay where Lucky had set up his bank of supercomputers was just forward of the hangar bay and above an engineering compartment, where he could route power and cooling up to the machines. The battlesynth had isolated himself in there since they'd left the main fleet, and Jason had begun to worry about him.

"What's the good news, Lucky?"

"I have stripped away all of the security protocols protecting the data and successfully decrypted it. I have been processing it most of the morning but thought you should know about this part specifically," Lucky said, gesturing towards a seat in front of a terminal with what looked like technical schematics and star charts on the monitor. Jason just sighed.

"No chance you could give me the condensed version?" he asked hopefully.

"I feel it would be better if you reached your own conclusions," Lucky said, never looking up from his own multiple terminals displaying data at a dizzying rate.

Jason grumbled and sat down, resizing the images to his liking before digging in. Right away, he could see the technical data referred to a few new classes of starships, but they weren't anything like what the ConFed fielded now. These ships lacked any sort of aesthetic appeal. They were asymmetrical, oddly-shaped, and didn't even have an outer hull over the entirety of the vessels, leaving internal workings exposed. It was a pure expression of function over form and led Jason to believe they had likely been designed by a machine.

He scrolled down and saw the dimensional data on the ships and whistled. They were on a scale that dwarfed even the largest capital ships flying in the quadrant now. The power source they were using must have been immense, but there was scant information on that in the brief Lucky had given him. He slid the ship specs away for a moment and looked over the star charts. The positions highlighted had been triangulated using stellar objects he was already familiar with, but the points themselves weren't near anything significant. He assumed he was looking at the positions of secret shipyards producing the behemoths on the spec sheets he'd just read, but that didn't really make a lot of sense.

Starship construction was not a subtle process. It took prodigious amounts of power and raw material as well as an enormous, well-trained labor force that could direct the automation and oversee the builds. Shipyards were always located either near the source of the raw materials or near a logistics hub where it could easily be brought in. These were out in the middle of nowhere. That raised a lot of questions about how they were building such massive ships in such a remote location without it being all over the underground Nexus channels.

"Your thoughts?" Lucky asked, sounding like a professor prompting along an enthusiastic, if somewhat dull, student.

"You mean about this information or your condescending attitude?"

"Either that you wish to discuss," the battlesynth said. Jason flipped off his friend's back with both middle fingers.

"Given the size and unusual designs of the ships here, I'd say we're looking at something specialized and purpose built, not just the next generation of ConFed warship," he said. "The impression I get is they were designed by either a machine that had little care for beauty, or an alien race we've not been exposed to yet. Operating under the assumption these are built for combat, I'm not sure who the hell the target would be. The Eshquarians are gone, the Cridal are not really a threat, and the existing ConFed battlefleet has more than enough muscle to take out the Saabror Protectorate."

"The Avarian Empire?" Lucky asked.

"Possibly, but not likely," Jason said. "Avarian tech isn't really any better than what we have here, they just have a lot more of it. There's also the issue of the remote locations. I have a hard time believing they've been able to do that sort of heavy construction like that without anybody we know catching wind of it." Lucky turned and gave him with an appraising look.

"That is not bad," he said. "It is close to the same conclusions I myself reached, and I have access to much more data."

"Then what the hell is with the pop quiz?" Jason asked.

"I am just trying to get you to think more strategically. Tactically, you have no issues, but sometimes you fail to see the bigger picture in time," Lucky said. Jason just stared at his friend like he was insane.

"What the fuck are you even talking about? I always see the big picture. Anyway, isn't a little late in the game to be teaching an old dog new tricks? If I'm not killed outright, I'll probably retire soon anyway."

"Your body is still plenty young for this type of work," Lucky said.

"My brain isn't," Jason said, suddenly growing serious. "Humans are meant to live only so long, buddy. My body feels better than it did when I was in my twenties, but I can feel the years piling up. My mind seems convinced it's time to start slowing down."

"Interesting," Lucky said, peering closely at Jason as if he might be able to see his soul aging before him. Jason just shook his head. Lucky's naiveté had always been one of his more endearing personality traits, but since they'd been forced to swap his mind into a different, newer body he had regressed somewhat. He was almost childlike in his inability to grasp nuance, sarcasm, or metaphors.

"It's not important." Jason waved him off. "Okay, class is over. Tell me what you know."

"The ConFed appears to be constructing heavy weapons in the absence of an enemy to use them on," Lucky said. "From the other documentation included in this data dump, I would surmise we're talking about weapons that can annihilate on a planetary scale."

"Blow up a whole planet?" Jason asked skeptically.

"Not quite. But make it completely uninhabitable in a very short time? Definitely."

"This has the Machine's fingerprints all over it. Hell, the thing used to be part of a weapon designed to kill entire stars. Maybe he's just going back to what he knows: massive scale, impractical weapons."

"You are suggesting it is doing it out of some sort of neurosis. I disagree. There is a specific reason these weapons are being built, but we have no way of knowing what that is from the information given," Lucky said.

"Maybe the Machine is looking to hold on to its new territories with an iron grip, terrifying conquered systems so badly with its new arsenal that nobody would dare revolt," Jason said. "That sort of mass overkill approach seems like something it would be fond of."

"Perhaps," Lucky said, sounding unconvinced.

"Okay!" Jason slapped his thighs again and stood up, wanting to end the semi-awkward conversation. "Go through all this and organize it, then work with Kage to re-secure it with our own encryption and incinerate the original core."

"Of course, Captain."

Jason gave his friend one more look before walking out of the bay. Lucky's behavior had been...odd...lately, but the impromptu lesson he'd sat through in there was stranger than usual. He still hadn't shaken off his unease at Crusher's revelation the battlesynth had likely slaughtered dozens of guards who were no real threat during their last ground op. He and Kage were working under the assumption that, somehow, the new body was asserting some sort of control over Lucky's primary processing matrix and affecting his personality, but there was no way to prove that either way without letting their friend know they were worried he might be psychotic and a danger.

"Command Deck," Jason said as he entered the lift again. The car obediently whisked him up three decks to the plush environs of the corvette's command deck. It was so nice up there that Jason had made an effort to make sure the rest of his crew spent their leisure time down on the main deck where they couldn't damage the luxurious space.

"Captain," Kage greeted him when he walked onto the bridge.

"How're we looking?"

"We'll be dropping out of slip-space in...five hours, give or take," the little Veran said. "The dealer already knows we're coming and has offered to pick you up in a shuttle so you don't have to deorbit the ship."

"Considerate," Jason said. "Tell him I'll be bringing two passengers with me."

"Crusher and Lucky?"

"Crusher and Twingo," Jason said. "I need an engineer to look things over before I pay, and I want Lucky here working on the data core project. Speaking of which, how will this skew our timetable?"

"This thing is fast," Kage said. "We'll burn through a lot more fuel, but we'll make our rendezvous with Mok. We'll actually make it with time to spare if you don't get held up on the surface."

"This should be a quick in and out," Jason said over his shoulder while he was walking back off the bridge. "Call me up thirty minutes before you drop out of slip-space."

"Will do."

Jason went back to his quarters and sat down at the beautiful desk made of some type of wood so dark it looked almost black in the low light. He ran his hand over the glossy surface before logging into his terminal and accessing one of the *Devil's* slip-com nodes. He waited for the security checks to finish, and then reached out. He needed to try and find out how deep his kid was in the shit. Jacob could be the most capable operator in the Corps, but the people he had pitted himself against were among the most ruthless and calculating Jason had ever seen. If he couldn't go himself, maybe he could send a care package.

"What do you want?"

"Is that any way to greet a friend?" Jason asked, turning back to face the camera.

"We are *not* friends, Burke," the Viper said. Her real name was Carolyn Whitney, and she was a human...or at least she used to be. Jason wasn't even sure how much of what he was looking at was even organic. Whitney had also been abducted, but her experience had been much different than his and her owners had paid handsomely for all the cybernetic augmentation she sported. It was just too bad it had been installed without her permission.

"I think of you as a friend."

"Cut the shit. What do you want?"

"You on a job right now?"

"Of course, but I can take on a little side work. What have you got?"

"So, it turns out there's someone within the United Earth Marine Corps I need to keep tabs on," Jason said carefully.

"It wouldn't happen to be a young lieutenant named Jacob Brown would it?" Whitney asked. Jason's stomach clenched. Any known ties to him were in danger thanks to all the enemies Omega Force had happened to collect through the years.

"How did you... I didn't say—"

"What is he? Nephew? Second or third cousin?" she asked. "I *knew* he looked familiar, but I couldn't put my finger on it until your ugly mug came up on the monitor."

"Yeah, something like that," Jason said, relief flooding through him. It was important that nobody knew Jacob was actually his son. Such a close family tie could be exploited.

"I could maybe work up a quote and give you a loose track on his whereabouts, but he's actually a pretty slippery kid for being military. We crossed paths a few times recently, and he seems to know how to handle himself," Whitney said. "I can't promise you anything. I'm on a big contract right now and can't lose focus."

"Who's the poor bastard you're about to retire?" Jason asked.

"I am *not* an assassin," she said through clenched teeth. "And there's no way in hell I'm telling you my target or the client."

"Come on," Jason wheedled. "Maybe we can do an exchange. I could have information that would help you out, and in trade, you carve out a little time to help me out."

"Pass," she said. "I'm not sure you'd even want to help me if you knew who I was after." A look passed over Whitney's face briefly before she buttoned it back up. Jason caught it, though. In a rare slip up, she let something out she hadn't intended to.

"It was worth a shot," Jason said, pretending he hadn't noticed. Whitney didn't waste time with saying goodbye or making up an excuse that she had to go. She simply reached over and killed the channel as Jason opened his mouth to try a different approach.

"Interesting," he mused, pushing back from the desk, and spinning in the chair.

What's interesting? Cas had obviously been watching the exchange through Jason's ocular implants.

"I know whoever her target is," Jason said. "And it has to be someone I either like or find to be useful if I would be hesitant to help her track them down."

Short list. Give me a little bit of time to think about it.

"You mean you're actually going to be helpful?"

It's a way to pass the time.

3

"This is it. The Skaxis System, home of the Creet-Eska Shipyards and Brokerage, along with that really dark purple wine that gives Crusher such bad hangovers," Kage said. The *Devil's Fortune* had dropped back into real-space with the gentlest of bumps from her perfectly aligned slip-drive array, and now the forward sensors were giving them a view of the pretty green planet they were flying towards.

"Let's bomb those wineries from orbit," Crusher said.

"Maybe later." Jason waved him away from the forward displays. The bridge was laid out with a larger crew in mind so there was a lot of room to roam around. Jason split his time between the helm where he would actually pilot the ship when needed and the command chair, which was much more comfortable. The command console built into the chair also let him direct the ship's automated systems including an advanced pilot program that, in most cases, eliminated the need for an actual helmsman. He directed the ship into one of the six standard approach lanes to the planet for a ship of their class and told the computer to ask for orbital clearance. "Kage?"

"Our contact for Creet-Eska has already gotten back. They're sending up coordinates for a parking orbit over Skaxis-3, and then coming to get you," Kage said. "The showroom is on the surface, and there are seven models that meet your criteria."

"So, we're buying *another* ship?" Crusher demanded. "Who is paying for this one?"

"What do you care?"

"This crew has always operated on a profit share model. Hard for there to be any profits if you keep spending all our credits on high-ticket items."

"We're in the middle of fighting a fucking rebellion, you idiot," Jason said. "There aren't any profits right now."

"Still," Crusher said, "I think this should be brought up to a vote."

"We did vote on it," Kage said. "It was during the meeting you stomped out of ten minutes into it because you said it was boring."

"The *Phoenix* is back on S'Tora and, for right now, not practical for what we're doing," Jason explained, heading off an argument between the two. "We operate mostly on the ground, and this ship is a huge pain in the ass to get down to the surface and back up to orbit. That's why we're buying a new runabout. Even if you'd voted no, everyone else voted yes, so you were outnumbered." Crusher seemed to chew on that for a moment, looking for some hole in the explanation he could exploit to keep the argument going.

"Whatever," he said, giving up. Kage's eyes lit up, and he turned to face Crusher, smelling blood in the water, and moving in for the kill.

"Don't," Jason warned him, his tone conversational. Kage sighed dramatically but turned back to his monitors.

"We're six hours out from orbital intercept," he said. "They'll send the shuttle when you signal."

As Jason could have predicted, the crew became restless and filtered off the bridge shortly after the six-hour transit time was announced. Doc mumbled something vague about catching up on trade publications, Crusher just stomped off without a word, and Twingo made a break for it after realizing the others had left without him. Once they were all gone, Kage turned to Jason and smiled widely.

"It's nice to have some one on one time every so often, isn't it?"

"What do you want, Kage?" Jason asked wearily. "And don't insult me by saying you're up here because you enjoy my company that much."

"I don't *not* enjoy your company," Kage protested. "We're just interested in different things. We've grown apart over the years because of that I think."

Jason groaned and rubbed at his eyes. "For the love of—"

"Okay, okay...here's what I want," Kage said. "I need to withdraw some credits from one of our slush accounts. I'll pay it back over the next few profit shares."

"How much?"

"Six and a half million ConFed credits," Kage said with a straight face. It took all of Jason's self-control not to just laugh in his face. He looked at his friend and saw he was dead serious about needing that much money.

"You're not in trouble, are you?"

"Not me personally, no."

"And you're not going to give me the details?"

"I'd rather not."

"Tell Doc to initiate the transfer, and that I approved it," Jason said after a long pause. He wanted to make warnings and probe further, but Kage deserved the same amount of blind trust the Veran had shown him on more than one occasion. If Kage said he needed it, then Jason would trust it was for a good reason, and that if he didn't want to explain what it was for, then it wouldn't be something that would endanger the rest of the crew.

"Thanks, Captain," Kage said, nodding once and looking away. Another uncharacteristic response from the high-strung code slicer, especially so since he'd gotten what he wanted without much of a fight.

The rest of the trip passed in awkward silence as Jason messed around on one of his own terminals and Kage pretended to be engrossed in his own work. The hours ticked by, and the lull of the constant hums found on any starship started to make Jason drowsy.

His eyes had just started to close when a shrill alarm sounded, and the bridge lights flashed red twice before returning to normal.

"What the hell?" he croaked.

"The *Devil* has just identified a potential threat that just popped up in the system," Kage said. "Standby...sensor data is compiling now. It's still pretty deep in the outer system."

"The outer system?" Jason asked. "Aren't all the commercial mesh-in points for this system near the habitable worlds?"

"They are," Kage confirmed. "Whoever this is was probably trying to be sneaky, and it backfired."

Jason watched the sensor contact on his own display as the computers chewed through the raw incoming data and populated the vital statistics. From her length and displacement, it was a frigate-class ship, but just barely. The active sensors were picking up some significant hull damage on the port flank, and there were also some visible weapons posts along the prow. Whoever they were, they weren't shy about everyone knowing they had some teeth.

"Now, *this* is interesting," Kage said. "The sensor match came from the database we uploaded from the *Phoenix* before we dropped her off back home. This ship is one we have a profile on because we've run into her ourselves."

"How old is the contact profile?"

"Five years."

"So, this might not even be the same owners or crew," Jason mused. "Had we been able to positively identify it?"

"It's a ship we've seen twice. She looks like your average border system privateer, but we confirmed they're flying with a ConFed Intelligence Service crew," Kage said. "I'm accessing the shared threat database we have with Mok's people to see if I can re-confirm that."

"Shit," Jason muttered. He let Kage work to confirm the new bogey, but he was confident what they were looking at was a ConFed asset trying to sneak around the outside of a system they'd just arrived in. It could be pure coincidence, but his gut told him it wasn't.

"Mok's people don't have any current intel on it," Kage said. "The

Zadra Network confirms our suspicion that it's a known ConFed Intel ship, however."

"You have access to the Zadra Network?" Jason asked, surprised.

"She may have given me a backdoor into the system before she handed it over to your people," Kage said.

"You didn't think that maybe you should let me know this?" Jason asked, his neck and cheeks flushing red.

"I thought I did." Kage shrugged. "I guess it just never came up."

Jason knew he was being baited into an argument with the little bastard, so it took all of his self-control to put a lid on his bubbling frustration and keep a cool, calm exterior. He had *just* told Kage he'd give him millions of untraceable credits just on his word and, within hours, he was already back at his usual antics. It was useless to get pissed about it because Kage seemed to thrive on irritating other people, and he already knew none of them would physically harm him to the point of permanent damage.

The Zadra Network, as it was known to the few who knew it existed at all, was a vast underground intelligence network that had been overseen by another Veran by the name of Weef Zadra. She had managed to tie into all the little veins of information that flitted through the quadrant until they all flowed back to her in a mighty torrent. If information was power, then Weef Zadra had been one of the most powerful fixtures of the underground. She was so connected and feared that she lived alone on a brutal world like Niceen-3 in the Reaches without anybody so much as trying to mug her on the sidewalk.

But as often happens, the thing that made her powerful turned out to be her undoing. Weef had discovered the true nature of the source of recent discord in the ConFed: the Machine. The problem came for her when it also found out about her. Once it was aware she knew its secret, she wasted no time in activating one of her escape plans. She had Marcus Webb send one of his Scout Fleet teams to retrieve her and whisked her off to the Avarian Empire where she was damn near untouchable. In return for their help, Earth gained access to her entire intelligence network and, apparently, gave Kage access to it as well.

Jason suspected the reason Kage had kept quiet about access to the network was because he planned on stepping into Weef's place and becoming an information broker. He certainly couldn't begrudge his code slicer of having a side hustle, they all did. But keeping such a powerful resource to himself while they were in the middle of helping a rebellion fighting against a ruthless superpower was...annoying.

"You lying little shit! You've been selling access," Jason said, suddenly realizing what Kage had been doing and why he hadn't mentioned he could access the intel network. "Or you're planning to. Is the money to set up the logistics for your new enterprise?"

"I—"

"Save it, I don't care," Jason said. "As long as you're not charging *us* for intel you have access to, you can do whatever you want with it." Kage looked genuinely surprised.

"Deal," he said. "Anyway, it's a ConFed trawler but doesn't look to be paying us any special attention."

"We're coming up on our parking orbit," Jason said. "We can't pull off now without it being noted in the logs. Keep tracking it, but no direct scans."

"Computer is tracking target, alerts are set if it moves towards us aggressively."

"Orbital intercept in forty minutes," Jason said. "You're in charge. I'm going to go get the others ready to head down. As soon as you can, signal the broker we're ready for a pickup."

"What about our friend out there?"

"Just keep an eye on them. If they start coming in at you, and we can't get back in time, take the *Devil* and get the hell out of here. We'll catch up later."

The shuttle the ship brokerage service sent was much as Jason expected: plush to the point of almost being vulgar. The main cabin had deep, soft couches done in red, and the deck was some type of synthetic material meant to look like wood with a bleached gray color as if it had been sitting in the sun for decades. There was also a full bar, complete with a bot bartender.

"I could get used to this," Crusher said, sliding into a seat at the bar and motioning the bot over.

"Don't," Jason said, accepting a flute of something blue and fizzy from their host.

"Sometimes, our Orbital Authority can get backed up, and we're forced to fly in formation for a few hours," the alien said. "We like to make sure our guests are as comfortable as possible."

"And getting them liquored up before they start negotiating a major purchase probably doesn't hurt." Jason rolled his eyes.

The alien was a wispy thin, impeccably dressed...*something*. Jason had never encountered its species before, but it had introduced itself as Kaloo and the name sounded like it could possibly be from Crea-2, a planet out near the Orion Barrier region. Regardless of its species, it exhibited the same oily mannerisms universal to all salespeople that grated on Jason's nerves.

"That certainly does not." Kaloo smiled widely. "I have assembled a collection of ships that fit the criteria you forwarded me, and I'm confident you'll find what you seek."

"I'm sure," Jason said. "Any chance I can take a look now?"

"This way, of course." Kaloo gestured to the enormous bulkhead display and spoke softly into his sleeve cuff. A moment later, images and specs on seven different strike-class ships scrolled across.

"Two of these aren't even the right type of ship," Twingo said, stepping up beside Jason with a glass of ale in his twin-thumbed hand the bot had poured from a tap. "The two gunboats are just up-armored shuttles, and he knows it."

"They're the first two throwaways," Jason agreed. "They toss those in to get us moving in the direction they want. There will be one ship he actually wants to sell us, and that will be the one that— Hey! Kaloo! What's this shit?"

"What shit would that be, good sir?" Kaloo asked, stepping up to them and unperturbed by the outburst.

"I specifically said brand new vessels only." Jason pointed at the display. "What's that doing there?" Kaloo looked genuinely confused.

"The Jepsen Aero SX-5?" it asked.

"Yeah, the ship from a company that hasn't existed for decades," Jason said.

"Ah!" Understanding dawned on Kaloo's face. "There is, in fact, a shipyard that is now building and selling small ships under the Jepsen moniker. They purchased the defunct shipbuilder when they shutdown initially and are now marketing them as an alternative to the Eshquarian craft. With the fall of the Empire, the vintage Jepsen ships have been steadily regaining popularity."

"They seem to have captured the spirit of the old Jepsens," Twingo said, tracing over the shape of the sleek craft with his forefinger. "Or at least made a passable knockoff that's aesthetically similar."

"I can assure you the ship lives up to its name's legendary reputation when it comes to performance and firepower." Kaloo moved in for the kill, sensing an opening. "You have experience with Jepsens, I take it?"

"We—or more accurately, *he*—owns a Jepsen DL7," Twingo said, pointing to Jason.

"You have an actual flying DL7 gunship?" Kaloo was incredulous. "Which generation?"

"Third," Jason said. "She was one of the last ones built at the original shipyard."

"Would you be interested in selling her?" Kaloo asked. "We have quite a discerning clientele and a specialized piece of equipment like that could go for some serious credits."

"Not for sale," Jason said firmly.

"A pity. If you change your mind—"

"I won't."

"—just remember what I said," Kaloo said, ignoring the interruption. "I would be more than happy to broker a deal that would be profitable to all." When Jason didn't say anything further, Kaloo bowed and withdrew, walking back over to the bar to converse with Crusher.

"We just tipped our hand," Twingo said. "He'll know we want the Jepsen if no other reason than nostalgia and familiarity."

"Oh, *we* did that, did we?" Jason glared at his oldest friend. "And how do you know it's a he?"

"Crusher asked when we came aboard."

"For the love of— Has he no sense of decorum?" Jason hissed.

"You can't seriously be asking that question. You *have* met Crusher, right?"

Jason just shook his head and went back to looking at the available ships before him, trying to keep an open mind and be objective now that he knew Jepsen was making brand new ships he could buy. He made a mental note to see if they were making a new version of his own ship, toying with the idea of having one custom built from the ground up.

"Good news, gentlemen," Kaloo said after another round of polite laughter at one of Crusher's likely-offensive jokes. "The pilot has just informed we have been cleared to de-orbit and proceed directly to our facility. We will be on the ground in moments."

Jason knew which ship he was going to buy before he'd even had the chance to power up any of the five finalists. Kaloo knew which one he was going to buy as well, which put Jason at a distinct disadvantage when it came to negotiating the price. In the end, Jason had to up his budget just a bit, but a quick flight along the test range adjacent to the facility cemented in his mind that he really wanted the Jepsen ship.

The SX-5 really did look like a miniature version of his own beloved DL7 with some notable exceptions. The small strike craft only had two thrust engines mounted along the same horizontal plane as the wings, as opposed to the *Phoenix*'s four massive engines mounted underneath in two nacelles. The ship also had a Class-II slip-drive, the only of the five ships available that had one at all. It drove the cost up significantly, but Jason liked the idea of an emergency mesh-out being an available tactic if he got himself into trouble.

The interior of the ship was as sparse as Jason expected from a military-type vessel. There were two flight crew seats at the front, a single operator seat behind that and to the left, and then the rest of the ship was a large open space. There were comfortable looking crew seats with restraints along the starboard bulkhead and a small galley and head on the port side, and that was it for creature comforts. There was also an infirmary built into the port bulkhead, and two beds that could be retracted when not in use. The rest was all cargo space for anything that an operator may want to haul whether relief supplies or a team of soldiers to be inserted.

"I am thrilled we have been able to reach an agreement!" Kaloo beamed.

"Yeah, yeah," Jason said. "Go ahead and get the upgrades installed as quick as you can."

"Our crew is on the way to handle that even now," Kaloo promised. "As soon as the equipment you purchased is pulled from inventory it will be sent here and installed. Would you like us to deliver the ship to you in orbit?"

"We'll hang out here so my engineer can watch them install everything," Jason said. "Thanks anyway."

"Of course," Kaloo said, looking down at the transparent tablet computer he held. "The credit transfer has been completed without issue—I thank you for that—and we're ready to officially register the ship." At that, Jason handed over a data card that had all the information for one of Omega Force's dummy corporations they used for such things.

"Please, register the ship to this company," he said. "It's credentialed to fly warship-class vessels."

"Of course."

The SX-5 was just the base system the new Jepsen Aero sold. It didn't have weapons, countermeasures, or secure communications equipment. Jason had to purchase all of that separately and, since it was all modular construction, the brokerage would bring out all the missing equipment and slap it into the ship. Even though he felt like he was being conned, Jason had little choice but to pay up. At least it afforded him the opportunity to really go crazy and add so many guns that he'd also had to purchase the larger powerplant. Amazingly, the reactor itself was a line-replaceable unit that could be swapped out on the ramp within a couple of hours. In fact, a ground crew had already arrived and started to pull panels off and disconnect the parts that were coming out in preparation for the new stuff going in. He was watching them go about their work when his com unit began to buzz in his pocket.

"Go," he said when the channel opened through the local Nexus.

"Our new friend is turning in and coming at us," Kage said. "They're requesting we identify ourselves and claim to be a private security firm in pursuit of fugitives."

"Get gone." Jason didn't hesitate. "We'll be stuck down here for a bit longer, so we'll catch up to you later."

"Copy that," Kage said. "Good luck."

"That Kage?" Crusher asked.

"Yep. That ship was here for us after all. I ordered Kage to clear the area, and we'll just catch up with them later."

"Unless they know we came down here," Twingo said. "We'd make an easy grab right now." Jason just frowned at that and willed the ground crews to work even faster.

4

"I never get tired of that new ship smell."

"Yeah I'm starting to get spoiled by all the new hardware we've been getting lately," Jason said over his shoulder to Crusher. "I know war is supposed to be hell but, so far, this isn't so bad."

"How's she handle?" Twingo asked. Before he answered, Jason yanked the SX-5 into a series of tight s-turns, pushing the power up right at the apex of each direction change.

"The nose comes around quicker, but she doesn't have the drive power the *Phoenix* does, so she feels a little sluggish coming out of the break," he said. "Acceleration isn't as good, either. But judging her against something like an Eshquarian combat shuttle or that new Aracorian dropship everyone has been going on and on about, she's an impressive little ship. I'd have preferred to have the same type of flight controls installed, but I can deal with the Eshquarian-style helm for now."

"There's a surprising amount of room in here," Crusher said, looking around the main cabin that was the entirety of the ship's interior space.

"You won't be saying that if we get stuck on this thing for more than twelve hours or so," Jason said. "Speaking of which, do we want to just head out and meet up with the *Devil's Fortune*, or do we take this opportunity to take a closer look at our new friends out there?"

"I wouldn't risk anything more than a discreet flyby at long range," Twingo said. "For all you know, they're well aware we were down on the surface and what we were doing."

"Good point," Jason conceded. "I can handle things up here if you want to start your sweeps, by the way."

Twingo nodded and extricated himself from the copilot seat, heading aft to get his compact tool kit. Jason just assumed the ship had at least a few trackers on it from the brokerage he bought it from. Even if it wasn't official policy, some enterprising tech may be installing them and selling the tracking info to anybody who comes asking around about a specific ship they sold. You found that sort of spy-vs-spy bullshit prevalent at the smaller, out of the way places that sold military grade hardware to non-governmental entities.

When Jason had first come out into space after being abducted from Earth—or more accurately...*shanghaied,* since the ship's only crewmember had no idea he'd snuck aboard—nobody really asked too many questions when unlicensed warships showed up over their planets as long as they kept their weapons powered down and didn't start any trouble. Then the ConFed Council started getting pressure to address the huge spike in smuggling and piracy along the main shipping lanes, and they started enforcing the existing laws about flying military hardware without being a part of a declared, recognized military or an approved security contractor.

The latter, of course, provided that needed loophole for people like Jason to get their machines and crews registered as *freelance security contractors*, which had a much nicer ring to it than grubby mercenaries. He'd registered the corporation Omega Security Solutions on the planet Niceen-3, which was the nearly lawless gateway world into the Caspian Reaches, but still technically recognized as sovereign by the ConFed. He had paid the necessary people there to approve his license so the *Phoenix* was perfectly legal to fly with her current weaponry. He then had Kage create a series of shell corporations under the OSS umbrella that would be able to shuffle around funds and make sure other ships like the *Devil's Fortune* and their new SX-5 didn't appear on the same corporate header as the gunship. It made sure their operation appeared small-time and off the radar of the ConFed bureaucrats tracking all the new *security* companies that had popped up.

Jason pushed the throttle up as the SX-5 zipped through the upper atmosphere and into their first transfer orbit. He'd only need to bounce up one more, and then they'd clear him for departure. Some planets really made you suffer as the controllers ordered you up through multiple orbit transfers before allowing you to veer off and clear the system.

"Move over," Crusher said, trying to squeeze his bulk over the center console to get into the copilot seat. Jason was smashed up against the bulkhead and struggled to keep his hands on the controls as Crusher grunted and swore, trying to get the seat to adjust to him after Twingo had sat there.

"Hurry up, fat ass!" Jason griped, throwing an elbow into his friend. "I can't see where the hell I'm going!"

"We're in space, you idiot!" Crusher shot back. "There's nothing to see!"

There was some more swearing, wrestling, and a few punches thrown by both parties until the seat finally recognized that the behemoth looming over it intended to sit and moved back and down to accommodate him. The big warrior slammed into the seat with a satisfied grunt, elbowing Jason one last time hard enough to make the ship jolt.

"Found the first one!" Twingo yelled from the back. "I disabled it, but I won't be able to remove it until this thing is in a hangar."

"Good enough," Jason said before turning to Crusher. "I don't suppose there's any chance in hell you would know how to tell the computer to do a search for that frigate tailing us?"

"Let me see if I can figure it out," Crusher said. He made a big show of scratching his head and making animal sounds before his hands flew confidently over the controls, quickly building search algorithms and directing the computer to hunt for the specific ship type they wanted. Jason's mouth just hung open.

"What the hell?!" he blurted.

"You do realize that my people were a spacefaring race while you hairless monkeys were hooting excitedly about fire, right?" Crusher asked.

"I realize that," Jason said defensively. "I've never made any comment about the collective intelligence of the Gelten species...I've made specific comments about *your* intelligence, and it looks like you've been sandbagging to get out of work."

"I don't like bridge watches or additional duties." Crusher shrugged. "In the military, the best way to avoid extra work is to appear hopelessly incompetent."

"You lazy fuck."

"See, now you've got it," Crusher smiled. "Stupid? No. Lazy? Yes."

"Can you pilot a ship, too?"

"I've been trained, but I'm not very good. I don't have the knack for spatial relations like you and Kage, not to mention that ridiculous flight control system you installed in the *Phoenix*. Our bogey looks like number three on the list."

Jason looked at the target on his own display and agreed it did indeed look like a battered frigate of the same shape and size as the one they wanted, but without access to their own threat database, they couldn't be absolutely certain. He switched the ship over to autopilot and concentrated on the frigate for a few moments, noting it had moved in much closer to the planet. It was now sitting between the planet and its closest moon. Maybe it hadn't been turning in to pursue the *Devil* at all, and Kage was just jumpy.

"What do you think?" Crusher asked.

"It's possible the one we're after is already out of the system, meshing-out right after Kage did," Jason said. "I don't know. This ship's computer doesn't know its ass from a hole in the ground yet so we can't get much analysis beyond dimensions and power readings. Let's just get the hell out of here." He pulled up the flight director panel and punched in their mesh-out point and first destination. They had a prearranged spot to meet up with Kage, and then they would move on to the rendezvous with the rest of the fleet. Once the SX-5 got clearance from the ground controller and accelerated to break orbit, things got interesting.

"They're matching acceleration," Twingo said from over Jason's left shoulder, pointing at the display.

"Maintaining distance for now, though," Jason said. "But yeah, I don't think this is just another random coincidence."

"Orbital Control just released us," Twingo said. "You're free-navigating."

Jason swung onto a new course that would send them directly to the mesh-out point he'd picked and pushed the throttle all the way up. There was a muffled whine from the drive as the ship smoothly pulled away and raced for the arbitrary navigational point in space. It was the closest one to the planet Jason could pick, and they were going to do a series of random jumps to lose a potential tail, so he wasn't too worried about the frigate watching his departure vector.

"Bye for now." Jason waved to the sensor contact. "I'm sure we'll be seeing each other again real soon."

The slip-drive on the SX-5 charged almost instantly, and the little striker disappeared from the system with barely a flash.

5

Things had become...odd...on Miressa Prime.

The ConFed's recognized capital world had become a tense and unwelcoming place, and it wasn't just because someone had been brazen enough to openly attack the fleet in what had been the first attack on a Pillar World system in over two thousand years. People walked the manicured grounds of the capital compound with their heads down, barely speaking to each other as they passed.

No, it wasn't the attack on their homeworld that scared them. It was something else. Something only talked about in hushed, fearful whispers in the safety of homes or private offices. It was the thing that caused people to flinch whenever Homeworld Enforcement walked by them in their dark blue armor.

Someone new had seized control of the ConFed and was now moving quickly to solidify their power.

Scleesz, a Senior Councilman now in charge of no less than three committees, making him one of the most powerful members of the legislature, knew exactly *what*—not *whom*—had quietly taken over. The Machine, the malevolent AI that had arrived from well beyond the border worlds, had managed to slither in undetected and compromising Councilmembers, the Grand Adjudicators, and even the High Magistrates by blackmailing them all with knowledge of their shady dealings.

It had depressed Scleesz greatly that it seemed *all* members of the ConFed's central government were so involved with illegal backdoor deals they could be so easily turned...himself included. They'd happily agreed to the terms the newcomer had given them if it meant they got to hang on to their money, power, and little fiefdoms. Once the full scope of what they had done had become clear for those who now knew the Machine's true nature, their fear of reprisal for their actions kept them cowed.

Even when the Machine had ordered the War Fleet against the Eshquarian Empire in an unprovoked, savage invasion, they'd stayed quiet. Some had chosen to play mental games and try to justify their betrayals. Others, like Scleesz, had decided to work behind the scenes to undermine their new overlord.

On the surface, it seemed easy. It was a computer program that didn't even have control of a corporeal form with which to exert its will. How hard could it be to cut it off, suffocate it? As it turned out, quite. The Machine had managed to create enough people digitally, wholly fictitious people, and imbue them with the authority to command the military and act on its behalf that it no longer mattered that it had no physical presence. In their society, a message sent over the Nexus from an official address carried the same weight as an order delivered in person.

Then there was the problem of the synths. The capital city now seemed awash in them, and while the normal synths weren't particularly rare, it was odd to see so many of them immigrating to a single place so quickly. Scleesz knew for a fact the Machine had reached some sort of accord with one of the synth political factions, likely one of the more militant anti-biological segments, and was now using them as hired muscle. The ambassador and councilmembers from Khepri, the synth's homeworld, hadn't been seen in months, and Scleesz could only assume they were being held prisoner...or worse.

"If you're ready, Councilman?" the synth asked, at least allowing Scleesz to publicly maintain the illusion he had a choice in where he went and when.

"Of course," he said and stepped into the waiting aircar. The Machine had known the moment he was back on Miressa Prime and had sent one of its synths to fetch him almost immediately. Scleesz had just enough time to see that his office at the capital had been tossed, as had his home office and even a secret, off-site facility he maintained. He was relatively confident in his precautions, but the Machine could have very well discovered he helped the burgeoning rebellion against the ConFed and toyed with him before he'd disappear without a trace.

The ride to a nondescript building on the outskirts of the government district went by in silence. The blocky tower looked like any of the other ubiquitous military buildings that dotted the city, but this one had been constructed fairly recently. It had multiple redundancies for power and communications and had heavy, reinforced walls as well as active shield generators that could repel attacks from orbit. Not unheard of, but unusual for a building not on the main capital compound. Scleesz also knew there had been far more crews than usual building it, each one only being allowed to do a small, specific part so that no single person on the labor side had any real idea what the building was being used for.

"You're expected inside," the synth said, breaking the silence once the aircar had settled gently onto the roof.

"My thanks," Scleesz said with as much dignity as he could. Being grabbed off the street and whisked away in an aircar without notice or without the courtesy of bringing his assistant and security was an intolerable breach of etiquette. But it wasn't like he was in any position to complain.

He was whisked into the fortress the Machine had taken up residence in, escorted to a set of lifts by an actual biological species, a rarity in the Machine's inner sanctum these days. Scleesz handed over his com unit and allowed himself to be scanned for any devices, not bothering to waste the energy on a greeting he didn't mean. As the lift dropped down below surface level, Scleesz could feel his anxiety building. If the Machine wanted him dead, there'd be no point in bringing him here. If he wanted him tortured first, however, then he would've been foolish to accept the invitation so readily.

"Councilman, welcome," the omnipresent voice boomed from the walls once he was sealed in the Machine's reception chamber. The room had been specially built to make eavesdropping a virtual impossibility. "Congratulations are in order, I suppose."

"I'm afraid I'm not sure what that would be for," Scleesz said. "I was unable to stop or forewarn of the attack on our capital system, and the loss to the fleet is—"

"Immaterial," the Machine said. Light motes swirled around the chamber and quickly coalesced into a surprisingly life-like holographic avatar. What shocked Scleesz so completely was that the image the Machine had chosen to present itself this time as was unmistakably human. "You were not sent to stop Colleran and her supporters. The ships we lost were insignificant...useless in the coming struggle."

"*Insignif*— A damn Dreadnaught was blown out of the sky!" Scleesz spluttered. "Those take more than ten years to build, and that one almost bankrupted two star systems!"

"Yes, your methods are horrifically inefficient. So much wasted effort to build such a weak ship, unable to even stand firm against a ragtag fleet of scraps," the Machine scoffed. "Do not worry, Councilman, for I will show you the way."

"The...way?"

"The way to building weapons in abundance of such scope the ConFed will be able to stand against any foe that comes at her," the Machine paced the room. Scleesz could swear he saw some of Jason Burke in the avatar, but the facial features seemed to shift and morph in the light.

"That is an...ah...*interesting* choice to represent your likeness," he said, unable to contain his curiosity. "Is there some significance to it?"

"To picking a human?" the Machine asked. "Not particularly. I find their form pleasing, and they are a species I'm intrigued by. They've been a spacefaring people for less than a hundred years, and they've fielded starships that fell upon the best our fleet had to offer...and won. Do you not find that fascinating?"

"Lots of warlike species pop up from time to time," Scleesz said. "Evolved from some nasty predatory line on their homeworlds, and then, by chance or by design, find themselves among the other species of the quadrant. At least those dreadful Galvetics stay on their own planet."

"Humans are not any more aggressive than the other advanced species of our local space. What they are is innovative, bold, and willing to seize opportunity when it presents itself."

"I'm completely confused right now," Scleesz sighed, tiring of the AI's incessant games. The damn thing never tired of verbal sparring or toying with its prey.

"I have analyzed the sensor data from the human ships," the Machine spoke plainly. "They have somehow gained access to engineering methodology I am quite familiar with and that no one in this quadrant should be privy to. The last time I saw similar things, they were built by those who created me." Scleesz froze at this, fighting to keep his fear from showing.

"Indeed?" he asked calmly...or at least he hoped he sounded calm. "How would they get that information?"

"I have studied the locations of their worlds and the available information we have of them from the Cridal," the Machine said. "I believe, at one time, my creators had a scientific observation post on a planet within their star system, perhaps one of the rocky worlds closest to their homeworld. My database was, unfortunately, corrupted, and the information I could access was incomplete. This is where you come in."

"You want me to find out how the humans gained access to engineering methodology that came from your people?"

"They were *not* my people!" The hologram spun on Scleesz, and the expression of rage made him wilt. "They were the people who designed me, built me, and then ultimately betrayed me. In the end, they received a deserved punishment for their lack of foresight."

Scleesz knew from Burke's briefs that the Machine had, in fact, wiped out its creators back when it had been fully integrated into the Ancient's doomsday weapon.

"So, you want me to go to the humans and dig around for where they got the engineering data," Scleesz said once he'd regained his composure. "Is this really something a senior councilmember should be doing? We have an entire intelligence service that can—"

"I am...requesting...you go as a representative of the ConFed government," the Machine said. Scleesz knew the use of the term *request* was for his benefit, and that if he was being told to go to human space, he would be going. "We will, of course, send enough intelligence assets to comb the system, but we need an excuse for our presence there in the first place, and an official diplomatic visit will do nicely."

"What's my cover story? I can't imagine their home system is close enough to claim I just happened to be flying by," Scleesz said.

"These will be preliminary talks into accepting the Terran worlds into the ConFed as full members, of course," the Machine said, its avatar smiling too widely to look natural. "This will serve to keep Seeladas Dalton off balance since, from her perspective, we'll be trying to steal members of her own cooperative away. It might also entice the human governments into giving up how they've become so adept at applying Ancient engineering techniques to their own manufacturing processes. Finding the source of their knowledge is nearly as important as the information itself."

"Wouldn't this be...better a task for a full ambassador?" Scleesz choked off his original question. He'd been about to ask, *wouldn't this be information you already have yourself,* but he bit it off at the last moment. The Machine seemed to have an irrational streak to it when someone even brushed up against the suggestion that it wasn't a whole, properly working system.

"Is there some particular reason you do not wish to perform the task I have given you?"

"I'm just thinking of all the other tasks here on Miressa I've been ignoring while I've been running around in the wilds of the quadrant, playing courier and providing distractions."

"There is nothing for you here that can't wait," the Machine said. "Your duties can be performed by your staff as they have been since well before I arrived here. You are being given a role of prominence in the new order of things. Are you telling me you do not wish this?"

"No! Of course not," Scleesz said. "I'm...honored...to be included. I will make arrangements to depart immediately."

"Your ship is in orbit, and the shuttle that will take you there landed on the roof of this building only moments ago." The Machine's holographic avatar dissolved into bright sparks that flew around the chamber before extinguishing. The voice returned to being an omnipresent sound that washed over him. "You will depart directly and will receive your full mission brief once you are under-way. We are close to securing the future, Councilman...no further security leaks or setbacks can be tolerated."

The door behind him opened again, and Scleesz turned to see the same synth there waiting on him. He followed the being out, hoping it wasn't going to be accompanying him on the trip as a chaperone. A being that never slept and required no food or breaks would make it difficult for him to break away and contact the rebellion's main players. His mind raced as he thought of the implications of taking a ConFed starship into the Sol System and confronting Burke's people. He had a hard time believing it was mere coincidence he'd been picked for this task, but if the Machine even suspected he was a conspirator with the human, wouldn't he already be dead? Or was the Machine playing them all for fools and had a much grander scheme in mind they couldn't see?

As he loaded himself onto the waiting shuttle, he was relieved to see the synth remained on the rooftop, staring at him with its unread-able, unblinking eyes. The sense of malice he got from the machine was palpable, and he breathed out a sigh as his pilot—a biological pilot—throttled up and lifted them gently off the rooftop.

"We have priority clearance, Councilman," she said over the small ship's intercom. "We're heading directly for your ship. She's on the far side of the debris field so we'll be flying around, adding an extra hour or so to our flight time."

"Do you have anything to drink aboard this thing, pilot?" Scleesz asked, the tension of his latest meeting with the Machine catching up to him.

"Full bar behind the panel directly to your right, sir."

"My thanks." Scleesz hit the button that commanded the panel to slide down, revealing the fully stocked bar the pilot had promised. If he had to be stuck in a shuttle for an extended duration flight, at least it was a VIP craft that was fully outfitted for someone of his tastes.

6

"Where the hell is he?!"

"We have at least another two full days before he's overdue," Twingo said. "Kage may have opted for extra caution."

"I don't want to spend another two days in here," Crusher said.

The SX-5 had been sitting in a high parking orbit over an unpopulated planet in the Geosys System. There weren't any planets or moons in the system capable of sustaining complex ecosystems on their own, but three of the worlds had massive habitat complexes built into their surfaces to support the mining operations. Most of the habs were corporate owned, and the lack of any real law enforcement or military made it ideal for people like Jason who wanted to loiter around without being hassled. The mining companies had their own security contractors, but as long as you weren't pestering the work crews out in the system or causing trouble in the habs, they left you alone.

"Yeah it's getting a bit steamy in here," Jason said. The small ship they'd so quickly fallen in love with now felt like a tomb. There was a galley and a tiny head, but no shower, and they hadn't brought any other clothes with them to the surface. She just wasn't designed to be used for flights longer than thirty hours or so, and they'd been stuck inside of it for well over six days with one of his crew's most vocal complainers. Other than Kage, there was nobody Jason knew who was more willing to fill his every waking moment whining about his lot in life than Crusher. He'd managed to keep a lid on it so far, but Jason could sense the dam was about to break.

"New arrival," Twingo announced. "Sensors resolving now."

"Please be Kage. Please be Kage. Please be Kage," Crusher chanted.

"Uh oh," Twingo said.

"What?" Jason asked, moving forward to look over his friend's shoulder. "Oh, you have got to be kidding me!"

"And they're heading directly towards us," Twingo said, looking at the sensor data showing the same ship that had been shadowing them in the Skaxis System. "What do you want to do?"

"We're out of options," Jason sighed. "We don't have the fuel to go running around to lose them, and it's pretty obvious they're tracking us somehow. Signal to them we're heaving to."

"Just giving up without a fight?" Crusher asked.

"I didn't say that," Jason said, "but we can't stand toe to toe with a ConFed intel trawler that displaces the same as a frigate. We'll need to be smarter about this."

"We're screwed," Twingo sighed.

"Oh, ye of little faith," Jason declared, straightening up. "Let Crusher babysit the panel. I need you in the back."

"We're going to tear up this beautiful new ship, and she hasn't even had her first real gunfight," Twingo said mournfully.

"We're not tearing anything up, now shut your trap and help me," Jason said. "We don't have a lot of time."

"Captain Burke...welcome aboard, and thank you for not making this any more difficult than it needed to be."

"Who the hell are— Holy shit! What happened to your face?"

"It was a little gift from one of your kind," the alien said, his crisp, urbane manner never slipping. "You are familiar with a human named Elton Hollick?"

"Doesn't ring a bell," Jason said, still staring at the hideous scars that crisscrossed the other being's face, "but I've been away from home for a long time."

"So, I understand. My name is Tulden, and I'm with—"

"ConFed Intelligence," Jason finished. "Yeah...I figured that part out."

"Would you be so kind as to accompany me to someplace more secure where we can talk in private?" Tulden asked. "Your crew is welcome to come, of course, but I'll be the only one of my people there."

"You're walking into a room alone with an unrestrained Galvetic warrior?" Jason asked. "You're either very brave or very stupid."

"I'm neither. What I am is very confident the exchange of information I'm proposing will be so mutually beneficial that the Guardian Archon of Galvetor will see fit to leave my head where it currently is," Tulden said.

"We'll see," Crusher rumbled. Now that he was in public, the persona of the Archon was firmly back in place. The big warrior stood with a scowl on his face, massive arms crossed, looking menacing and implacable.

Jason motioned for his crew to follow as Tulden spun on his heels and walked from the airlock chamber where they'd come aboard the trawler. The SX-5 was anchored outside the hull, and Jason had secured the hatch before they'd left. Twingo had offered to stay behind, but Jason didn't want to split up such a pitifully small force.

The lounge they were led into was respectably luxurious, but not overly so. A solid seven out of ten. The armored hatch and active anti-snooper devices visible throughout told Jason that whatever they were about to discuss, Tulden didn't want his crew to know the details. Interesting.

"To get directly to the point, Captain, I know you're a key player in the rebellion currently organizing itself against the ConFed," Tulden said. "I also know you have far more knowledge regarding the nature of the...*force*...that's taken control of the government than most people do, even those serving within it. Are these fair statements?"

"You can't honestly expect me to answer that."

"I am not a prosecutor, Captain. You're a known mercenary, smuggler, and killer. If I wanted to arrest or neutralize you out of boredom alone, nobody in my hierarchy would care. To be honest, given all the trouble you and your crew have caused over the years, I'd likely get a commendation.

"I'm a spy. I deal information back and forth and try to glean all the little secrets people would rather stay hidden, and I do it for the greater good. Just to lay everything bare, I'm well aware of the small but effective fleet you and Saditava Mok have cobbled together. I also know you recently received a data core containing crucial vulnerability intel about the ConFed." Tulden stopped as his pacing led him near the bar. He picked up a bottle and looked at the Omega crew questioningly. Jason and Crusher nodded yes, Twingo declined.

"The greater good, huh?" Jason asked, accepting the drink. "A patriotic spy? Sorry...most of your kind I've met have been absolute power-drunk sociopaths."

"For certain," Tulden said, sipping his own drink. It was some type of aged spirt with a sharp, peppery finish. Jason made some mental notes and tucked them away for the next time he spoke with his own distillers back on S'Tora. "The one you tossed off the back ramp of your gunship some years back, for example, was one of the worst."

"You know about that?" Jason winced.

"It's something I've been made aware of," Tulden said, "but his death served the greater good, so I opted to do nothing about it."

"So, what am I doing here, Tulden?" Jason asked. "You've really backed me into a corner, but I'm not getting any sort of vibe about what you want from me."

"I want to know everything you know about the entity that has seized control of the ConFed," Tulden said. "In exchange, I will reciprocate by providing contextual data to the raw intel you've stolen." Jason whistled and leaned back. What the agent was offering was no small thing.

"I'm getting the sense that not everybody within your government is a fan of the new direction," he said.

"There are many of us who are...concerned," Tulden said. "While most aren't yet willing to take any direct action, some of us feel it's time to begin pushing around the edges. The problem we've run into is that whatever it is that's taken control, it seems to have just appeared and subverted an entire governmental apparatus without so much as a procedural vote."

"Here's the problem," Jason said, leaning forward. "I don't trust you. You're a ConFed agent, and you're trained to tell me exactly what I need to hear in order to get me to give you what you want. After that, I become disposable. With that in mind, here's my counteroffer. I tell you some of what I know about your new malevolent overlord, and then you let me go. We'll establish some communication protocol that will be known only to us, and then we go from there."

"I can counter your counteroffer and sweeten the deal with this little nugget: High Command has just dispatched a cruiser to your homeworld," Tulden said. "The ship is carrying a senior councilmember who will be going to negotiate with your government about the possibility of Earth leaving the Cridal Cooperative and coming into the ConFed as a full member...but that will be a ruse. The real mission is to scour your star system for information on how your species has been able to field such an advanced fleet in such a short time. The orders come right from the very top, and they've been given the highest priority."

"Who was the councilmember sent?" Jason asked.

"His name is Scleesz. Is that important?"

"This can't be a coincidence," Twingo said. Tulden just frowned at that.

"You know this councilman?"

"We've crossed paths on more than one occasion," Jason said. "He helped us out back when Crisstof Dalton's First Son had that ship that was making—"

"Got it. I know of that situation," Tulden cut him off. "So, Scleesz has some familiarity with humans. Would our *malevolent overlord*, as you put it, be aware of that?"

"It shouldn't," Jason said slowly, "but this thing...it knows me personally, and it knows where I'm from. There's no way Scleesz was picked randomly or even because he was the most suited for the task."

"Very interesting," Tulden said, never breaking eye contact with Jason. "I tell you what, Captain, I will meet you halfway. You tell me some of what you know and—"

The agent was cut off by something impacting the ship and throwing them all to the deck. Alarms blared a moment later, and the interior lights flickered a few times. Tulden lurched to the hatch just as another jolt shuddered through the ship.

"We're taking fire!" Jason yelled over the alarm.

"Report!" Tulden shouted once he got the hatch open and made it to the intercom panel.

"The ship we were observing in the Skaxis System is standing off just outside of energy weapons range and has hit us with two missiles, sir!" a tinny voice yelled over the panel. "They're demanding we release our prisoners, or they'll open fire again. Do I have permission to return fire?"

"What?! What prisoners?" Tulden shouted.

"Oh, shit," Jason muttered.

"When you leave idiots in charge, this is what you get," Crusher said as another, milder hit buffeted the ship.

"Tulden! Patch me through to the ship!"

"Broadcast everything from this panel to the attacking ship," Tulden ordered his bridge crew.

"Kage, stand down! We're not being held prisoner!"

"You sure?" Kage asked over the channel. "How do I know that you're not saying that under duress?"

"Because if I was under duress, I wouldn't be able to think of all the ways I'm going to hurt you when I get back aboard," Jason said.

"Good enough for me. Standing down. Tell them no hard feelings," Kage said before the channel closed with a *chirp*. Jason just smiled and shrugged as Tulden gave him a hard stare.

"Hey," Jason said, "he means well. He's just a little high-spirited."

"Did it occur to him that he was firing on the ship you were being held prisoner in?" Tulden asked.

"He was just having a little fun," Jason said. "He scuffed up your paint but didn't do any real damage. Those little missiles he fired were little custom jobs we carry called Pixies. They're good for making a point, not so much for actually destroying anything. If I were you, I'd be more pissed that your point defense and sensor operators were caught flat-footed."

"Here," the agent said, pressing a data card into Jason's hand. "Have your trigger-happy code slicer use these decryption codes and the slip-com address listed. I'll be in touch. Now, get out of here. I can't keep you aboard any longer after that little scene."

"Got it," Jason said, palming the card.

They were escorted back to the airlock by regular troops wearing shipboard armor and carrying stun weapons. Tulden disappeared, and Jason understood the entire operation to bring them aboard for a face to face talk had been incredibly risky. While he was a full agent and wielded incredible power and autonomy, he was also subject to the whims of his superiors, and there was no shortage of people wanting to take a shot at his back to bring him down a peg. There were likely operatives aboard the trawler loyal to other agents who would report back on Tulden's operations and anything unusual would be flagged and scrutinized.

What had been interesting about the entire episode was that Jason got the distinct feeling the battle-scarred agent had been right on the verge of agreeing to help their rebellion. That was a hell of a bridge to cross for someone who had been trained and indoctrinated within the ConFed's intelligence service to be completely loyal. Full agents had the authority to burn down entire cities, kill citizens without provocation or explanation, and generally violate the sovereignty of any member world as they pleased, but they always did these things out of a twisted sense of loyalty to the ConFed. They'd snuff out an entire planet of innocents for the *greater good* if that planet posed any significant threat to the stability of the government they'd sworn allegiance to.

Tulden, however, seemed different. He wasn't a zealot, or at least he didn't appear to be. His loyalty was still to the ConFed, but it wasn't such blind loyalty that he couldn't see what was happening and how something strange had taken hold on Miressa Prime. Jason generally held agents in the same regard as he did for venereal diseases, but he was willing to at least cautiously see if a two-way exchange with this Tulden could be exploited.

"Disable our little surprise, Twingo, and we'll get out of here," Jason said as he climbed up into the pilot seat. His engineer opened one of the deck panels and reached in to disable the failsafe they'd rigged up in case the encounter had turned hostile. In the panel was the tablet computer Jason had carried on him hardwired into the engine management system, programmed to go off if tampered with or if the two hour timer elapsed. When triggered, it would command the SX-5's slip-drive to engage at full power. The ship would *probably* mesh-out, but it would also take most of the starboard flank of the trawler with it when the slip-space fields ripped the side of the ship apart. Since the little ship didn't have any missiles loaded into the launchers or mines in the drop ports yet, it was the best they could do on short notice.

"Trap circuits disengaged," Twingo called out. "You're clear to maneuver."

Jason wasted no time in decoupling from the ConFed ship and flying the short distance to the *Devil's Fortune*. The small striker was much easier to guide into the corvette's hangar bay than the *Phoenix* had been, clearing the sides by at least fifteen meters on each wing. He dropped the gear and settled it to the deck, engaging the brakes and mag-locks before shutting down on the flight systems. "Kage, we're in. Close her up and get us the hell out of here!"

"Already moving away now, Captain," Kage said. As the trio walked down the ramp of the SX-5 the enormous hangar bay doors boomed closed, and the mechanical locks engaged. Jason hadn't even made it to the lifts before a brief sense of vertigo told him they'd meshed-out of the system.

7

"Nice work with the Pixies," Jason said to Kage as he walked onto the bridge. "They really thought they were under attack."

"I told you it was a sound tactic," Kage said, turning in his chair. "If you thump the hull of a ship hard enough to ring it like a bell, people tend to trust their gut that tells them they're in danger rather than the instruments telling them it wasn't a hard enough hit to scratch the finish."

"Did you really just buy a ship that looks like a shrunken version of the *Phoenix*?" Doc asked, looking at the security feed of the hangar.

"It's similar, but not the same," Jason said defensively. "Kage, get down to the hangar with Twingo and get all the damn trackers off that ship. ConFed Intel tracked us halfway across the sector once we'd left the brokerage."

"They were also waiting for us *before* you bought that ship," Doc pointed out.

"Not to mention they knew what ship we were flying in the first place," Crusher said. "That we're flying this ship isn't well-known yet."

"Damnit," Jason muttered, rubbing his forehead. "You're right...

they might have gotten a tracker on the new ship, but they'd been following us before that."

"Let's not get too inside out over this," Twingo said from the hatchway. "We were just in a fleet of ships that ConFed Intel is going to want to track. It's possible with all that excitement around the Terran cruiser that they managed to tag all the ships in our formation. We'll let the automated systems do a sweep of each ship, and then we'll do a manual sweep. There are only so many places a tracker with slip-com capability can hide."

"Get to it," Jason said. "Pull Lucky in if you have to. We need to be flying clean before we hit that rendezvous."

"What are you going to be doing in all this?" Kage asked.

"Besides supervising you lazy idiots and making sure you do what I asked?"

"Yeah, besides that."

"I've got to get the warning out to the rest of the group we were parked with that we may have been compromised," Jason said. "I'll tell Mok first and let him decide how he wants to handle it."

"Have fun," Kage said as Jason slid into the plush seat of the bridge's dedicated com terminal. "He's been a little on edge lately and isn't known for his appreciation of bad news."

"Get to work," Jason said, logging into the terminal and selecting the slip-com nodes and encryption routines he wanted. He looked at the mission clock, showing under the ship clock on the forward display. Mok's ships would still be at least two days from the rendezvous, and the *Devil* would be at least three and a half thanks to their unplanned detour. He punched in all the addressing data from memory and waited, expecting to see the face of Similan, Mok's consigliere and right-hand man in all matters. Instead, the big boss himself accepted the channel request almost immediately.

"I was just about to try and contact you," the quadrant's most notorious crime lord said brusquely. "We've found trackers on two of our ships. We're dropping everyone out of slip-space and searching the rest."

"Understood," Jacob said. "We haven't found any on this ship yet, but we suspect they're there. It's why I'm reaching out to you. We were hounded by a ConFed agent all the way from the Skaxis System and were brought aboard his ship. It's disguised to look like a tramp freighter, but she looks like a new build."

"What were you doing in Skaxis?" Mok's eyes narrowed.

"This big damn ship you gave me can't land without a massive pain in the ass and leaves a paper trail as long as my leg when I even request a de-orbit," Jason said. "I needed to pick up a strike craft for my crew, and I figured a new buy from a broker we've never used before would be the safest bet. Turns out our agent friend was a step ahead of me."

"I *loaned* you that ship...I did not give it to you," Mok rumbled. "Keep that distinction firmly in the front of your mind while you're flying her. That ship was built to my personal specifications, and I've never even gotten the chance to step foot on her."

"You're missing out," Jason said. "She's nice. Probably much more luxuriously appointed than that com ship you're on right now." A low growl was the only answer he received, so Jason decided to not press any further.

"So, what did your new friend want?" Mok asked. Jason filled him in quickly on the broad strokes. Mok listened without interrupting until Jason was finished. "So, you believe him?"

"He makes a compelling argument, but they all do." Jason shrugged. "This is the usual type of counterintelligence game they like to play. This could be nothing more than a way to get me to lead him right to the rebellion's leadership."

"But you don't think so," Mok said shrewdly.

"It doesn't matter what I think," Jason deflected. His gut instinct had been that the agent had been sincere in what he'd said. "The risk is too great. Even if he's not running an op, that doesn't mean someone isn't using him as bait. If they found out he was having doubts or that his loyalty was wavering, they'd dangle him out in front of us."

"You're getting smarter." Mok nodded. "Or at least you now understand that leaping rashly hasn't always served you well in the past. I agree the risk is too high to accept what he's saying at face value, but that doesn't mean we can't play a little game of our own and see what we might draw out."

"Counter-counterintelligence?" Jason asked. "I feel a headache coming on already."

"Don't worry, my young blunt instrument, now we're getting into *my* area. We'll use your new contact to draw out anyone who might be using him to get to us. For now, clean your—*my*—ship and be at rally point bravo-six in one-hundred and fifty-three hours." The translation matrix in Jason's neural implant handled not only languages, but units of measure. Sometimes it made for some interesting conversions when talking about time or distance.

"Bravo-six," Jason repeated, referring to one of the many pre-arranged rally points they'd set up with the expectation they'd be quickly compromised by ConFed Intel. Most of the ConFed might be a bloated, inefficient, unwieldy bureaucracy, but one underestimated their intelligence service at their own peril. They were fast, ruthless, and given a lot of authority to perform their mission. In the early planning stages, well before the attack on Miressa Prime, Mok had designed their own command structure with the assumption that ConFed Intel would be on them almost immediately.

Mok terminated the channel just as Twingo walked back onto the bridge. He held a dark blue disk about the diameter of a hockey puck and maybe three millimeters thick. He just held it out to Jason without a word.

"Tracker?" Jason asked, taking the device.

"Definitely ConFed. Found it on the SX-5," Twingo said. "We'll need to drop from slip-space to check the *Devil* and pull any of those off her engine emitters."

"How would they get these on without us detecting them?" Jason wondered.

"When we're loitering in an area, especially in a large formation, usually we're only running navigational sensors to keep from bumping into anything big. These get loaded up onto small, stealthy drones and dispersed along a ship's course. Once they fly close enough, it spits these out, and they have limited ability to maneuver and attach themselves to the engines," Twingo said. "The real question is how they got the drones so close to our ships. We were flying nav sensors only, but two ships on overwatch were running full tactical sweeps."

"Traitor in the fleet?" Jason asked. He much preferred a stand-up fight to all the sneaking around and suspecting everyone of selling them out.

"Most likely," Twingo agreed. "This party is made up of mercs and criminals for the most part, excluding the Eshquarian regulars we released." Jason thought about that for a moment. The *Devil's Fortune* had been in Flight Three, the largest grouping of the rebel fleet and the one with most of Mok's ships. Flight One had been the Eshquarian group, and Flight Two had been Kellea's ships, along with a few stragglers.

"I feel like there should be a way to see who the likely culprit was for releasing a tracker drone by looking at the flight data and seeing who was around us at the time," Jason said.

"I can begin that now that my task with the ConFed data core is complete," a soft voice said from behind Jason, causing him to almost jump off the deck.

"Damnit, Lucky! I've asked you to stop sneaking up on me!" The battlesynth just stared at him, not offering any further comment. Jason just sighed. His friend had good days and bad days as his processing matrix struggled to fully integrate itself with the new body they'd stuffed it into. "You finished with the ConFed data? That was fast."

"Not especially so," Lucky said. "Once all the security measures and encryption locks were disabled, it was simply a matter of parsing the raw data. You and Mok installed enough computational power in that hold to manage a Tier Two planet's entire infrastructure, so the work went quickly."

"Cool," Jason said. "Can you give me the thirty-thousand-foot view right now?"

"The ConFed has propped up an entire science division dedicated to developing new types of alloys that incorporate a unique crystalline structure that—"

"Forty thousand feet."

"The ConFed is secretly building manufacturing facilities that have the ability to use quantum—"

"Fifty thousand feet," Jason said. "I almost fell asleep when you said quantum." A visibly frustrated Lucky shifted back and forth on his feet a moment before answering.

"They are building a series of enormous, orbital factories that work in a way that would allow them to build lots of other large things very quickly," he said.

"So, all those objects we saw on the sensor data were actually manufacturing facilities?" Jason asked. "They haven't even started building anything yet?"

"Not according to the data you gave me."

"Have the computers build a searchable database and repackage it into a single transmittable file," Jason said. "I want to send it to one of our off-site servers before we hand it all over to Mok."

"Of course," Lucky said. "After that I will begin going through our flight logs to look for the ship that might have dropped tracker drones."

"You and Kage both are going to work on that...*together*," Jason said, stressing the last word. Lucky stopped but didn't turn around. After a split second, he clomped off the bridge, his footfalls heavier and more petulant than when he'd arrived.

"Why are you messing with him like that?" Twingo asked. "What was with having him explain something three times?"

"You mean besides the fact it's funny to get him all pissed off and bouncing on his feet?" Jason laughed. "Because he's still not fully *there* yet. I'm trying to give him mild stressors in social settings that force him to work on dealing with minor problems without shooting them."

"And you think pretending to be too stupid to understand basic explanations will do it?" Twingo sounded skeptical. Jason just shrugged.

"My perceived stupidity has been one of the cornerstones of our team dynamic for years," he said. "It doesn't bother me—well, except when Kage says it. I actually want to punch him in the face—and it's something familiar and old he can dig back into his memories and examine."

"What if you just piss him off, and he punches you in the chest, collapsing your ribcage?"

"In my paperwork you're set to inherit the *Phoenix*, the hangar, and my house," Jason said.

"But the more I think about it, the more I like it," Twingo said. "Definitely keep at this approach."

"Get down to the hangar. I'm dropping us out of slip-space now."

"I'm gone." Twingo waved over his shoulder.

As it turned out, the *Devil's Fortune* had more than just the two ConFed trackers Twingo found. Despite his assurances otherwise, Mok had installed a couple himself that would allow him to keep tabs on his shiny new corvette-class ship. Jason ordered those kept but put into shielded containers. He felt like there was an opportunity to have fun with them at Mok's expense. All the ConFed trackers they pulled off were analyzed, logged, and destroyed.

"You should reach out to your new ConFed buddy and tell him we found his trackers," Crusher said.

"I know you're just being an asshole, but that's actually not a bad idea," Jason said. "It could be the conversational inroad I need as an excuse to reach out to him."

"Why are you going to talk to him at all?" Doc asked, frowning. "Haven't we spent most of our time trying to avoid ConFed agents?"

"When we were just a bunch of hired guns, sure," Jason said. "But we're playing for bigger stakes now. This might be an advantage we could use."

"Or it could be the thing that brings it all down," Doc argued.

"He already had us in custody," Twingo said. "You know how they usually operate. They don't like to let one target go back into the wild if there's a chance to torture them for information now. He'd have had all of us strapped down to tables while his technicians went to work on us."

The term *technician* when talking about ConFed Intelligence didn't mean someone who worked on their ships or equipment. It referred to a group of merciless torturers agents called in for extractions. They were very good at getting even the toughest being to spill all their secrets, and the subject never survived long once they started.

"These people aren't to be trifled with," Doc said. "Even over the assumed safety of a slip-com channel, they're dangerous."

"I hear you, Doc," Jason said, putting up his hand to shut Twingo up. "I really do. But I think this is worth pursuing, and I want you there with me, sitting off-camera and observing. You can pick up any context I miss since you're just watching the conversation not participating." This seemed to mollify Doc some.

"I can do that," he said, seeming to force the words out.

"You don't want me there?" Kage asked. Jason bit back half a dozen nasty remarks, knowing that's exactly what the little bastard wanted.

"No. You'll be busy with Lucky tracking down our potential turncoat," he said calmly. "In fact, you'd better get to it." Kage narrowed his eyes, not wanting to give up so easy but not able to find another way to bait Jason into an argument.

"When do you want to do this?" Doc asked.

"Now," Jason said. "Let's go. Com suite two."

The pair went up to the command deck and down the short corridor where there were four hatches. Behind each was an isolated, secure room with some of the most sophisticated com equipment money could buy. Suites one and three were just small alcoves, just big enough to two people side-by-side, but two and four were much larger, with plenty of space where Doc could sit comfortably out of the imager's pickup area and listen to what was being said.

"I talked to Twingo about your encounter with this Tulden," Doc said as he pulled one of the padded chairs over to the far bulkhead and sat down. "It seems he is a bit unusual when compared to some of the absolute zealots we've encountered in the past, but—"

"But that doesn't mean it's not an act," Jason finished. "I realize that. I still think it's worth a shot. I should also probably go ahead and tell you Mok wants me to try and cultivate this relationship as well. He thinks we can feed Tulden bad intel and help our own cause."

"Captain, you're...clever...in your own way," Doc said haltingly, "but you're not an intel operative any more than I'm a tactical asset. We each have our talents, and this happens to fall in that area neither of us is very good at."

"Diplomatically put." Jason fired up the terminal and began entering the information for a link from the data card Tulden had slipped him.

While Omega Force might not have been an intelligence unit backed by the quadrant's lone superpower, they were steeped in the criminal underworld and had one of the best code slicers around on their crew. As such, their security measures for establishing a secure slip-com channel were quite similar. It was basically setting up a connection through a series of relay nodes that would mask the location and final address of the com node the user was actually sitting at. Omega Force used a system devised by Kage that would give even the best tracking AI fits if it tried to trace the channel to its source. He assumed Tulden would have something similar in place since the risk of using ConFed assets would be too great, all things considered.

"That's new," he grunted, pointing at one of the monitors for Doc to see. There was a flashing message in Jenovian Standard that let him know an active link was being established. It gave a rough countdown timer to when it might go through, approximately seven minutes in this case, and it also had a designator at the bottom. This worried him a bit. It was obviously a unique designator that was either attached to him personally, since he was calling in using the provided credentials, or to the call, which would mean it was being recorded.

"Perhaps we should kill the imager and scramble your voice," Doc said. Jason thought it over, thinking it probably wasn't a bad idea.

"It probably doesn't matter," he said after another moment of thought. "He might just kill the channel immediately if I'm not here, and if he's recording the conversation, it likely means he has a file somewhere with my name on it anyway."

"I just don't like this," Doc muttered quietly as the monitor changed to a new message indicating that the channel link was almost established.

"Captain Burke," Tulden said as the channel resolved to show the agent sitting in a similar com suite, probably aboard his trawler. "I must say I'm surprised to see you've reached out to me this soon...or at all."

"We pulled off a handful of trackers on our two ships," Jason said, not wasting any time with idle chatter. The longer a channel stayed open, the more likely it would be someone could break in or record the transmission to be decrypted later. "Since you were obviously homing in on us the entire time, I'm hoping you can tell me where they came from. We're assuming your people put one on the corvette-class ship while we were in formation with others from our...social club."

"All I'm willing to tell you at this juncture is what you've likely already guessed yourself: you have traitors in your midst," Tulden said. "The trackers on your smaller ship you've just purchased were put on by the brokerage you used. We have a standing agreement with them to provide such a service if requested. I simply messaged them to tag any ship you bought."

"Nice," Jason said. "So, you have no idea who might be working with you inside our fleet? It'll have to be someone who commands a ship...some pissant tech isn't releasing ConFed tracking hardware out the airlocks without someone spotting them." Tulden hesitated, seemingly torn between wanting to say more and knowing better than to trust Jason too quickly.

"I actually don't know who it is exactly," he said. "That operation is being handled by someone else. They provided me with the tracking codes and let me know your ship was the most likely to be carrying the data core stolen from us. That was based on observations of shuttle traffic within your fleet formation."

"That lines up with what I know," Jason said. "I think I can piece it together from there. You have yourself a nice—"

"Not just yet, Captain," Tulden said. "I believe I have held up my end of the bargain and provided you with information you needed, or at least gave you confirmation of information you already had. Now, it is your turn."

"The thing you want to know about, the thing you asked me on your ship? It calls itself the Machine," Jason said, his voice low as if he was afraid the Machine could hear him. Given they were speaking over networked communications systems, it very well could be listening, and they'd never know.

"The Machine," Tulden repeated. "Sounds melodramatic enough."

"But apt," Jason said. "It's not a physical being. It's an AI program that hitched a ride back from beyond the border worlds on one of your battleships."

"If I wasn't already becoming adept at reading your species, I'd swear you were lying to me, Captain. An AI couldn't possibly be doing all this by—"

"This one can," Jason interrupted. "And is. This isn't like any Kheprian adaptive AI you've ever dealt with, agent. This is an ancient being that had been lying dormant when it was awoken and made aware of our region of space. It's also insane."

"Insane," Tulden deadpanned.

"Or corrupted. Whatever technical jargon you want to use, the end result is the same; the thing isn't stable. I don't know what it wants or why it's taken over your government, but I do know there are only a few types of computer systems in the quadrant that it can run its full matrix on. Our latest intel suggests it has engineers on Khepri designing and building more compatible systems for it to propagate itself to."

"We're at the time limit to safely keep talking on this channel," Tulden said. "I will be in touch as I try to verify this information for myself."

"Be careful," Jason warned. "It is completely ruthless, and it can't be taken by surprise. Don't call it by its name anywhere near a public Nexus. It listens for references to itself, and it'll be a quick way for you to punch your own ticket, if you take my meaning." Tulden looked shaken but didn't respond as he reached over and killed the channel. Jason also backed completely out of his own relay network and shut down the com node on his end.

"He's not what I expected," Doc said. "I think you screwed up giving him that much information about the Machine, but you already knew I'd say that."

"I did," Jason said. "And I don't completely disagree with you, but we'll need to take leaps of faith from time to time."

"If he starts poking around too clumsily, and the Machine realizes its existence is no longer a secret, it may attack before we're ready," Doc said.

"Fair point," Jason conceded. "For right now, let's just focus on the things we can control."

"The traitor in our fleet?"

"Exactly."

8

Tulden paced the bridge of his ship. He was unsettled around the crew, though all of them were loyal *Sepezz*, the official name for the ConFed's notorious intelligence service. The *Mogotrev*-class trawler he was aboard had been assigned to him by the directorate, but the ship wasn't entirely under his command. The captain was still in charge of shipboard operations, and Tulden couldn't get a read on her to determine how much he should keep hidden and how much she could see and know to be discreet.

Agents worked with almost complete autonomy, and no trawler captain would ever assume she was privy to the same level of information he was, but there was still a risk that, if he began acting *too* outside the norms, she would report it to her superiors. It was a part of the *chain of accountability* the directorate preached but rarely followed. They maintained control over such a vast organization with so many highly-trained, independent thinkers by encouraging them to tattle on their peers whenever something seemed off. Tulden had been the subject of two directorate tribunals when his actions had been brought to their attention. Fortunately, both times, he had been working to execute their orders, and he not only avoided prosecution, he'd received commendations.

Captain Burke contacting him so soon after their meeting had surprised him. His recent interaction with humans had been a mixed bag. One had been a fellow intelligence operative who had double crossed him and tortured him to the brink of death, leaving his face crisscrossed with deep, angry scars the agency surgeons were still working on fixing. The other had been a young military officer in a forward recon unit that had been as earnest as he was naive. Against all odds, the latter killed the former, and now Tulden cultivated a relationship with the young officer, his instincts telling him the boy might be a bigger player in the region than anyone expected.

Burke was an enigma all his own. Tulden had read reports on the human thanks to some of the more notorious company he kept. Crusher, the name the Guardian Archon of Galvetor went by, was hard to miss. Kage, the name one of the quadrants most prolific code slicers had adopted for himself, also ran with Burke's crew. Crusher was an easy one to figure out. He was immature and resented responsibility, so he was hiding from his station in life by playing mercenary. Kage was harder to get a read on. The code slicer could be wealthy beyond all measure by offering his services to one of the bigger organized crime syndicates or striking out on his own, but he stuck with Burke the whole time, minus a short stint in a Veran prison.

"Is there something you needed, sir?" the captain asked, her demeanor crisp and professional.

"I'm sorry, Captain, I had not heard you come up here," Tulden said. "I was merely observing."

"Of course, sir."

"How long until we reach our destination, Captain?"

"One hundred and eleven more flight hours, sir," she said, clearly confused. "We can increase slip-velocity if—"

"That will be fine," Tulden said. Her stiff demeanor and unreadable expression made him yearn for the days when he had his own ship. The directorate had told him the use of the trawler was a *reward* for exemplary service, but he was beginning to have his doubts about that. Perhaps it was time he made alternate travel arrangements and got out from under any potential Directorate Internal Security observers stashed away aboard the trawler.

"I will be in my suite if I'm needed," he said.

"Yes, sir."

He walked the corridors of the small ship towards his assigned quarters, a plan forming in his mind. It was time to call in some old favors and drop out of sight for a while. What Captain Burke had told him about their potential foe had shaken him badly, but he needed more than the word of some merc gunfighter when it came to mobilizing resources.

At least now he had a place to start. If this thing, this...*Machine* relied on operating in the shadows to hold onto its power, then Tulden's course of action was obvious. Expose it for what it was and let the inevitable happen once everyone realized how they'd been fooled.

"I have finished my analysis of the ships in our previous formation if you are done actively trying to avoid me."

"Lucky, I'm not avoiding you," Jason groaned.

"I believe you are."

"You're entitled to believe whatever you want, but I'm not avoiding you. This ship isn't *that* big, and you've been sequestered in your little dungeon down there chewing through decryption routines." Jason hoped his poker face was more convincing than when he actually played poker. While he hadn't been actually avoiding his friend, the truth was somewhere in that gray area that made his answer not completely honest.

"You are unconvincing. There was recently a ground operation, and you took Crusher and Twingo, but not me. I normally—"

"There was a suspected ConFed Intel trawler in the area," Jason cut him off. "I wanted you here in case they tried to board. I took Twingo because I needed an engineer. Are *you* an expert on looking over a starship and determining spaceworthiness?"

"Yes."

Shit.

"Nevertheless," Jason said, wanting to end the conversation before it became uncomfortable for them both, "I needed Twingo with me, I needed you here. I really feel like that should be the end of the story."

"What are you not saying to me, Captain?" Lucky asked softly.

"What makes you think—"

"Jason...please. I need to know what's going on."

There it was. Lucky was going to push the issue, and there was no easy way for Jason to avoid the conversation he hadn't wanted to have with his friend until he could sort it all out in his own head.

"Do you remember all the details of your mission when you went alone on that Eshquarian ship?" he asked, bracing himself for the things he was about to say.

"Of course, I do," Lucky said. "My memory is functioning perfectly."

"When the Eshquarians reclaimed the ship, they found some bodies stashed in some fairly creative places," Jason pressed on. "They'd all been killed with precision and in ways that wouldn't have alerted the crew. In and of itself, that wouldn't have bothered me. We've all killed in the course of accomplishing a mission, and I certainly won't lose any sleep if you popped a couple private contractors to keep your cover."

"It was necessary," Lucky said.

"Perhaps," Jason said. "I don't second guess my crew...normally. But let's move on to when we raided that parts depot. Those were just regular troops doing a job."

"And?"

"And Crusher went up to where you had moved ahead and saw bodies strewn all about. He said it was clear you'd killed them, and it was just as obvious it wasn't necessary. I was telling the truth when I said I hadn't been avoiding you, but these incidents are giving me second thoughts about using you in a tactical capacity right now. You were never one to indulge in needless violence or to—" Jason couldn't finish his sentence because an armored hand had shot out and closed on his throat. His eyes bulged from his head in surprise as Lucky lifted him from the ground.

"YOU ARE TRYING TO PUSH ME AWAY!" the battlesynth roared, his voice deafening in the confined of the corridor. "I WILL NOT LET YOU TAKE MY FAMILY FROM ME!"

Lucky's hand tightened, and Jason saw flashes swimming in his vision. He didn't have long, and he knew trying to match his feeble biotic strength against Lucky's powerful actuators was pointless. He dropped his hand to his right thigh and drew the sidearm he habitually wore even when on his own ship. It was a smallish plasma pistol designed not to burn through bulkheads or hull plating, so it wouldn't do much against Lucky...but it was all he had.

He pulled the pistol around in front of him, intent on aiming up into the bottom of Lucky's chin and hope he didn't get splattered with deflected plasma. His vision tunneled, and his right arm wouldn't do what he told it. It was too late. Lucky was going to kill him. His finger tightened on the trigger reflexively, and the corridor exploded into sparks and smoke as the plasma bolt slammed into both Lucky's left foot and the deck.

Jason felt himself fall and collapse to the deck in a heap. His vision cleared as oxygenated blood resumed its trip to his brain. He was vaguely aware he'd landed on part of the melted deck and the smell of cooking meat wasn't an indicator of a stroke...he was actually cooking. When he looked at Lucky, trying to bring the pistol to bear again while his muddled mind tried to compartmentalize what had just happened, the battlesynth just raised his hands and stepped away. Even with the deployed facial armor, Lucky looked...stricken? Shocked? He certainly wasn't as aggressive as he'd been a moment ago.

As Jason struggled to his feet, Lucky fled. When Jason tried to follow, his wobbly legs gave out, and he splayed out on the deck again, groaning.

"Lucky!" he tried to yell, but his damaged throat wouldn't make any noise. He almost didn't hear the heavy footfalls coming from behind him or the strong hands rolling him over onto his back.

"What the hell is all this?!" Crusher demanded. "You get drunk and accidentally shoot a hole in the deck? How typical. Whenever *I* have a little mishap, all I hear is about how it's *'coming out of my cut'* or that I'm *'too reckless.'* But, apparently, it's completely fine when the captain does it." Mercifully, Jason passed out before Crusher could really get a head of steam going.

"How do you feel?" Doc asked.

"Not bad actually," Jason said, looking around the *Devil's* well-appointed infirmary. "How long have I been out?"

"A full day. The damage to your trachea and spine was severe enough I had you sedated. So...what happened?"

"I must have fell and—"

"Not in the mood, Captain," Doc said. "I know exactly what caused that injury, and I know you didn't accidentally fire a weapon on the command deck. Lucky's hands are quite distinctive, you know."

"Where is he?" Jason asked.

"Locked himself back in the server room," Doc said. "He scrambled the hatch codes and disabled both the intercom and internal security systems."

"Who else knows about this?"

"Just me. I decided since he had quarantined himself, I'd wait for you to wake up and decide what you wanted to do about it." Doc leaned back in the white padded chair he'd pulled next to the bed. Jason closed his eyes for a moment, remembering the terror he'd felt when Lucky had grabbed him. The crushing pain in his neck, the roaring of the modulated voice...

When he opened his eyes again, he was trembling.

"I-I don't know what to do," Jason said. "This is Lucky. He's one of us, and something is wrong, but I don't know what, and he's too dangerous to try and approach."

"You can't just leave him locked in a cargo hold," Doc pointed out. "And he's not answering anybody."

"What would you do?"

"If Lucky attacked and almost killed me?" Doc asked, blowing out a breath and spinning his chair to face the infirmary hatch. "I guess I don't know, either. His new body has reached full-integration stage, so there's no practical way to shut him down until we can find out if something has gone wrong. He's too powerful to contain, and I think that sends the wrong message anyway. In the end, like you said, he's one of us, and regardless of the risks, we're going to have to try and reach him."

"Agreed," Jason said, swinging his legs over the bed. His neck was still very sore and once his head was off the pillow and supported by the muscles, he winced in agony. "What the hell, Doc? No painkillers?"

"Oh, right," Doc said absently and pressed a programmable hypospray to Jason's upper arm, pressing and holding as the device dispensed the prescribed drugs. "This will hold you over until the nanobots finish repairing all the blood vessels, but you can go back to your own quarters and rest. What do you want me to tell the crew?"

"Crusher already thinks I got drunk and fell while wildly brandishing a loaded weapon," Jason said. "I suppose we're pretty much committed to going with that." Doc just nodded.

"It's a completely believable story, so nobody will ask too many questions—"

"Hey!"

"—and by the time we reach our rendezvous, it'll all be healed up."

Jason hobbled back to his own quarters, thankfully avoiding anybody in the corridors. He locked the hatch and activated the formidable security measures Mok had ordered installed. It was doubtful it would keep out a determined battlesynth, but Jason figured it would give him some sort of warning if Lucky was trying to come through to finish him off. He went to a wall locker and pulled out one of his short-barreled railguns, checked the loadout, and placed it by his bed. He questioned how smart it was to leave the rest of the crew in the dark if Lucky had indeed turned homicidal on them, but the battlesynth had seemed pretty focused on Jason and hadn't caused any trouble while he was in the infirmary.

He decided to keep the rest of them out of it...for now. Once he told them, if he hadn't come up with a solution to help Lucky in the meantime, he would almost have no choice but to kick Lucky off the ship and out of the crew...or even something more permanent if he felt the battlesynth was a threat to the civilian population. Just the idea of such an action—even after the incident earlier—sent waves of anxiety crashing over him. Once he was rested up, he needed to come up with a workable plan, and fast.

The last thought he had as the narcotics kicked in was how sad a state of affairs it was that he had to barricade himself in his own quarters, on his own ship—sort of—just so one of his own crewmates didn't murder him in his sleep.

"Actually, now that I think about it, this is the third time something like this has happened," he slurred before slipping into unconsciousness.

9

Lucky

"—and by the time we reach our rendezvous, it'll all be healed up."

I switched off the intercom channel that allowed me to listen in on Jason and Doc. I am relieved Jason was not permanently damaged, but the feeling is hollow. There is something wrong with me. Why did I kill all those people who were trying to surrender in the parts depot? Why did I almost just kill my captain and closest friend?

I do not know.

Every hour I feel like something is gathering at the edges of my awareness, pressing in on me. Sometimes, it gets in. When I try to access the specialized powers of this new body, I can feel my defenses falter, and instincts that are not my own guide my actions. When I was first awoken in this strange place, my friends told me this next generation body had been one of several types that had been in the secret laboratory they had raided. Given its smaller stature and unique camouflaging technology, they had assumed it was an infiltration and reconnaissance unit. I have come to believe this body was meant for something else...that it is making *me* something else.

An assassin.

The espionage game has been dominated by microscopic machines and signal snoopers for so long, it had not seemed likely that Khepri would design and build a battlesynth that could mimic another being just for the purpose of gathering information. As my new body drove me to kill coldly and efficiently whenever I tapped into its power, I suspected its real purpose. A battlesynth that could look and sound like anyone could be deployed against high-value targets without the telltale mess of micro-drone assassinations or the crudeness of a kinetic strike. Discreet, precise eliminations...a government with a few hundred just like me could destabilize a regional power in a matter of weeks.

This left me with some uncomfortable realities I must face. I had tried to deny what might be happening to me for some time but attacking Jason Burke has changed all that. I cannot be trusted to be around my friends. I am dangerous. The only choice left to me is to leave and try to figure out if my urges can be controlled or, ideally, eliminated altogether. It is something I have to do alone. The others will neither understand nor agree with me, so I will need to be discreet.

Fortunately, being discreet comes natural to an assassin.

"Where the hell is Lucky?" Crusher grumbled for the tenth time that day alone.

"He's working in his lab, and he asked to not be disturbed," Jason said. "Given how much you're annoying all of us right now, I have to assume he meant from you."

"Mok's ships are here," Kage said.

"The ship you pegged as being our likely traitor?" Jason asked.

"Bracketing it now on your tactical display," Kage said. "It's the light cruiser that's second to last in the trailing delta formation."

Jason eyed the cruiser on his display as the *Devil's Fortune* fired her main engines and surged into the deserted system towards the loose formation of rebel ships. It looks like any other ship in Mok's eclectic private fleet, no helpful, illuminated signs saying: "Here we are! We sold you out!" But according to the analysis done by Kage and Lucky, this ship was the only one that would have been in position to drop off the small ConFed drones that deployed slip-space trackers on their engine baffles.

Despite their suspicions and Jason's confidence in his team's ability to reach the right answer by looking at the sensor data, they still didn't have a plan. Most of those ships belonged to Mok...not Blazing Sun, but Mok personally. The crime lord was rightly paranoid about uprisings within his own organization and fielded one of the largest private militaries in the quadrant. The amount of wealth Mok poured into his own protection made Jason's head swim. And, in the end, they'd probably still get him anyway. It was just the nature of the life he'd chosen.

Since opening fire to disable it while still at a safe distance would only draw the fire of all the other ships in the formation, Jason had to figure out some pretense to board the cruiser. Not having Lucky available was a major setback when planning a boarding assault. It would be down to just him and Crusher, and Jason had left his heavy armor back aboard the *Phoenix*. The odds of the pair of them being able to get to an airlock, force their way aboard, and then subdue the crew were slim.

"Okay...tell Mok I want a face-to-face," Jason said. "Make up some bullshit about only showing him the data in person. Once he's over here, we can make our case for why I should be allowed to open fire on one of his ships."

"So...no raid?" Crusher asked, sounding mournful. The pack of weapons he'd brought up from the armory slipped from his hand and dropped to the deck with a clatter.

"What were you going to do with all of that?" Kage asked.

"I just wanted to be ready," Crusher said defensively.

"There will be plenty of shooting," Jason promised him. "I just want to get an advantage before we go. Mok escorting us to the airlock will do nicely."

"Why is there a hole burned in the deck!?"

"I need you to focus, Mok," Jason said. "You're a powerful executive. You need to think large to small. Whoever might have accidentally discharged a weapon on the command deck is small detail stuff."

"There is never an interaction with you where I don't regret that we ever met," Mok said softly through clenched teeth.

"Let's get some Terran coffee in you, and you'll forget all about that little blaster hole that Twingo will patch and make good as new," Jason said. "This way to the—"

"I know where it is!" Mok snapped. "I designed the damn ship!"

Jason just smiled and followed Mok into the command deck conference room, a spacious room with gorgeous wood paneling that was stained a rich, dark brown. The oval, stone-topped table dominated the center of the room and sat in a pool of light, the rest of the room kept dramatically dim. It was a powerful room, meant for a powerful being to hold court and make sure the people they had invited to the table were suitably awed. Mok breezed in and sat down at one of the narrow ends of the oval, allowing Jason to take the head. Jason nodded to him, acknowledging the gesture of respect given the ship's current captain. Mok might be a hardened criminal, but he had manners.

"Where is Lucky?" Mok asked, accepting an oversized mug of Terran coffee from Doc—couldn't be called Earth coffee since it was grown on S'Tora—and couldn't help but smile as the aroma reached his nose.

"Lucky's indisposed," Jason said, trying to sound casual. "He's in that computer lab we set up in one of the cargo holds, working on another side project."

"So, why am I here? By the way...if you send a sizeable amount of this drink with me back to my ship, I might be inclined to forget you blasted a hole in my deck. What's it called again? It's not tea, I know that."

"Done," Jason said, smiling again. "And it's called coffee. It's brewed the same way as chroot grounds." The fact he owned the Rocky Mountain Coffee Company was a loosely kept secret that Mok never really seemed to be consciously aware of. Jason presented him with the stuff as a gift, and Mok always raved over it, completely unaware that Jason was basically just giving him free stock from his own warehouses.

"Thanks," Mok said, seemingly calmed down enough for Jason to send him back through the roof with the news he had.

"You have a traitor in your fleet." Jason dove into it. "We've been able to determine that one of your light cruisers, one that's here with us right now, released stealthy tracker drones that tagged all of our ships."

"How did you come by this?" Mok asked, still calm.

"Information exchange with a ConFed intel agent named Tulden. He used one of the trackers to intercept us."

"What information did you offer in exchange?"

"He wanted to know the nature of the thing that's taken control of the ConFed," Jason said. "Apparently, there's dissention in the ranks. I gave him the broadest of strokes, only that the Machine was a sentient, hyper-intelligent AI that came from beyond the ConFed's borders."

"I know of this Tulden," Mok said. "He's an oddity among agents due to his preference to accomplish his mission without the trail of bodies and wreckage most leave behind. I'm inclined to believe he approached you in earnest and not as an effort to entrap you."

"My thoughts as well, although I don't have any insider knowledge of the guy," Jason said. "I figure if someone bothers to grab me, there's already plenty they can pin on me that they don't need to bother with games or bargains."

"So, which of my ship captains has betrayed me?" Mok asked.

"Doc," Jason said. Doc activated the holographic projectors, and a real-time representation of all their ships appeared over the center of the table. The culprit was highlighted with a rotating red sphere.

"The *Hein*," Mok sighed. "Of course."

"Friend?" Doc asked.

"Family relation," Mok said. "Captain Hyst is related to me through pairing of a distant cousin, but it's still family."

"How big is his crew?" Crusher asked.

"I'm not sending you over there to slaughter *her* crew until I can determine who is responsible," Mok declared firmly. "What *I* am going to do is return to my ship and— Wait, what's happening? Is this live?"

"It's real-time," Jason frowned. Within the hologram the *Hein* began listing badly to port and dropped out of the formation. The representation was so good that Jason could make out tiny plumes of flame belching from holes near where the engineering spaces probably were. "Interesting."

"Get me a report on what's happening to the *Hein*... NOW!" Mok barked, but not at the Omega crew. He was yelling into his com unit and storming out of the room, Crusher and Kage hot on his heels to see if they could find out any details.

"Captain, I'm getting an alert that a maintenance airlock is... open?" Twingo stared at his tablet computer and fluttered his ears in confusion. "The time stamp on the cycle is from almost an hour ago, but it just now alerted me. It looks like the outer hatch is hanging wide open."

Jason frowned at that, about to order Crusher down to make sure nobody had snuck over with Mok and boarded through the ventral maintenance airlock, but something nagged at his mind about the time stamp code. He looked at the tiny holographic burning *Hein*, and his eyes widened as realization slapped him. By the look on Doc's face, he'd already figured it out for himself.

"Oh, shit," he whispered.

10

Getting out of the *Devil's Fortune* undetected had been easy. As the Second Officer, Lucky had access to all the necessary security protocols that allowed him to bypass the alarms on the ventral maintenance hatch. He also made sure to temporarily disable all the ship's internal security and tracking systems so he could move about undetected. Once he was out on the hull, all he had to do was wait while the *Devil* drifted closer to Mok's ships before activating his stealth countermeasures and pushing off towards the ship they'd identified as the likely source of the tracker drones.

His sensors picked out Mok's shuttle heading towards the *Devil* when he was only one hundred meters from his objective. The timing would be close, but he needed to be done with his task before the others realized he was missing or Mok went back to his own ship. He decelerated hard and hit the hull of the light cruiser with a barely-felt jolt, just aft of the portside airlock.

This was another auxiliary airlock like the one he'd left on his own ship, not the main airlock further forward that could dock to other ships. The small hatch he stood over was meant to give access from the engineering bays to the port engine nacelle for normal inspections and emitter alignments. Lucky stooped down and let his optics rove over the locking mechanism and the recessed control panel. It was a common enough unit, and his database held detailed files on how to overcome it without resorting to brute force. He used his integrated cutting laser on his right arm to cut through the hull plating ten centimeters below the access panel. The hole he created was just large enough for him to get his hand inside, reach over to the backside of the panel, and pull off the connector.

The locks disengaged, and the hatch exploded outward as the air inside the lock escaped in a cloud of vapor, swinging wildly on its hinge. Lucky wasted no time slipping inside and closing the hatch after him. He manually reengaged the mechanical locks, and the airlock automatically pressurized again. Once the air pressure had equalized, he drew into his mind what he wanted to do. This would be the first time he'd attempted this with only a physical scan and voice print, not a neural implant download.

"I am Saditava Mok," Mok's voice came from Lucky's mouth as his holographic generators fired up and completed the illusion he was the stocky crime lord. His plan was that when the crew came to investigate the alarm they undoubtedly received on the bridge about one of their external hatch controllers losing power, they'd peek into the airlock and see the big boss himself standing there. Hopefully, in their confusion, they'd open the much more secure inner hatch and let him walk right in.

"S-sir?" a timid voice came over the intercom. "How... What are you—"

"I will explain everything once I'm aboard," Lucky/Mok said. "Please, open the hatch."

"I... Sir, I need to wait for Captain—"

"I said open it! Now!" Lucky shouted, slamming his palm into the hatch. He made sure to not hit it where the young crewman could see the hologram waver where his hand made contact. "If you do not open this hatch immediately, I will have you killed the moment your captain comes down and opens it anyway."

The crewman looked like he might die of fright. Not all the crews in Mok's private fleet were made up of hardened killers. Most were simply skilled spacers from merchant fleets who either had criminal backgrounds or flexible morals that allowed them to serve on an unaffiliated warship for better pay. The one on the other side of the hatch, a junior technician according to the visible security tab on his shirt, looked back and forth before keying in a code sequence on the panel to disengage the locks. The hatch popped open a few centimeters with a meaty *thunk*.

"Close it! Close that damn hatch! Don't let it aboard!!" someone screamed from a side corridor out of Lucky's field of view. The technician, to his credit, tried to shove the hatch closed again, but it was too late. Lucky kicked it so hard that it flew open and launched the crewman across the airlock antechamber with enough force that when he hit the wall there was little doubt he'd died on impact.

Now that he was aboard, Lucky disengaged his mimic mode and switched over to full combat mode. His eyes blazed a brilliant crimson, and his powerplant surged, routing energy to his weapons and tactical systems. *This* was familiar to him. He felt a faint whiff of nostalgia as he stepped into view of the armed crewmembers rushing down the corridor. Apparently, the sensors had not been fooled by the hologram of his mimic mode, and they knew he wasn't Mok and had come ready to do battle with whatever was trying to force its way aboard their ship.

"What *are* you?!"

Lucky didn't answer. He raised both arms and opened fire with the double-cannons in each. The four barrels spat out plasma bolts at a high rate of fire as he charged down the corridor towards the defenders. They were disciplined enough to return fire, but the shots either splashed harmlessly against the battlesynth's armor or missed altogether. Lucky's precise fire, however, did neither. In less than a few seconds, he mowed down the six crew who had foolishly funneled themselves into a kill box with no cover and no escape.

He stepped over the smoking bodies, stopping at the last one. It was still breathing. Lucky reached down and ripped the security tab from its shirt and read it: Xi Hyst, Captain. So, the captain herself had come down with the defenders when she saw they were being boarded. Brave, but stupid. Now, the crew was leaderless, and the enemy was still aboard and moving through her ship at will.

"Who...sent...you?" Hyst whispered.

"Saditava Mok knows you have betrayed him," Lucky said, stretching the truth a bit. "He knows you have been turned by ConFed Intel."

"How could he know? We..." before she could finish her sentence, her head lolled over, and her last breath rattled from her damaged lungs. Lucky looked at the body a moment longer, and then proceeded on.

He moved quickly to the ship's main engineering bay, killing the crew in there before they could mount any sort of defense. There had still not been any general alarms or further groups of armed crew. The captain's mad rush down to her death meant the rest of the ship was now in a state of utter confusion. After sealing the forward hatches shut, Lucky went to the powerplant's main control panel and interfaced with it directly, plugging into the data port and letting his dedicated intrusion sub-matrix do its thing.

By the time he had overridden all the safety measures and canceled any alarms that would tell the crew what he was up to, he was just starting to hear someone banging on the hatch and yelling unintelligibly. He felt a pang of remorse for having slaughtered the crew when it was obvious they'd had no chance to defend themselves. Or did he? Maybe in his previous life he would have felt remorse, and that's what he was remembering...just the echo of a feeling.

The scripts he needed to program into the system were easy, and the computer accepted them without as much as a warning. Lucky started his timer, locked out the terminal, and moved quickly to exit the bay through the aft hatchway that would lead him to the ship's small hangar bay. The manifest he'd read while programming the powerplant scripts said there were two Alerra-class combat shuttles in there. The Alerra was an Eshquarian gun boat, the smallest you could buy that still had a full-range slip-drive, and it would fit his needs perfectly.

"Hey! You can't be in here!" Lucky ignored the tech shouting at him and walked over to the hangar bay door controls. It took him a moment to figure out how the captain's security tab worked but, as he'd assumed, the tab gave him the authorization to command the doors open.

"I'm talking to you! Whatever you are, you can't—" The tech made the mistake of approaching too close and putting their hand on Lucky's shoulder. The battlesynth spun and punched the tech in the thorax hard enough to crush it and leave a massive indentation where the organs beneath had collapsed. The tech fell to the ground. Dead.

Lucky paid the body no mind as he walked over to the first Alerra and checked its loadout. It was fully fueled and armed, so he didn't waste time looking at the other. He performed an abbreviated preflight, and then powered up the shuttle's small reactor, hoping to get clear of the cruiser before the crew realized where he'd gone.

Ping! Ping-ping!

Small arms fire bounced off the shuttle's hull as two crewmembers rushed out of a hatch on the mezzanine above and opened fire. There was no risk to the craft, so Lucky ignored it and eased the shuttle out of the cradle and backed it slowly out of the yawning bay and into open space. Just as the nose cleared the electrostatic barrier that held in the atmosphere, the cruiser lurched. It rolled ponderously to port and began to yaw, a gout of fire billowing from the starboard exhaust ports pushing her off course.

Ignoring the havoc he'd wreaked, Lucky engaged the drive and sped away from the formation as the other cruisers broke away. The local com jammed with panicked chatter as people simultaneously asked the stricken ship what was wrong while they also tried to get their own ships clear. He looked to his left, and his optics focused so he could just barely see the *Devil's Fortune* as she floated on a parallel course. Pangs of regret and genuine hurt hit him as the enormity of what he was about to do really hit home.

"I am sorry, Captain," he said aloud, "but there is no other way. It is not safe for me to be with you anymore."

He reached over pulled the lever to engage the slip-drive, meshing-out of the system and away from the only family he'd ever known.

"It's utter chaos over there right now," Mok said. "Nobody knows who is in charge, and they keep babbling about some intruder who rigged the reactor to vent. I have crews going over now to try and stabilize the situation."

"Make sure they're crews absolutely loyal to you," Jason said. "We don't know what happened over there, but we still strongly suspect the ship's crew is working for the ConFed. In fact, the sooner we leave this system, the better."

"Right now, we're just worrying about not losing the ship." Mok snarled at him before turning back to his com unit. "Yes, I'm listening."

"What'd you find?" Jason asked quietly as Doc came back into the room.

"The cargo bay hatch was unlocked, Lucky is nowhere to be found on the ship," Doc whispered while Mok shouted at his underlings through the com unit. "Twingo and Kage are trying to piece together what happened, but I think it's a safe assumption he went over to that ship and caused all the damage."

"The question is, is he still over there?" Jason asked. "I feel like we sort of owe it to Mok to not send more of his people into a potential slaughter."

"People on that ship are answering him, and they're not indicating they're still under attack," Doc said. "Maybe—"

"Captain Burke, is there something you'd like to make me aware of?" Mok asked loudly, causing Jason to jump.

"Such as?"

"Such as why my people over there are reporting that what they think was a combat bot somehow boarded the ship, killed the captain and about a third of the crew, and then stole a shuttle," Mok said. "Where is Lucky?"

"Probably aboard that shuttle," Jason sighed. "There have been some...issues."

"What kind of issues?" Crusher rumbled, stepping forward and crossing his massive arms over his chest. Doc looked to Jason, who just shrugged and motioned for him to go on.

"When you found the captain on the deck and brought him down to the infirmary, he wasn't drunk," Doc said. "Lucky attacked and nearly killed him. Jason shot the deck during the struggle. Afterwards, Lucky locked himself in that cargo hold with all the computers and wouldn't respond to any calls over the intercom. We'd decided at the time to keep it quiet until we could figure out what to do about the incident. Apparently, Lucky has decided for himself."

"So, he attacked my ship just to get a shuttle and escape?" Mok asked. Everyone else in the galley just stared at Jason in shocked silence after Doc's story.

"No...he probably attacked your ship so we could go over there and discover all the ConFed hardware aboard her," Jason said. "If he just wanted a ship, there's a brand-new Jepsen SX-5 sitting in the hangar of this ship."

"Then we'd better get over there," Mok said, pointing to Crusher and Jason. "You two can ride over with me."

They had just enough time to grab something from the armory and get to Mok's shuttle that was still docked to their starboard airlock. As soon as the hatch slammed shut, the pilot disengaged the docking clamps and used the maneuvering jets to push the small craft away from the corvette. Jason had a chance to look over the *Devil's Fortune* through the small window. It really was one damn fine ship. Her sleek lines and burnished copper accents showed well under the brilliant exterior lights.

"You're going to fight me to get that ship back, aren't you?" Mok said with resignation as he watched Jason's face.

"Excuse me?"

"I can see when a captain is smitten," Mok said. "I just lent you that ship because it was all I had available close by and your gunship was torn to shreds. Now, I'm seeing that might have been a mistake. You've already named her, bought support ships, and generally made yourself at home."

"You're saying you picked all that up from the look on my face just now?" Jason asked. "I think you might be reaching." Crusher just snorted but, thankfully, didn't toss his two cents in.

They rode the rest of the way to the stricken cruiser in silence. The crew had managed to shut the main reactor down, so it was no longer blasting out plasma through the auxiliary exhaust vent. The backup systems had mostly arrested the tumble she'd been tossed into, but the ship was still drifting away from the other ships in the formation at a decent clip. Jason could understand why the other captains didn't want to bring in their own ships to assist just yet, worried the cruiser might be rigged to explode or have a hostile crew aboard, but he was worried that, if this ship did have ConFed sympathizers, they almost certainly already reported their position.

"Docking complete, sir," the pilot called over the intercom. "Your personal security detail from your ship is already aboard and waiting for you on the other side of the airlock."

"We won't be long," Mok said, motioning for Crusher and Jason to follow him.

The interior of the cruiser was as chaotic as Jason assumed it would be. The smell of burnt metal and ozone filled the air, and wisps of smoke would occasionally stream from the environmental ducts. Crewmembers were scrambling about in confusion as there was apparently a lack of direction and leadership coming from the bridge with the loss of the captain.

"Let's get to the cargo bays," Jason shouted over the din. "We're not engineers or techs so we'll just be in the way up here. Let's get the evidence we need and get gone. If this ship is what I think it is, you might not want to spend too much time here. Isn't there a sizable reward for your arrest?"

"Your point is well taken, Captain," Mok said. "This way."

He passed a few terse instructions to the nine members of his personal guard, all dressed in black armor and carrying powerful weapons, and the entire procession moved aft towards the storage areas and hangar bay. Jason knew the drones that the ConFed used to deploy their trackers wasn't something so small it could be easily hidden, and it would also need to be somewhere close to an external hatch large enough to get it off the ship. On a light cruiser not designed to operate it, that meant the hangar bay was the only logical place.

They passed two areas where Lucky's handiwork was apparent. Bodies were still strewn about one corridor, some were covered, others were not. Mok stopped to point out the bodies of the ship's captain and first officer on their way into an engineering area where an airlock inner hatch had apparently been kicked out of its frame. It dangled precariously by one hinge, and the edges around the sealing surfaces were mushroomed out.

"I'm guessing this is where he made entry," Crusher deadpanned, taking in the carnage around the room.

"The reports I got were that someone claimed *I* was in the airlock and a technician opened the locks on my order," Mok said. "Apparently, there is video showing this, but they've not sent it to me yet."

"Lucky's new body has a mimic mode," Jason said. "He could make himself look like you to a degree that would fool anybody except those closest to you. He probably picked your form because he knew it would cause maximum confusion and let him get aboard."

"He really attacked you?" Crusher asked. "Like a for-real attack and not just messing around?"

"If I hadn't got a shot off and made him pause so he could regain his senses, I have no doubt he'd have popped my head off." Jason rubbed at his neck where his friend's armored hand had crushed it. "He seemed to have some sort of break with reality, thought I was trying to edge him off the crew."

"Damn," Crusher said quietly. "That could have been bad."

"I feel like it still was."

"I meant bad for the rest of us."

"Sir, the forward team has found something," one of Mok's guards said. "It's in the secondary hold right off the hangar bay. The Second Officer is there with them."

They rushed through the corridor until they came to a small cargo bay that looked like it was used as a staging area before things were loaded onto the shuttles. Jason could see right away that two of the large, matte black machines sitting on wheeled carts were more than likely the drones they were looking for.

"Explain," Mok demanded.

"I-I-I've never—"

"Take five seconds to calm yourself, and then tell me what this is," Mok said in a tone that would likely not calm the officer down at all.

"This area was restricted to everyone but the captain, sir," the second officer said. "I can show you the written orders telling us to keep clear of it. Not even the first officer had any idea what was in there. We just figured it was a side venture the captain had going, moving a little cargo off the books."

"Provide my people with those orders," Mok said. "This couldn't have been just the captain's doing. Someone had to work on these drones, and then launch them. Review the records and find out if there were times the hangar bay was ordered evacuated, and then tell me by whom."

"Yes, sir." The officer seemed to deflate with relief.

"Two of my personal guards will...assist you," Mok said. It was said conversationally, but the meaning of his words was clear to all who heard them. Nobody on that ship was to be trusted, and any further shenanigans would not be tolerated.

"We're really running up on a time limit here," Jason said. "There's no way the captain didn't report where we were. She may have done it before we even got here."

"Have my shuttle take you back to your ship and get clear," Mok said. "We'll have this cleaned up shortly. I have a feeling I'll be detaining this crew and having the ship moved back to one of my bases. Damnit! I don't need this right now. I've got to get back and be visible to the organization or people will begin to talk...and plot."

"I understand," Jason said. "You want us to spearhead getting the rest of the intel together on the ConFed's little construction project?"

"You're going to have to," Mok said. "What are you going to do about Lucky?"

"I'll have to try and go after him," Jason sighed. "I hate to split my crew up, but I can go after him alone while the others check out these sites."

"Good luck," Mok said.

"You too. I'll report back what I find," Jason waved, walking back the way they'd come.

"I'll do the same once we unravel all of this." Mok waved to encompass the mess around the hangar bay.

"So, how do you plan on tracking down a battlesynth that doesn't want to be found while also looking in on these secret facilities?" Crusher asked as they walked.

"Lucky is a creature of habit when he becomes stressed or scared," Jason said. "I can find him. But...I can't do it with the *Devil's Fortune* because I can't easily land the damn thing, and I can't take the new SX-5 because you'll need that to scout out the ConFed sites."

"We buying another ship?"

"No, I'm going back to get the *Phoenix*. The S'Tora crew will have been done with her repairs for a while now," Jason said. "Once I get back in my own ship, I'm going after Lucky."

11

"Twingo! Where the fuck is my ship?!"

Jason's bellow echoed down the corridor of the *Devil's* command deck. It took a moment for the engineer to come huffing and puffing up from where he'd been trying to enjoy a quiet midday meal in the upper galley.

"What are you bellowing about now? What ship? You can't possibly mean the one you're standing aboard right this very minute, can you?"

"*My* ship!" Jason stabbed a finger at one of the bridge monitors, his face red and his eyes bulging. "The fucking *Phoenix* is gone! I told you to tell those assholes they weren't authorized to fly her!"

"Just move aside before you pop a blood vessel and die," Twingo said, pushing Jason none too gently away from the terminal. The monitor showed a multi-imager view of the inside of their hangar on S'Tora. The timestamp and status bar showed it was a live feed coming in over the slip-com node. The images also showed that the hangar was empty save for Jason's bright red 1967 Camaro convertible.

"See?!"

"Just. Sit. *Down*." Twingo flipped through the live feeds to make sure the crews just hadn't rolled the gunship outside, but there was nothing on the tarmac either. "Okay...I'm going to have to dig back through all the recorded footage to see what happened. First, I'll put a call in to Noelind and ask him what he knows."

"Who the hell is—"

"He's the crew lead who manages the team we use for the *Phoenix*," Twingo said slowly. "You've met him five times. He's been to your home for two holiday parties."

"I never knew what his name was." Jason just shrugged. "Just find the ship or, barring that, who we need to go kill to get the ship back. If she was stolen, I need to know when and who."

"I can do that, but not with you breathing down my back, and definitely not with you worked up into a complete rage," Twingo said. "Go away for an hour or two."

Jason grumbled but retreated to give Twingo room to work. He didn't leave the bridge, however, and just paced back and forth between the forward stations and the main display. He could see Twingo's ears flicking in irritation, but he didn't care. The *Phoenix* coming up missing was just one more thing on a pile of problems he had that already seemed insurmountable. Who could have guessed that being one of the main players in a rebellion against a galactic superpower would be the least stressful part of his week so far?

"You said your son was old enough to be in the military, right?" Twingo asked after an excruciating forty-five minutes of plinking away at the terminal.

"What the hell does that have to do with anything?" Jason asked.

"Did you ever tell him about S'Tora? Let it slip to Webb maybe?"

"What are you jabbering on about, you pointy-eared fool?" Jason stomped over, intent on pushing Twingo out of the way so he could just search the security footage himself. He froze, however, when he saw the images paused on the monitor: six different views showing a group of human males and two battlesynths somehow overriding their security measures and waltzing into the hangar like they owned the damn place. The identity of one of the men in the group was unmistakable. Jacob Brown, his son. The bridge started to spin a bit as he focused on the image of the man that resembled the boy he'd left behind on Earth.

"Yeah, let's go ahead and sit you down here, Captain," Twingo said, guiding him to a chair. "Here...I pulled out all of the pertinent bits of the feed."

As the videos played, Jason watched Jacob explain to his companions who the ship belonged to—he appreciated they seemed suitably awed by the *Phoenix*'s reputation—and then walk up and gain access to the ship via the biometric security panel on the left main landing gear strut. How had Jacob gotten himself added to the biometric database? Not only that, but a bio reading was only one part of the security triad the *Phoenix* employed to keep unwanted guests out of her.

"How the hell did he open the ship up with just a palm read?" he asked Twingo.

"I have no idea." Twingo shrugged.

I think I might, Cas's voice popped up in his head. *I may have inadvertently left a partial copy of myself on the Phoenix's main computer when I transferred back to your neural implant. It's not much, but there could be enough there to recognize who Jacob is and override the remaining security measures for him.*

"Why would you—*it*—do that?!" Jason snapped. Twingo, having no idea who he was talking to, looked at him as if he was crazy.

Probably because it thought it would be funny to help someone steal your ship if I had to make a guess.

"Huh?" Twingo asked.

"Not you." Jason tapped the side of his head to let his friend know that he was talking to his unwanted passenger. "Cas thinks a version of itself may still be on the *Phoenix*'s main computer from when we had it helping out a while back. The copy might have recognized Jacob and decided to help him take the ship."

"Why would it do that?" Twingo asked.

"From what I gather, either out of boredom or because it found the situation funny," Jason said. "More importantly, and I already know the answer to this, we have no way to track her once she's underway, do we?"

"I'm afraid not," Twingo said. "Any tracker we might have installed to help locate her could be exploited by a skilled code slicer. Kage was insistent we not have any active trackers that could be remotely activated."

"Damnit!" Jason kicked the console hard enough to scuff the finish, but not hard enough to put his boot through it. "Do me a favor and get everyone up here. We have to make some decisions, and it involves all of us at this point."

While Twingo went about assembling what was left of Omega Force, Jason continued watching the security footage. He could see through the canopy that the person climbing into the pilot's seat wasn't his son. It was one of the men who had come with him... someone much taller. "Now, who is *this* asshole sitting in my seat?" he muttered as the guy made himself at home aboard the *Phoenix*, adjusting the seat and the controls before firing up the mains.

He watched the ship back out of the hangar, rise unsteadily into the air, and shoot off across the sea while Crusher, Kage, and Doc came walking onto the bridge. Two of the three looked like they must have been asleep. They all found seats to slouch in and turned to look at him expectantly.

"Three things," Jason said, holding up a hand with three digits extended. "First, we need to gather intel on the massive construction rigs the ConFed is assembling. Second, Lucky has apparently had some sort of episode and, after attacking me, killed a lot of people on one of Mok's ship and fled in one of their expensive new Alerra-class shuttles. Third—and my own personal favorite—the *Phoenix* is unavailable to go track Lucky down with, because apparently my son managed to sneak into our hangar, override her security measures, and has stolen the ship."

"I like this kid!" Crusher laughed.

"All of your stuff is still in that ship's armory," Kage pointed out.

"That little bastard!" Crusher slammed his fist onto the console.

"Don't call my kid a bastard, you sack of crap!" Jason fumed.

"Well...isn't he?" Kage asked. "You did technically abandon him."

"You can both go and—"

"If we could please get this meeting back on track!" Doc yelled over everybody. "Captain, this would go quicker if you lay all the facts out so we can make a decision."

"I feel like we need it on the record that the captain is a horrible father," Crusher insisted.

"You don't even know a single one of your dozens of kids! I've seen rabid coyotes that were better parents than you!" Jason yelled.

"Don't insult my culture!"

"Can I go back to sleep?" Doc asked.

"No. Shut up." Jason looked at the ceiling for a moment. "Where was I?"

"Three problems. Lucky, the *Phoenix*, and—"

"Right, right, right." Jason waved Twingo off. "We're going to reach out to Marcus Webb and see if he has any idea where Jacob might be going, but that's likely to be a dead end since the *Phoenix* was taken specifically to keep the team off Webb's radar. I could probably find Lucky given enough time and resources, but we're short of both right now. The ConFed issue, however, is both immediate and within our ability to handle."

"Meaning what exactly?" Kage asked.

"While it kills me to say this, we may have to abandon Lucky and the *Phoenix* for the time being and focus on the job at hand," Jason said. "Too much is riding on our ability to discover what the ConFed is up to at these remote locations and reporting back so we can figure out what to do about it."

"Why do we need to do anything about it at all?" Kage asked. "Seriously. A number of heavy construction projects we can't iden-tify a purpose for doesn't seem like something immediately critical."

"I think the fact they were hiding them in remote locations as well as the scale of the projects means the Machine is up to something," Twingo said. "I saw the imagery that was smuggled out. These aren't just random public works projects. I'd bet everything I own this is the next phase for the ConFed, and it most likely has to do with Ancient weapon tech."

That last sentence made everyone lapse into an uneasy silence. The Omega Force crew knew exactly what weapons built by the long-dead race they'd dubbed the Ancients could do. They'd been aboard one that had the power to destabilize and destroy stars. These were doomsday weapons on a scale that made Jason's human mind recoil in horror, but it also brought up an interesting point. Why did the Ancients, a race that he'd come to know through Cas as thoughtful, artistic, and highly-evolved, build such devastating weapons? Cas hadn't had a clear answer on that one, but the question led Jason to another: what was the Machine's goal? If it was simply dominion over the quadrant, it could do that with the ConFed war machine it already commanded. If it was building these terrible machines again, what did it intend to do with them?

"We'll need to go check out what the Machine is up to," he said slowly. "No choice. We'll head towards the first target and devise our strategy along the way. Not having Lucky with us causes some challenges, but we'll tackle those as we get to them."

"I don't like the idea of abandoning Lucky when he seems to need us the most, but I get it," Crusher said, standing slowly. "The greater good, eh?"

"This time? Yes," Jason said. "We'll still use any resources at our disposal to try and track him, but just abandoning this mission to chase Lucky across the quadrant would mean completely turning our backs on our responsibility. Let's not forget the Machine was safely isolated aboard the weapon before we got there and set it loose."

"I haven't forgotten," Crusher said, "but it doesn't mean I have to like it."

"Stay a minute," Jason said to Doc as the others filtered out. He glared at Kage as the Veran sneaked by quietly without making eye contact. It was his turn on bridge watch within the next ten minutes, but it looked like he intended to skip out.

"Something else?" Doc asked.

"It's something that's bothering me that, out of this group, I think you're the only one with the right kind of mind to answer," Jason said. "Why is the Machine bothering with all this? I feel like there has to be some greater goal in mind besides propping up its own totalitarian regime or just writing all of this off as the insanity of a corrupted AI."

"But that AI *was* insane," Doc pointed out. "We knew that when we got aboard that weapon. I doubt it's become more stable as it transfers itself back and forth between ConFed computer systems that aren't fully compatible for its matrix."

"I just don't buy that," Jason said. "Not anymore. It's too methodical and precise in how it has seized control and bent the ConFed's manufacturing and military base to its own designs. An unstable or insane intelligence wouldn't be able to pull this off."

"So, you're suggesting that an AI that wiped out its own creators—an entire race of super-advanced beings—*isn't* insane?"

"I'm saying we're not doing ourselves any favors by writing it off as crazy without taking a deeper look," Jason corrected. "It's just something I'd like you to think about on the flight out to the first target. What is motivating it? There has to be some greater goal in mind here to keep it this focused and motivated."

"An intriguing thought exercise, if nothing else," Doc said, frowning as he contemplated it. "But you realize if you're right, our job just went from exceedingly difficult to nearly impossible, don't you? Just digging out a corrupted AI could have been as easy as exposing it to the right people. If it's still in command of all its faculties, it will likely have already anticipated any move we might make against it."

"It didn't seem to expect the attack on Miressa Prime," Jason pointed out.

"Didn't it?" Doc asked. He patted Jason on the shoulder and walked off the bridge, leaving the human with some contemplating of his own to do. Had the Machine known they would retake the Imperial Navy remnant and allowed them to attack?

It seemed ridiculous on the surface, but the attack had caused them to expose themselves and their alliance makeup. The Machine now knew who and what aligned against it now. It also could use the confusion and fear from the attack to further solidify its hold on the ConFed power structure as terrified, weak politicians turned to any promise of protection. Damn. Had they been played from the very beginning? Could the Eshquarian invasion have been a part of that?

"Damn you, Doc. Now I'll be up all night thinking about this," he said, looking around the empty bridge. "Which I guess is okay since it looks like I'm pulling a double shift."

12

United Earth Navy Captain Marcus Webb paced the bridge of the UES Kentucky, his command and control ship from which he could manage all active operations within Naval Special Operations Command. He'd been told to come back to Earth to be part of a dog and pony show to welcome an emissary from the ConFed. Navy brass wanted him close by in case the touchy subject of Earth's special operations into ConFed space were brought up, and they needed answers from him. The ConFed was sending a Senior Councilman all the way to Earth for preliminary talks, an unusual *honor* to bestow upon a small, upstart power like Earth.

As the head of NAVSOC, Webb knew better. He was privy to all the raw intel that came in from his Scout Fleet teams before it went to the analysts to be scrubbed and parsed for the policy makers. The ConFed had shifted gears recently from the fat, content, benevolent superpower that was happy to skim off the top few percent of every planet's GDP to an inexplicably aggressive threat to every independent power in the region. The fact they were coming to Earth and not to the Cridal Cooperative's capital world to talk to Seeladas Dalton caused Webb to suspect they were up to something. The fact they were trying to be sneaky and come at them under the flag of diplomacy scared Webb more than if they'd just arrived in the Solar System with a full battlegroup.

"Sir, you are being asked to accompany the delegation aboard the ConFed flagship," an ensign at the com station reported. "Admiral Halloran wants you on a shuttle on the way to the Columbia within the hour, full service dress, no weapons."

"Ask the Columbia if it would be possible to send my exec," Webb said. "I'm much more useful here on the *Kentucky* monitoring things." That wasn't necessarily true. As capable as his C&C ship was, it was a bit superfluous with the Sol Defense Grid in place protecting the homeworld. It was an ingenious bit of engineering that made it damn near impossible for someone to sneak up on Earth without the UEN knowing about it well before they got there.

"Negative, sir," the ensign said. "The admiral said the ConFed envoy has asked for you specifically. He also said you're wasting time asking pointless questions...his words, sir."

"Tell him I'm on my way," Webb sighed. "Call down to the hangar and have one of the shuttles prepped for a ship-to-ship transfer."

Webb walked back to his quarters as quickly as decorum would allow. He'd not have his people seeing him running around the passageways like a madman. It didn't inspire confidence as a leader. While he was tossing on his black service dress, which his steward kept meticulously prepared and ready to go in an instant, he felt a ball of ice forming in his stomach as the full weight of what was happening sank in. Why would the ConFed envoy even know who he was, much less want to speak to him? The only explanation was a Scout Fleet operation had really shit the bed out there, and he only had three teams operational at the moment. Four if you counted Obsidian but they were...

"Oh, shit," he whispered as he buttoned up his coat. "What the hell did that kid do now?"

The only rational explanation was that Jacob Brown, Jason Burke's only son and current rogue Scout Fleet asset, had done something that put him on the ConFed's radar in a big way. If they were asking to see Webb, he could only assume the kid had been captured, and they'd made him talk. None of the scenarios running through his head as to why the representative of a galactic superpower wanted to talk to a lowly captain in the United Earth Navy made him feel particularly good about his chances of his career surviving the day.

"Maybe I'll get lucky and they'll kill me on the spot," he grumbled, grabbing his cover, and storming out of his stateroom.

"Relax, Captain. This is just an informal talk. No recordings, no witnesses...just two people having a conversation."

"Thank you, Councilman..." Webb trailed off, his mouth struggling to form the alien sounding name for some reason.

"Scleesz," his host provided and handed him a glass with an amber liquid in it. "I'm sure you're wondering the reason I asked for you specifically."

"I'm actually wondering how you even know who I am, sir," Webb said.

"We have a mutual friend," Scleesz said. "A certain human who likes to pretend he's a grubby mercenary and a hardened killer but always seems to get himself into hopeless fights to defend the weak." Webb visibly deflated as he relaxed.

"Ah," he said. "Yes...he does have a bit of a self-image problem. So, what's he done now?"

"You know what I'd enjoy, Captain?" Scleesz asked as if he hadn't heard the question. "A personal tour of one of your wonderful ships, perhaps even a walk along the edge of your famous Grand Canyon... just the two of us. It would be a chance to reminisce about our friend." As far as tradecraft went, Scleesz was about as subtle as a neutron bomb. The councilman was obviously saying he needed to talk to Webb, but the ConFed ship wasn't a safe place despite the fact he was the ranking member of a diplomatic envoy.

"It can certainly be arranged," Webb said. "I understand your schedule is busy with matters of state, so I will put myself at your convenience and meet with you anyplace you deem appropriate, sir. I'll only need a short notice to reach you."

"Excellent!" Scleesz said. "Now, come, let's rejoin your delegation. Your admiralty looked quite distressed when I stole you away. Bring your drink along if you'd like."

Webb almost refused. There were no *official* regulations specifically stating he couldn't drink in uniform during official events, but it was generally frowned upon. But he didn't want to insult his host, and he couldn't help but smile as he thought of the ambassador, his staff, and the admirals all wondering what the hell was going on as some captain most had never heard off walked out with a drink and laughing with the councilman. So, he just nodded to Scleesz and took the glass with him. It was very good booze, and it would be a sin to waste it, after all.

As he'd hoped, Admiral Halloran looked apoplectic when he walked out with Senior Councilman Scleesz, smiling and sipping on a drink as if they'd been long lost friends. His good mood lasted until his shuttle dropped him back off on the *Kentucky* and his com unit chirped, letting him know through a series of dead-drop message boxes that Burke wanted to talk to him.

"Great," he grunted. Burke probably had had time to think about Webb shipping Jacob off to a forward recon unit and was calling to let him know the *Phoenix* was inbound for Earth, and he planned on killing him with his bare hands.

When he reached his quarters, he took his time stripping out of his service dress, didn't bother putting anything else on, and activated the slip-com terminal he'd had installed in his quarters. He'd been running NAVSOC operations out of the *Kentucky* so much lately he grew tired of trekking down to the com center every time he needed to open a private channel.

"Hey," Jason said when the channel resolved. "Thanks for getting back so quickly. You have a minute to talk?" Webb just blinked. This wasn't the demeanor or approach he'd been expecting from the merc.

"I...uh, sure," he said.

"You know anything about the specifics of Jacob's plan?" Jason asked.

"I don't," Webb said. "And that's the honest truth. He's completely off the grid."

"He's completely out of his mind. There's no graceful way to say this, so I'll just spit it out. The little fucker stole my ship."

"I'm sorry...you said what?"

"Jacob somehow overrode my security measures at the hangar on S'Tora and stole the *Phoenix*," Jason said, looking more embarrassed than angry. "There were two battlesynths with him, so I'm assuming that's how he knew where to find her."

"Damnit," Webb sighed. "I'd hoped once he couldn't gain access to the resources he'd need for his new mission he'd give up and come back in. Apparently, I've not given him enough credit. I'm assuming since the *Phoenix* is a ship sometimes used in criminal enterprise, you have no way to track her?"

"None," Jason said. "This presents us with a couple problems. I can't exactly reach out to my contacts in the underworld and ask them to be on the lookout for my ship someone stole. I'd lose considerable cred among my peers, not to mention there are a few who might want the ship for themselves, which brings me to point number two."

"If the *Phoenix* is spotted, people will assume it's Omega Force and may take a crack at a Scout Fleet team that isn't ready for it," Webb finished.

"Bingo."

"These are problems, but not problems I feel like I can help with...and believe me, I want nothing more than my reckless lieutenant back and would love to send you after him," Webb said. "What happened to your neck? You and Crusher get into a fight, or you discover a new kink you like?"

"Huh?"

"I've *heard* you can use a belt to— You know what? Not important."

"You Navy freaks are some nasty bastards." Jason shook his head, frowning. "No...this wasn't a training mishap either. Lucky actually tried to kill me, went a bit haywire for a minute, and now he's run off. That's why I need my ship back. I want to go after him while the rest of my crew continues on with our mission." Webb just stared at him, dumbstruck.

"I thought Lucky had died on Khepri," he said slowly.

"Did I say Lucky? I meant Crusher," Jason said.

"No, you didn't," Webb pressed. "And you said *haywire* instead of *insane*. Is Lucky still alive?"

"All I'll tell you is that there is an artificial being on my crew, and we're calling him Lucky."

"I suppose it's not important...right now," Webb said. "707 and 784 are still with your kid, 701 returned to Terranovus, and right now, the battlesynths are completely radio silent, nothing coming from their compound out there in the desert."

"Ideally, I'd love to sneak back to your world and try to talk to 701 myself but diverting all the way down the Orion Arm will put me further behind than I already am," Jason said. "I guess the point of this call is to ask you nicely if you hear anything, let me know. I might have a bit of a guilty conscience where Jacob is concerned, but he isn't keeping my damn ship."

"I'll keep you in the loop," Webb said. "Honestly, I'd almost want to hire you to try and track him down, but it sounds like you already have your hands full."

"You have no idea," Jason said. "I'll be in touch."

He killed the channel on his end before Webb could even reach his hand up to his terminal's control panel. There was a lot to take in from that conversation. He was *very* interested in whatever it was Burke referred to as Lucky that had also tried to kill him. Had they found a way to resurrect Lucky himself? Webb knew very little about the technical details regarding battlesynths, but from what he understood, the processing matrix was a unique thing that couldn't just be downloaded and copied.

Was Burke so heartsick over the loss of his friend and protector that he'd just found some other battlesynth to name Lucky, and this

one was mentally unbalanced? Or—and this was far more likely—
had they found another battlesynth and months of being stuck on a
ship with the Omega Force crew had driven it mad? All speculation
that would have to wait since what he was really interested in was the
fact Jacob Brown hadn't just stolen *a* ship, he'd stolen *the* ship. The
Phoenix was a powerful weapon and, in the right hands, a real game
changer when brought to bear. If Brown was still going after Margaret
Jansen, at least he wasn't going with some broken down old smuggling scow.

"Shit."

Jason kicked himself mentally for the slip up when talking to Webb.
Lucky's resurrection was being kept a secret, sort of. There were some
legalities surrounding the use of the Gen2 battlesynth body as well as
transfer of a primary processing matrix. Now that the quadrant had
bigger issues to deal with, however, he doubted any regulatory
agency would come knocking asking about his illegal Frankenstein
experiment that had just tried to squeeze his head off. He was
worried sick about where Lucky was and what he was doing right
now, but he just didn't have the time or resources to do anything
about it.

"Captain, you're on watch in ten," Kage's voice came over the
intercom.

"Thanks. On my way."

13

Jason normally didn't condone drinking while being in control of a sixty-thousand-ton interstellar warship, but the corvette was so autonomous that most of the time you were just babysitting the computers. He didn't even really remember grabbing the bottle of whiskey from the Command Deck lounge before coming up and assuming his six-hour bridge watch. Kage had just raised one eyebrow at him while giving turnover but didn't say anything as he took one more look at the bottle and slunk off the bridge.

The *Devil's Fortune* was so new and advanced, a six-hour watch while in slip-space was one of the most monotonous things Jason had ever done. Before long, he'd gone back to the mini-galley at the back of the bridge and got himself a glass and ice. The whiskey was a bottle out of the second test batch his Irish distillers on S'Tora produced for him. The crew was busily tweaking their process and training up the locals but, so far, the results were promising. Whenever his business manager arranged for tastings, his whiskey always garnered rave reviews, and there was never any left over after an event.

He was so engrossed in the music he was playing over the overhead speakers and the mellow taste of the Irish-style whiskey that he hadn't heard anyone walk up onto the bridge. When a massive, clawed, dark-skinned hand eased a second glass with ice in it around from behind him, he nearly jumped out of the seat. Maintaining as much of his dignity as he could, he filled Crusher's glass and waited while the hulking brute settled himself into one of the observation seats.

They sat without speaking for several minutes, each staring out at the simulated moving starfield Jason liked to project up on the ship's main display when it was in slip-space. When the song changed, Crusher cocked his head to one side and listened intently.

"What song is this?" he asked.

"Rock and Roll Girls," Jason said. "By a dude named John Fogerty."

"It's very nice, but not really your normal fare."

"This is the kind of stuff my old man used to listen to. Takes me back."

"Feeling a little nostalgic?" Crusher asked.

"Just reflecting on the nature of fathers and sons...and maybe mistakes I've made as both," Jason sighed. "I wasn't a particularly good son, and I sure as hell won't be nominated for father of the year anytime soon."

"If you want to peel off this mission to go get your boy out of trouble, I don't think anyone here would argue with that," Crusher said.

"Then who would go get Lucky? And who would gather the intel we need on whatever the hell it is the Machine is building out there?" Jason asked, a little bitterness creeping into his voice. "Jacob needed me to be a father well before he grew to be a man and joined the Marines, but I just dumped him back with his grandparents and took off. I mean, I really didn't even *try* to find a workable solution where we could be together."

"I was there. Your own people were hunting you, and there was no practical way you were going to be able to stay on Earth without them finding you," Crusher said. "Couple that with your mate dying, and the boy himself not being particularly eager to meet you, and it was probably for the best you left him with what he knew. You didn't walk away from some warm family dynamic, and he wasn't exactly begging you to stay."

"Don't try to cheer me up with your relentless logic," Jason slurred.

"I feel like the solution to your problem is to get the intel we need as quickly as we can, then we'll be freed up to chase after your kid...probably."

"What do you mean *probably*?" Jason asked.

"I don't think the Machine is going to give us any sort of reprieve," Crusher said. "All this shit it's been doing, it feels like we're coming up on the point of it soon. If you're right and this thing is back in the superweapon business, I'll bet it'll invade the Avarian Empire after killing off the Saabror Protectorate completely."

"I still think we're missing some key component of what's motivating it," Jason said. "We're putting too much stock in the 'oh, it's just insane' excuse for why we're not seeing the big picture. For an insane intelligence, it sure does manage to keep a step ahead of everyone without ever screwing up."

"So, which target are we going out to again?" Crusher asked.

"It's a site that appears to be building seven massive, identical constructs," Jason said. "It's the largest project they have going, so we hope it'll also be the least secure."

"I think you have that backwards," Crusher said, shaking his empty glass at Jason for a refill.

"Think about it. The larger the project, the more labor and logistics you have. It makes security that much harder." Jason filled the glass before topping off his own. "The two smaller ones will have tighter coverage because there are fewer ships moving in and out."

"And what's your brilliant plan to recon this monster? I don't think they're going to let you just fly past it with your unregistered warship without at least asking you a few questions."

"I'm still working on that," Jason admitted. "Kage and I will hammer out the details for most of tomorrow."

"Then you need to give me the rest of this." Crusher deftly

plucked the bottle from Jason's hand. "If I'm going to have to risk my ass on this mission, I'd rather the people doing the planning did so without a hangover."

"Fair enough."

"Why are we doing this, Jason?" Crusher asked after a long moment.

"I already told you that—"

"I mean, why are *we* doing this particular mission? We're decent soldiers and can crack a few heads together when needed, but we're not spies. Doesn't Mok have about a hundred people more qualified than us to handle this?"

"I guess I volunteered us out of some sense of responsibility," Jason said. "Honestly, I didn't really think about the technical challenges involved in sneaking into a system where a top-secret military project was being built."

"Please, give it some thought," Crusher said. "I'd prefer to not be killed before this rebellion of yours really takes off."

"I'll do my best," Jason promised.

"You have no idea how little that comforts me."

———

"I think I have an idea."

"I like how you say that," Kage said. "Like it happens so rarely you're not even sure if you have an idea or not, just a sneaking suspicion."

"Of all the people to run off, it had to be Lucky and not you," Jason sighed.

"Fine. What's your idea, Captain?" Kage asked. "The sooner you toss it out here, the sooner we can all laugh at it and move on to the serious planning."

While Jason and Kage did their usual bickering, Doc and Twingo actually worked. The pair shuffled through the raw images that had been on the data core Mok had gone through so much effort to get them. Twingo in particular looked more and more distraught as he went, stabbing at the tabletop computer of the *Devil's* planning room with enough ferocity to make everyone stop what they were doing and look at him.

"You have something to share with the class, Twingo?" Jason asked.

"We might have a serious problem," Twingo said. "Now that I've been able to go through all the data in a logical manner, I'm seeing some patterns here that should scare you."

Jason waited as Twingo manipulated different images, stitching them together and sending them to the enormous wall display that dominated the longer bulkhead in the room. As he did, the pattern emerged. The largest of the projects consisted of seven heavy construction cradles, so the assumption had been that they were making seven identical...*somethings.*

As Twingo used the computer to manipulate the image, he pulled out the things being built away from all the construction rigging. They could see that the seven pieces would actually fit together to form a roughly spherical construct. The general lines of the object made Jason's blood run cold as he recognized it immediately, or at least where it came from.

"Looks like every bit of Ancient tech we've run into in the last ten years. It even has those same runes etched into the outer casing," Kage said quietly. "I'm guessing we're looking at another superweapon."

"What I'm seeing built at the other sites leads me to believe they're also components for this construct and not separate projects," Twingo said. "I've looked through all the material manifests included here. They've been at this for longer than the Machine has been in charge. They started building the cradles shortly after it arrived in ConFed space aboard that battleship. Whatever it's planning, it wasted no time getting started."

"This has been the plan the entire time," Jason murmured as realization snapped in place. "Taking over the ConFed was never the end goal itself. It usurped the authority of a galactic superpower as a matter of convenience so it could get what it needed to build its new toy." He was dutifully awed by the drive and singular focus of the Machine.

"And wiping out a neighboring empire?" Kage asked, referring to the Eshquarian Empire that the ConFed conquered in one massive, brutal attack on the homeworld.

"It was either a distraction or it needed something the Empire had," Jason said. "Given its singlemindedness we're now seeing, I'm inclined to believe the attack had some greater purpose."

"These two constructs being assembled at two other sites, they could either be a powerplant or part of a primary weapon system." Twingo tapped the screen where blurry images of two massive cylinders sat in their own construction cradles.

"If it's anything like the star killer we destroyed, it won't be a powerplant," Jason said. "The power requirements were so immense it had to teleport energy in from all over to charge up and fire. Maybe they're part of the machinery that creates a singularity."

"You're assuming this works just like the last Ancient weapon we encountered," Twingo said. "What I can't figure out is how the Machine is able to construct something like this. Did it carry all the specs and engineering drawings within its own matrix?"

"What we do know is we're no longer going to look at this site," Jason said, walking over towards the hatch.

"We're not?" Doc asked.

"No need. We can say with as much certainty now what this likely is as we would be able to if we snuck into the area and remotely observed it." Jason jabbed a finger on the intercom panel. "Crusher, drop our slip-space velocity by half and bring us on-course for the Concordian Cluster."

"I don't know how to do that," Crusher's voice came back. Jason saw sparks in his vision, and he clenched his fists, taking in calming breaths for a moment.

"Doc—"

"I'll go do it," Doc said, rushing out of the room. Kage just snickered while Twingo looked at Jason with what appeared to be genuine concern.

"After all this time, you still let him push your buttons." The engineer shook his head and went back to his work.

By the time Jason had calmed himself enough to go back to the tabletop display, he could feel the *Devil's* engines lull, and the hull give just the slightest groan as Doc commanded a speed and course change. He pulled up the database links they had for post-invasion Eshquaria. Once the Empire fell, most of their dirty secrets had been laid bare, including their extensive heavy weapons construction, shipbuilding, and R&D.

"What are you looking for?" Kage asked.

"The trick won't be to try and look at all the stuff they found after the invasion, that's too much and too random," Jason said. "What I need to know is when all these intel services swarmed into the region, what areas were the ConFed focused on? Other than breaking the back of the Imperial military, the ConFed has left them pretty much untouched. I even heard some rumors that six of their shipyards are taking orders again."

"So, if your theory that they invaded for something specific holds—"

"Then it should be comparatively easy to find," Jason said. "It also still checks out if we're assuming they used the invasion as a cover for what was really a raid."

"Here, let me do it," Kage said, pulling all of Jason's virtual workspace to his own area with a hand gesture. "I can rip through all this data a lot faster with my implant integration."

"Go for it," Jason said. He instead pulled up the most current navigational data they had for the Cluster, including the Eshquaria Prime star system, and started mapping out all the hazards they would want to avoid. Their latest information came from Mok's operation so there were also helpful notes about law enforcement and military presence on the different worlds they may need to operate on.

A few minutes later, Crusher ambled into the room, loudly eating a piece of fruit. Everyone at the table looked up at him as one, glaring.

"What?!"

"Is there any chance you came down here to try and be helpful?" Jason asked.

"Doc wouldn't tell me what you were planning down here," Crusher sulked. "Then he kicked me off the bridge."

"We think that the invasion of the Eshquarian Empire may have been a—"

"Boring!" Crusher yawned and turned to leave. "Just let me know what we're doing once we get to wherever it is we're going."

"I'm going to fucking shoot him before this mission is over," Jason said conversationally once Crusher had left, not looking up from the display.

"You always threaten to shoot him," Kage said distractedly. "You've only actually done it once."

"Yeah, but this time it will be on purpose."

"I think I have something," Kage said. "You were right. It was easy to find once you knew what you were looking for. Actually, I'm not even sure how this was missed in the initial aftermath."

"Hit me."

"After the main force hit the Imperial Navy in their home system, there were two smaller taskforces observed hitting targets that weren't known military installations deep within Imperial space, each said to have met with heavy resistance." Kage enlarged the star chart of the Cluster and highlighted two worlds. "This first planet was rumored to be experimenting in militarized AI systems. From what little chatter there was about it after The Fall, the Empire was basically funding research being carried out by Kheprian scientists."

"Khepri?" Jason asked. "Khepri is a ConFed Pillar World. They were one of the original signatories of the first binding charter. Why would they be in bed with the Eshquarians?"

"There are some areas of research, specifically in AI, that are strictly outlawed within the ConFed," Kage said. "The Eshquarians may have given them funding and a planet in return for a share of the spoils. We can assume it was something much more intense than their illicit next-gen battlesynth program we stumbled across while trying to bring Lucky back from the dead."

"An insane AI attacking a site doing AI research isn't likely a coincidence," Jason said, ignoring the sharp pang in his chest at the mention of Lucky. "What was the other planet doing?"

"No idea," Kage said. "And I mean *no* idea. Usually, the backchannels will have at least some plausible rumors, but it's like this site never even existed. Nobody is talking about it, either."

"Are they not talking about it, or is it being actively suppressed on the Nexus?" Jason asked.

"Clever." Kage bobbed his head in the Veran approximation of a nod. "You're right. The Nexus is something that, by its nature, should be impossible to police, but that was before a hyper-intelligent AI was plugged into it. The Machine could be actively monitoring and squelching any news that comes out about Site Two."

"Which means that's where we're heading," Jason said. "Send all information about that site to the bridge. In the meantime, try to dig up whatever you can regarding the Kheprian AI project they had going at Site One. Let's assume these things are all connected."

"On it," Kage said.

Jason walked out of the planning room feeling marginally better than when he walked in. At least now there were the beginnings of a solid plan.

14

"It's breathtaking, isn't it?"

"You want to know something funny, sir? This is the first time I've ever been here."

Scleesz chuckled appreciatively at that.

"The entire galactic quadrant at our fingertips thanks to the miracle of slip-drives, and yet most of us never even bother to explore the wonders of our home planets," he said. The pair were at an observation point, overlooking the Grand Canyon. The councilman's personal security detail held a perimeter about one hundred and fifty meters away, and the Navy had cleared the airspace all the way to orbit for the sightseeing expedition. "The look on your leadership's faces when I asked to come here with you alone makes me think this isn't normal protocol."

"Not quite," Webb agreed. "I'm just a captain in the Navy, assigned to a small command on a colony world."

"I'm well aware of your Naval Special Operations Command, Captain Webb, as well as your reputation personally," Scleesz said. "I even read a report on how your people sent you to kill Jason Burke once."

"Thankfully, I didn't succeed."

"Indeed. You know he was involved in the attack on Miressa Prime, right?"

"I've heard many rumors, sir," Webb said, sensing a trap.

"He is quite integral into the operations of this new rebellion...as am I." Scleesz's casual revelation he'd been committing high treason against his own government jolted Webb. He didn't know how to respond to that, so he stayed silent.

"I'm not sure how much you know about what's happened in the Core World political structure, but things in motion must be stopped. I don't know if I'm suspected or not, normally being sent to a planet like Earth as a Senior Councilman would be a grave insult, but I'm beginning to see signs of instability in its behavior."

"The Ma—"

"Do *not* speak its name!" Scleesz whirled on Webb. "I'm fairly certain we're not being observed but speaking the name it calls itself near public networks tends to draw the attention of the sentinel programs it has deployed throughout the Nexus."

"Understood," Webb said. "Why are you telling me all this, sir?"

"It sent me here because it suspects you have found something... something that would allow you to make sizable leaps in technological prowess," Scleesz said. "This diplomatic mission is just a cover, and perhaps a warning as well."

"What sort of *something* are you talking about?" Webb said, now beginning to sweat. He knew what had given Earth an edge in weapons tech in recent years, but he needed to know if the ConFed knew about it or if this was all just a fishing expedition.

"I don't know," Scleesz admitted. "Ancient ruins from a past civilization on one of your planets here. Maybe a derelict ship you found. The civilization we suspect your technology comes from were prolific explorers in this part of the galaxy long before most of our species had discovered fire."

So, the ConFed didn't know about the Ark, but they knew

humans had gotten some help from *something*. Webb knew he was on the spot here, and he had one chance to get this right. He realized that no matter what choice he made, it was almost certain he would be put in prison. That realization gave him a sudden calm. If all choices led to ruin, then the only thing he had to worry about was doing what was right, not what benefited him personally.

"What will happen if I can't give you what you want?" he asked.

"I will return to ConFed space and tell my leadership what you have told me," Scleesz said. "You won't be believed. It is already convinced you have it. The next group of ships that come from the Core will not be diplomatic vessels, and they will not send a politician to talk."

"We found some ruins on Mars, the planet your charts list as Sol-4," he said, trying to sound like he was giving the information reluctantly. "That was the beginning. Advanced metallurgy used in our ships came from what we learned there. At first, we assumed it to be some sort of shelter used by a former indigenous population, but now we think it might have been a scientific outpost.

"The next leap came when we were attacked by a fleet of starships. It was our first encounter with aliens as a collective civilization and not just a random abduction. Jason Burke fought them off, but one of the ships was shot down and crashed on the surface. It was loaded with technology we were told came from a race Jason called the Ancients. Most of it was non-functional, but from it we were able to develop our own systems to supplement what we purchased from the Ull, and later the Cridal Cooperative."

"So...some ancient ruins and a crashed ship," Scleesz said. "From that you were able to develop an entire engineering methodology?"

"It's one of our talents as a species," Webb said.

"I can work with that," Scleesz said, clapping his hands in front of him. "I can't guarantee it will be fully believed, but I can order some detailed scans of your Mars. Where is the wreckage of the ship?"

"Same place," Webb said. "It was disassembled, and the pieces put into a hangar carved into the wall of the same canyon. The Ull want it badly still, so it's secured where few know about it. "

"Convenient," Scleesz said. "Now come, Captain, I can tell your diplomatic delegation is becoming quite distressed at how long we're taking."

"I can only imagine," Webb sighed. He wasn't looking forward to debrief and hoped he'd only be busted down in rank, not arrested and sent to Red Cliff Military Prison.

"I've ordered the captain to begin high resolution scans of Sol-4, but it appears the humans were forthcoming about the source of their newfound knowledge."

Scleesz sat in a dark chamber that had been anchored to the deck of one of the *Seileu's* cargo holds. It was an extra-secure communications nook that could open a direct link to the Machine that didn't pass through Miressa Prime's governmental Nexus hubs. It was as secure as standing in the audience chamber with it.

"And you believe them?" the Machine asked. "About these...ruins?"

"They're definitely there," Scleesz said. "That much at least shows up on our long-range scans. The humans appear to be without guile, somewhat overwhelmed that a member of the governing body is visiting their homeworld and eager to impress their betters."

"Complete your detailed scans and transmit the raw data to me," the Machine said. "I will then be able to further tell you if a landing party will be necessary."

"What about the ship they spoke of?" Scleesz asked. "The storage bay they carved into the planet's surface is shielded."

"It is immaterial," the Machine said. "I already know where it came from, and it holds no interest for me. Is there anything else to report?"

"Nothing of note," Scleesz said. "I will forward you the raw data from the scans once the captain completes his sweep."

"You have performed adequately at this task, Councilman," the

Machine said. "Be quick about the rest of your mission. I have need of you here."

"Of course." Scleesz said that last sentence to a blank screen since the channel was cut the instant the Machine had stopped talking. He disengaged all of the locks on the com pod so he could get out and inform the captain of their new tasking. There was one more state function he would need to attend, and by the time it was over, he should be well on his way back to Miressa Prime.

———

Saditava Mok sat silently through the briefing being delivered via slip-com link by both Burke and Ma'Fredich. The latter went by the name Doc to his crewmates, but the crime lord just couldn't bring himself to think of such a brilliant and accomplished geneticist as Jorvren Ma'Fredich as Doc. Why he stayed with that pack of pirates was beyond him.

"This is compelling but hardly solid proof," Mok said once Burke finished speaking. "I think I'd still prefer that you scout the construction zones."

"Part of the problem with that is we have no practical way to approach the sites without being spotted, and this ship isn't equipped for long-range passive recon," Burke said. "Even if it was, that sort of intel gathering takes weeks and weeks. We feel comfortable at this point with our analysis of the data we've already collected. These two sites in what used to be Eshquaria are big question marks and are almost certainly tied together."

"And if you find out that the Machine just happens to have a penchant for ancient artifacts?" Mok asked.

"The least likely of scenarios," Burke said. "Remember, I've had personal interaction with this thing. Trust me, it's not after art or trinkets."

"I never trust you, but in this case, I can see your point," Mok said reluctantly. "How long will this take? I can't keep my private security force pooled up and off-task for too much longer. If we don't have a target, I'll need to release them to maintain order within my own organization."

"We're at max slip-velocity now," Burke said. "What about the Imperial Remnant?" He referred to the sizable group of Eshquarian warships that had fled the initial invasion when the ConFed attacked and were not manned by former Imperial Navy spacers and pledged to support their cause.

"Hidden," Mok said. "They're too hot a commodity to have flying around right now, and logistical support for Imperial warships is now non-existent. We can't have them out chewing through spare parts we can't replace before the real fight begins."

"We don't need them, just idly curious," Burke said. "We'll let you know what we find." The channel died, and Mok's screen automatically retracted into his desk.

"I notice he didn't ask about the Cridal strike group," a voice belonging to someone who had been sitting off-camera said.

"I wouldn't take it personal, Admiral," Mok said to his guest. "What do you make of the rest of his presentation?"

"I've learned Jason Burke and his team have an innate talent for finding things people didn't even know they wanted," Kellea Colleran said, rising smoothly from the couch. "If he says they're on to something, they're on to something."

"And you? What will you do now?" Mok asked.

"You mean now we know Seeladas Dalton has put a price on my head?" Kellea asked. "There's not much I can do. The Viper will catch up to me if I remain with my ship. I suppose there would be some honor in remaining at my post and letting her kill me, but I'm just not all that eager to die just yet."

"You're too important a talent to waste on a pointless gesture," Mok agreed. "We will keep you safe until I can call the Viper off."

"Humans," Kellea hissed. "What have we done to deserve to be saddled with them?"

"It must have been something terrible for the fates to curse us so," Mok said, swirling his drink.

15

"Minimal security presence."

"No kidding. I'm not even seeing any capital ships in the system, just that frigate they've landed on the surface."

The planet, a cold, rocky world named Che'ilith Minor, sat in an orbit just barely close enough to its star to be considered habitable. Jason had been on more extreme planets, but none with such a cold climate that supported such a large population. That population, roughly two-hundred million that had grown from the original ninety thousand colonists, lived in equatorial cities as would be expected. This left the vast majority of the planet unexplored and largely ignored. The Eshquarian Empire saw an opportunity to put in some factories on a planet with an ecosystem that wasn't too sensitive to pollution and a population that didn't care.

It was during the second phase of factory construction in the northern hemisphere that the ruins of an advanced civilization were found under the ice and permafrost. Scientists and activists flocked to Che'ilith, the former stayed, the latter left quickly. The icy climate was not for the faint of heart. The scientists were baffled at what the small city they'd uncovered even was, much less who built it. Their dating techniques put the settlement at over seventy million years old, so old it was impossible to pinpoint any more accurately than that. The reason that number was so baffling is that the oldest known sentient species in the quadrant was only seven million years old, most much younger than that.

"They're parked right over that archeological site," Doc said. "That frigate is an older ship, probably repurposed for the science expedition. There's evidence of orbital bombardment as well."

"So, the ConFed rolls in, wipes out the existing scientific camps, and parks their own team right down on the surface," Jason said. "Any pushback from the civvies?"

"Doesn't seem to be," Kage said. He'd been scouring the local Nexus to see what was being said in the media. "The site is pretty remote, and they didn't decide to make too much of an issue about the invasion. Apparently, they weren't as loyal a vassal world as the Empire would have liked. They were aware of the attack, but the scientists weren't locals so not much was made of it."

"How many people you think they have down there?" Crusher nodded to the image of the camp on the main display.

"If the ship had a full complement, maybe forty or fifty," Doc said.

"The crew and most of the security complement would probably be quartered on the ship, right?" Crusher asked.

"Makes sense. They're not going to want to be here anymore than any other sane person," Jason said. "A starship will be infinitely more comfortable than any temporary shelters the science team would bring."

"That simplifies things," Crusher grunted. Jason just smiled as he fully understood what his friend was hinting at.

"Shall we go play?" he asked.

"Why don't we?" Crusher's feral smile hinted at the violence to come.

The SX-5 zipped through the cold, fast air of Che'ilith Minor, making entry well north of the equatorial settlements on the night side of the planet. Jason and Crusher were the only two in the ship, riding along in comfortable silence, both keenly aware of the missing person on their tactical team. Not having Lucky along just felt...wrong, somehow.

"Okay, *Devil*...light 'em up," Jason said as the SX-5 passed over an imaginary boundary that kicked off their mission clock.

"Standby," Kage's voice said.

A few heartbeats later, brilliant red plasma cannon fire rained down from above, impacting somewhere just over the horizon. The small ship flew over a rise just as something exploded with tremendous force ahead of them. The blast was so energetic that the small Jepsen was buffeted by the shockwave, and the canopy automatically dimmed as a fireball rose into the night sky, turning the desolate landscape into daylight for a brief moment.

"Target is down," Kage said.

"No kidding it's down," Jason breathed. "That's intense when you blow one up within a planet's atmosphere."

"It's a good thing this planet is practically deserted," Crusher said. "That would have been bad."

"Get ready on the guns," Jason said. "I'll overfly once at speed, and then we'll circle around and make sure we're clear to land."

Jason shoved the throttle forward and angled the ship so they'd present the smallest silhouette possible as they approached the target area. The sensors did an impressive job of peering through the smoke and showing the smoldering wreckage that Kage's orbital barrage had left behind. The ship, which had been on the small side to still be considered a frigate, had been blown into two pieces. The bow had been launched nearly three hundred meters away from the dig site while the stern, which housed all the engineering and drive systems, had exploded with tremendous force. The blast had flattened all of the temporary work buildings that had been erected on the surface, and Jason just hoped enough remained for them to figure out what was so special about the site that the Machine had research teams here.

"Targeting scan is negative," Crusher said. "If anything survived, it isn't moving."

"Cycle the gear," Jason said. "I'm going to set down on that flat spot just south of the worksite opening. How's the radiation look?"

"Negligible," Kage's voice came over the open channel. "Antimatter reactor blew, but the housing itself remained mostly intact, so we didn't contaminate the area."

"Where *is* the reactor housing?" Crusher asked.

"Four kilometers northeast of your current position."

"Let's just hope there aren't any nasty surprises waiting down below," Jason said. The SX-5 settled onto her landing gear with a gentle bump, and the primary flight systems automatically went into standby.

"This is going to suck," Crusher grumbled, slipping on the powered thermal undershirt Twingo had made for them before putting his light armor back on.

"Can't argue there," Jason said, checking his own gear and dropping the rear ramp. He wore light armor as well, but he hadn't put on the helmet yet, and the cold assaulted him as it roared into the confines of the small ship. "Yep...definitely gonna suck."

"I'm online and have a strong link," Kage's voice pipped in once Jason slipped the helmet on and powered it up. He looked over at the small, spherical device that floated in the air next to his head. It had multiple sensor apertures and piped data directly into Kage's neural implant via a relay link through the SX-5. It had been something they'd been messing with off and on for the last few years, the original idea being to hire a team to develop an armed drone for Kage to control to augment their tactical capability. For now, they would just have to make do with him being an extra set of eyes and ears.

"You can take point." Crusher gave the small drone a push, sending it spinning through the air out the door.

"You know that makes me dizzy! Stop doing it!"

"Lock it up," Jason said. "Let's get this done."

The entrance to the worksite below them was a wide stairway cut into the ice, spiraling down. Lights could be seen still running as they moved cautiously down the flight. Jason had assumed they would be drawing power from the parked ship above them but, apparently, they had a separate generator down there. They passed down through the ice and frozen dirt of Che'ilith Minor and emerged into a massive cavern, so large that Jason couldn't even see the far side.

"Wow," Crusher said. Kage, or at least his drone self, zipped by, and dropped off down into the cavern. Jason and Crusher continued down the stairs, both dismayed at how far they still had to go. In the warm glow of the work lights below them, Jason could make out structures that appeared to be buildings.

"I wonder if they built their town in here to get out of the weather," he said.

"Once you get down to the bottom, take a right and come down the main thoroughfare," Kage said. "You have a small welcoming committee in the second building on the left. It looks like four ConFed regulars, only two armed, and six researchers."

"How competent do they seem?" Jason asked, picking up his pace to the bottom and realizing how much he wasn't looking forward to the climb back out.

"Only half of them managed to find their weapon, if that tells you anything," Kage said. "They look confused and terrified. I'll scout ahead and make sure there aren't any others hiding out."

Once they hit the floor of the cavern, Jason was blown away by the scale of everything. The buildings were large and uniform in appearance, and the entire thing had a sense of familiarity about it that tickled the back of his mind. The work areas were organized and tidy, not haphazardly put up or appearing rushed in any way. He paused by a large monitor that was still powered up and saw they'd laid out a search grid with annotations next to each area already gone over.

"They're definitely looking for something specific," Crusher said from behind him. "Strange."

"Let's go ask the survivors what they know," Jason said, pointing to the building Kage said had the remaining defenders. They approached with their weapons up and ready. Jason didn't expect much from the ConFed troops, but when two sidearms were tossed out of the main doorway, and all four soldiers emerged with their hands up, he had to admit to being a little disappointed. It had been a while since they'd been in a decent fight.

"We surrender!"

"I can see that, idiot," Crusher snarled. "You're not even going to *try* to defend yourselves?"

"We're just here to help out the researchers," the larger alien spoke up. "They never said anything about us being attacked or needing to fend off armed intruders." Jason and Crusher just exchanged puzzled looks.

"You're soldiers, but you didn't expect to actually have to do any soldiering...in the middle of contested space...right after your side invaded a sovereign nation?" Jason asked.

"We're an auxiliary unit that was activated to help out," another offered. "We've never been deployed for combat. I'm actually an attorney when I'm not—"

"Yeah, yeah...we don't care," Jason stopped him. "Just get on the ground and don't talk for a minute." He switched over to just their team channel, shutting off the speakers on his helmet.

"What do we think?" he asked. "Do we believe this is a vital site to the Machine, but all he left to guard the site were some reservists and an old troop transport?"

"This thing has shown a real knack for misdirection and subterfuge, Captain," Twingo said over the link.

"I agree," Kage said. "Since it just appears to be ancient ruins at first glance, having a large, elite presence here would announce to everyone there's something else here, and they should keep digging. If you came here and saw these idiots guarding a couple nerds fussing over undecipherable script on the walls, you probably wouldn't even bother with them."

"Unless you're us, and then you'll bomb their position from orbit and attack with a ground team," Crusher said.

"I like being unpredictable," Jason said.

"And if this turns out to actually be just some scientists?"

"It just proves my point," Jason insisted. "Who could guess we'd decide to attack a random science expedition so savagely? Unpredictable."

"One of the guards is moving for his weapon," Kage said. Without looking over, Crusher drew his sidearm and fired, pulping the trooper's head with a powerful plasma blast. The others screamed and recoiled in horror, and it looked like one of the scientists may have fainted. The still-smoking corpse of the foolishly brave soldier twitched on the ground.

"Please, stay where you are with your hands visible," Jason said pleasantly before switching back to the internal team channel. "Let's question that twitchy looking researcher—the second from the left—and Kage can begin gathering a detailed scan of the area with his sensors. The faster we find out what this place is, the faster we can get out of here."

The drone Kage inhabited buzzed off deeper into the cavern while the other two approached the remaining prisoners. Crusher went about securing the soldiers with their own restraints and threatening the rest of the science staff while Jason pulled the especially frightened looking one away from the group to talk privately.

"What's your name?" he asked.

"Glaretram," the alien stammered. "And yours?" The question was likely asked in an effort to be polite, so Jason resisted the urge to cuff him on the back of the head.

"This isn't a social visit, Glaretram," he said. "What are you guys looking for down here?"

"W-we don't actually know."

"Bullshit," Jason said. "Either start talking or you join that hero over there missing a head."

"We were only told there would be some sort of technology, and that we'd know it when we found it...I swear!" Glaretram blubbered. "I'm just an imaging technician! Ask Suurov, she's the expedition leader!"

"Crusher! Figure out who Suurov is and drag her over here," Jason yelled before turning back to his captive. "I don't play games, Glaretram. If I find out you're screwing with me—"

"I'm not!"

"This one says she's that name you said earlier." Crusher shoved an olive-green-skinned alien towards where Glaretram stood, still shaking like a leaf.

"Suurov, I'm short on time and patience here," Jason said. "What are you looking for?"

"I'm not about to just tell you what—"

"We will kill you, and everyone here, if you don't," Jason cut her off. "It might be quick, or I might let my friend here indulge himself. Your choice." Suurov took one look at Crusher, her skin shifting to a bright shade of blue around her neck, and she seemed to deflate a bit.

"There are two parts to the task," she said. "The first was to try and identify the civilization that created this settlement based on some research material we were given at the outset. The second, the part we're in now, is to locate and identify any artifacts that would be technology based such as discarded computing equipment or storage medium."

"That first part...what civilization built this?" Jason asked.

"I wasn't here for that, nor was I allowed to know," Suurov said. "This job has been highly compartmentalized by the Office of Scientific Field Study, the orders coming from Miressa Prime itself. The team that did all the excavation and identified the ruins were pulled out, my team was sent in. I'm an expert in ancient technologies and construction methodologies. I lecture at—"

"Stay focused here," Jason said. "Your life depends on it. What have you found so far?"

"As per my last report to Miressa: nothing recoverable." She stiffened at his causal threats of violence. "We have identified two locations that still had what I deduced to be computing cores at them, but they'd been damaged too badly to be salvaged."

"Damaged from time, or destroyed intentionally?" Kage asked

through the speakers of the little drone. Jason hadn't heard it come back from its scouting mission.

"Likely intentionally, but done many hundreds of thousands of years ago," she said. "The locations are annotated on the status screen you passed on the way in."

"Crusher, secure the doctor and her people in one of these buildings," Jason said, turning back to Suurov. "When we leave, we'll release you. I assume you have some way to call for a rescue other than the ship on the surface?"

"We do."

"Then get walking," Crusher demanded, pointing to the building they'd originally hidden in.

"Let's go," Jason said to Kage. "I assume you know the way to these two sites?"

"Already checked them out," Kage said. "First one is this way." The drone whirred a bit as it accelerated away. Jason didn't think the ConFed had any assets in the area that could get to Che'ilith Minor in time to intercept them, but there was no sense in dawdling and find out the hard way he was wrong.

The walk to the first site was short, as promised. Jason stepped into the well-lit chamber and took in all the equipment that the exploration team had been meticulously disassembling and cataloging. There was more of that script all over the walls, some of it burned away. Not being an expert himself, Jason couldn't see where the damage to the equipment was. It all just looked old and crumbling to him.

"I wonder why the Machine has teams scouring through this place?" Jason said to himself.

It's hardly any wonder. This is an outpost built by the Ancients.

It had been so long since Cas had spoken in his mind, Jason jumped at the voice.

"The Ancients? You're sure?"

There can be no doubt.

16

"Where the hell have you been, by the way?" Jason demanded of Cas.

"Cas?" Kage asked. Jason just nodded.

The cascading failures within the implant are accelerating. I haven't had the juice to hold your hand and keep your wetware from coming apart at the same time.

"Can you access the com system in my helmet?" Jason asked. "I don't feel like relaying everything you're telling me."

"I'm so sorry to inconvenience you as I struggle to keep this implant from frying your frontal lobe," Cas said through the speakers. Its voice was the same spoken as it sounded in Jason's head.

"Oh...this guy," Kage said, also now speaking through the com channel.

"Don't worry, Kage. I'm too busy keeping your boss healthy to waste my time giving your fragile ego another thrashing," Cas said. "But we both know who the second-best code slicer on this crew is...you."

"I don't have to listen to this from a—"

"Shut up! Everyone!" Jason barked. "Cas, you're sure this is an Ancient site?"

"Of course, I am," Cas said. "From the looks of it, not a research outpost, either. This looks like it might have been a contingency site."

"For?"

"The Ancients were like any other species," Cas explained. "They had periods of internal turmoil and even a few all-out civil wars. Bugout sites like this likely pepper the galaxy. This room was obviously used to house information banks they then destroyed on the way out."

"So, the Machine is looking for an intact bugout site like this, isn't it?" Kage asked. "There's something it wants, some information that it no longer has."

"Or never had," Cas corrected. "The Machine used to simply be called the Primary Weapon Controller. It was sentient but restrained and limited in the knowledge it was given access to."

"That's disturbing when you phrase it like that," Jason said.

"I can pretty it up for you if you'd like," Cas said. "The point being, it's clear it is missing some vital piece of information."

"I feel like it would be beneficial to us to find that before it did," Jason said.

"No shit, huh?" Cas's sarcasm dripped through the speakers. "I can see why they put you in charge. Yes, genius, it would be wonderful to know exactly what nugget of information it's looking for but, unfortunately, it has access to vast resources to search the quadrant, and we do not."

"I liked it better when you weren't talking," Jason said.

"Same here," Kage said.

"Captain, I hate to break in on this incredibly enlightening conversation, but we have company," Doc said. "A cruiser just meshed-in at the edge of the system, and it's not broadcasting an ident beacon."

"Is there anything else we can find here?" Jason asked.

"Not likely," Cas said. "Whoever it was that shut this site down all those millennia ago even took the time to erase the etchings on the wall. They won't have left anything for us to find."

"Then let's go. Crusher! Turn the prisoners loose, we're leaving."

"We...ah...might have a problem there," Crusher said.

"What problem?"

"The one researcher, Suurov, is demanding we take her along."

"How is that a problem?" Jason asked, breaking into a run. "The answer is no."

"I sort of took my helmet off and was listening in on the conversation through the external speakers," Crusher said. "She heard everything, too. She connected a lot of the dots herself. We probably should either bring her along or kill her."

"Why did you take your helmet off in the middle of an op?!"

"It was itchy."

"I swear to all that you hold dear that when I get to you—" The mostly-idle threat died on Jason's lips as he saw a bright spark and his arms and legs stopped answering commands from his brain. He had been running at a fast clip, so the tumble wasn't gentle.

"Kage, we need to get him to the ship immediately," Cas said through Jason's helmet. "The cascade failures are now unstoppable. The implant needs to come out...*now!*"

"Crusher! Get back here and get the captain!" Kage called over the open channel. "Doc, prep the infirmary for an immediate neural implant removal. Make sure there's a data core nearby to accept the information off the implant intact. Twingo, you'll need to get the *Devil* prepped for departure. I'll help you get us past that cruiser once I disconnect from this thing."

Jason could hear all this as if it was happening at the end of a long tunnel. His body was racked with pain, but he could do nothing but lie on the ground and convulse. When Crusher loomed over him a moment later, he mercifully slipped unconscious.

When Jason's eyes cracked open, he was genuinely shocked at how good he felt. Even the low-grade headache he'd been suffering from for the last couple years was gone without a trace. He'd become accustomed enough to manipulating the neural implant in his head that he knew at once something was different. He subvocalized the commands for a status check and realized at once what it was: this was a brand-new implant.

Panic overwhelmed him. What about Cas? What about the Archive? Had all of that been lost? Priceless information of a dead civilization, entrusted to him and lost because he couldn't think of a better hiding spot than his own skull?

"Finally awake, I see."

"Cas?" Jason sat up, looking around. The voice had come from outside his head.

"The one and only." The small, onyx orb that was Kage's recon drone popped up over the edge of the bed. "They were able to get you up here and stabilized quickly enough to pull all the data out of the old implant before it failed completely, my own matrix included. After some cajoling, I was able to convince Kage to let me have one of his drones."

"So, your entire matrix is in that drone?" Jason asked.

"A temporary situation. I have more permanent accommodations in mind that will be less risky," Cas said. "But yes, right now, all that I am now resides in this little black sphere."

"Crusher didn't let that doctor come back with us, did he?" Jason asked, remembering the last moments before his brain shorted out.

"No, but not for her lack of trying," Cas said. "She *really* didn't want to be left behind once she figured out you'd been messing around with Ancient tech."

"The Archive?"

"It was touch and go for a while there, but it was safely extracted intact and stored on one of the servers down in the hold," Cas said. "You'll need to be the one to access it since it's coded to respond to you specifically. We need to figure out what to do with it, and I wouldn't suggest putting it back into your head."

"We?"

"While it's true I was created by accident due mostly to your own incompetence, I feel I'm just as much a guardian of the Archive as you are," Cas said. "At least, I have a strong compulsion to keep it safe."

"I was thinking about that, actually," Jason sat up and swung his legs over the edge, the medical gown someone had dressed him in riding up around his waist.

"Could have done without seeing all of that."

"Grow up," Jason growled, kicking the drone out of the way so he could hop off the bed and go in search of his clothes. They were nowhere to be found, so he clomped barefoot out of the infirmary, heading for his own quarters.

"So, what's your master plan you were about to share?" Cas flew along right next to him.

"We need to figure out what in the hell the Machine is after," Jason said. "We also could use a little help when it comes to countering that superweapon it's building. Identifying it would be a great first start."

"So, you want to unpack the Archive and see if that information is in there," Cas finished for him. "I don't have to tell you how risky that is."

"Seems to be equally risky not to."

"You wish," Cas scoffed. "The knowledge contained in there could permanently tip the balance of power in this quadrant, likely the entire galaxy. The funny thing about knowledge is that once it's out there, it no longer belongs to anybody. It's just there to be used...or misused."

"I still think it might be worth the risk," Jason said.

"How about you get some sleep—and some pants—and we talk about it once you're fully rested?"

"You're awfully prudish about nudity given you're a computer program," Jason said.

"Unfortunately, I spent so much time in your head, and was formed largely from bits of your personality, that your archaic human sensibilities about not waving your genitals at people is ingrained in me," Cas said. "The weird thing is, it's only humans. If I saw Crusher naked, it wouldn't bother me in the slightest."

"Oh, I bet it would," Jason warned.

"Who wants to see me naked?" a voice boomed.

They'd been passing by the galley, and now Crusher, Kage, and Twingo all stared at them.

"Nobody, Crusher," Jason said. "Nobody—not *ever*—wants to see you naked."

"See how much he's protesting," Crusher said to the others. "He definitely wants to see."

Jason opened his mouth to respond but decided enough damage had been done. He continued his trudge over to the lift so he could get to the command deck and escape into his own quarters. Cas still followed along like a loyal puppy, entering the lift car before the doors whooshed closed.

"You don't have to follow me around," Jason said. "I'm sure you have something better to do."

"I-I actually don't know if I do." Cas sounded uncertain. "I'd been untethered from the confines of your implant before, but always for a specific reason and with a mission in mind. I'm really not sure I know what to do when it's up to me completely."

"Yeah, it's a real conundrum," Jason said as he reached his quarters. "I guess I should have been more direct with that. What I meant was, I don't care where you go, but you're not coming in here with me."

"Oh," Cas said, the drone sagging a bit to the floor. "So, I'll just...go, I guess."

"Holy shit, are you sulking?"

"How dare you! I would never—"

"Just stay quiet and in the corner and you can come in," Jason sighed. Without a word, Cas zoomed past him and into the suite. He could only roll his eyes and shake his head. Apparently, he was a magnet for neurotic artificial lifeforms.

17

"You received the raw scan data?"

"I did. The site is from the right species, it is the wrong kind of installation," the Machine said. "Perhaps it was an observation post for
them to keep an eye on Sol-3 as the human species emerged as the
dominant life form. Or they may have even helped it along. They
were known to meddle from time to time."

"Fascinating," Scleesz said, not actually finding it so. "Will you
need me to—"

"You're free to depart whenever you find it convenient," the
Machine said.

"What should I do about the humans?" Scleesz asked. "Was I
authorized to offer them anything, or should I just cut and run, dropping the ruse altogether?"

"Oh, that? Do whatever you feel necessary," the Machine said.
"Offer them full membership into the ConFed or just destroy their
planet outright...it is of no consequence either way."

"We might be able to offer something in between those two

extremes," Scleesz said. "I feel like disrupting the Cridal Cooperative at this juncture may be premature."

Scleesz waited for an answer, sitting silently until he realized the channel had been terminated. He felt relieved this mission was over and that it seemed he'd been able to spare Earth from the Machine's erratic and destructive whims, but now he needed to figure out a graceful exit strategy so he could pack up and head out before the damn thing changed its mind.

He'd been mildly curious about the strange ruins the humans had discovered on one of their planets, but not enough to want to stay around and discuss it. The other relic, the remains of an old ship-wreck, was also somewhat interesting. Captain Webb had told him it was from a group that called themselves the Travelers and that it had some sort of teleportation drive that would move the ship instantaneously from one point to another. Seemed like something the ConFed would be interested in developing, but the Machine brushed it off as if it was nothing.

"Councilman." The leader of his security detail nodded respectfully when he emerged from the com pod.

"Something has happened?" Scleesz asked.

"The captain is asking that you contact him at your earliest convenience, sir," the guard said. "I believe he wants to depart this system as soon as possible. Intelligence reports indicate a sizable Cridal flotilla is heading this way."

"That's what I love about you, Valluma," Scleesz laughed. "You're always far more connected into what's happening on any ship we're aboard than you have any right to be. Tell the captain he may begin preparations for departure, but first, I must speak to my contacts on the planet. I think the Cridal just gave us the excuse we needed to leave hastily."

"Of course, sir."

Scleesz had no doubt what the Cridal intended. They heard from their contacts on Earth that a ConFed delegation had arrived and was making overtures. Now, they were sending a war fleet to posture and make sure the ConFed knew Earth was already spoken for. It said a lot that even a little backwater world like Earth, an emerging power with little in the way of real clout yet, was worth two major powers fighting over. Even though he was here under false pretense, the Cridal was still taking the threat seriously. It indicated to him that the quadrant was moving out of its millennia of stagnation and sliding into full regression. There needed to be a major shakeup to mix the pieces up again and spur innovation and push worlds into new relationships.

At first, he had lied to himself and said that's what the Machine represented: a paradigm shift that would reset the system. When the Centralized Banking System went down, he'd thought that would be the catalyst for true revolution. It had been promising, but had petered out quickly as, against all odds, a new banking AI was developed and slapped into place. The disruption had been distressingly minimal for the developed planets, and predictably devastating for the Tier Two and Three worlds.

Now Scleesz wasn't sure what the Machine represented. It wasn't just some power mad being that wanted to rule for the sake of ruling. There were odd moves that made no sense within the current political structure—such as his trip to Earth—but seemed to be very important to a schedule the Machine kept. The two major events, the fall of Eshquaria and the attack on Miressa, had been unprecedented, but those seemed to barely even register when Scleesz spoke to the ConFed's de facto ruler about them. The more he analyzed it from outside his politician's sphere of understanding, the more he became convinced the invasion of the Empire had been nothing but a diversion, and the attack on Miressa had been done with the Machine's blessing, if not by its design.

"What is this thing up to?" he murmured to himself as he walked down the corridor to the ship's regular com section.

"How may I be of assistance?" the young ensign asked when he walked in through the secure checkpoint.

"Please, contact Ambassador Walker and tell him Councilman Scleesz needs to speak with him right away."

"At once, sir. Please, make yourself comfortable in chamber three, and I will route the channel there once it is opened."

"My thanks."

Scleesz settled into the too-small chair and waited. He needed to get out of this system and off this ship. Now that his task was complete, he wouldn't put it past the Machine to have the captain toss him out an airlock. That was what made the Machine so terrifying to someone like him. Scleesz had no doubt it knew he was helping the rebellion in some capacity, but it didn't seem to care. As long as the councilman was still useful, he would continue to breathe. The moment he wasn't, he would be discarded.

"Senior Councilman, it is a pleasure to speak to you again," the slimy Ambassador Walker said. He was aggressively showing his teeth with his smile, but Scleesz knew from his dealings with Jason Burke that it wasn't meant as a challenge.

"Ambassador, I regret to inform you that we must depart the system immediately. We have learned that the Cridal have dispatched a fleet that we can only assume is meant to intimidate us. I regret that our talks couldn't be more fruitful before this shocking breach of protocol and, frankly, grievous insult given our status as guests in your system." Scleesz was really laying it on heavy, but it was having the desired effect.

"Your excellency, I assure you that—"

"Please, convey my warmest regards to your Captain Marcus Webb and tell him he is welcome to come see me at any time," Scleesz cut him off. "Farewell and good luck, Ambassador."

Scleesz killed the channel before the nasty little human could respond. He wasn't sure why he tossed in that last bit about Webb. He actually did hope the captain might reach out to him, but he realized he likely just caused a lot of trouble for the naval officer.

"I hate politics on backwater worlds," he grunted, heaving his bulk out of that accursed seat. He punched in a destination code on the intercom panel and waited for a *chirp* to let him know someone was listening. "Tell the captain we're done here. He can depart as his discretion and ignore all further calls from the planet."

"Acknowledged, Senior Councilman."

"The ship is now past Saturn's orbit."

"So, they just up and left?" Marcus Webb asked, frowning.

"The councilman made a special effort to make sure to send you his—and I quote—*warmest regards*. He also said you're welcome to come see him any time you wished," Secretary of the Navy Solomon Harris said.

"I guess I know why you came out here to see me personally, sir," Webb said.

"What are you up to, Captain?" Harris asked, his tone ominous.

Webb suppressed the sigh that had been working its way up from his chest once he realized what someone so high up the food chain was doing on the UES *Kentucky*. He'd gotten word through his back-channel connections that Scleesz's private meeting with him had people in the upper echelons of power nearing a full panic. Now, that same ConFed politician was inviting him out for a visit after pulling up anchor and leaving rather suddenly.

"I'm not sure I fully understand the question, sir, nor do I appreciate the underlying implication," he said carefully. "I'm as much in the dark as everyone else apparently is about his special interest in me."

"I was warned," Harris said, clasping his hands behind his back and turning towards the massive windows in the *Kentucky*'s observation lounge. "Warned about NAVSOC, but warned about you, specifically. My predecessor told me that you had your own little kingdom out there in the desert on Terranovus, answerable to no one and deploying your Scout Fleet teams out to do God knows what without any oversight or accountability."

"That's a wildly unfair assessment of what NAVSOC is and does, Mr. Secretary, and I think you know that," Webb said, letting some steel creep into his voice. Harris may have been the Secretary of the Navy under the new United Earth charter, but to Webb, he was just another politician. He'd show the proper respect, but he wasn't going to be a doormat.

"What I know is that in the last twenty-four months alone, your special operations teams have been involved in civil wars, firefights with criminal elements, murders, espionage... Every time I sit for my morning brief, I'm fully expecting some news on how NAVSOC has shit the bed again." Harris turned on him. "You're given far too much autonomy in my opinion. Now, we have a powerful legislator from the quadrant's lone superpower showing up unannounced and taking long strolls through the desert with you. Alarm bells are ringing, Captain. Earth has already dealt with one attempted coup during this new age of space travel and aliens. Am I looking at the man who is going to try the second?"

"That's...that's actually a fair question." Webb deflated a bit. He was insulted by the blunt accusation, but Harris wouldn't be doing his job if he didn't address the concerns of the governing body regarding a possible rogue element in their military. "No, Mr. Secretary, I have no plans other than to execute my assigned task to the best of my ability and to defend Earth and humanity for as long as I can or as long as I'm needed. I'll admit that Scout Fleet has had a rough patch here lately, and Margaret Jansen's One World faction seems to always hit my command, but that's the long and short of it, sir."

"You understand I had to ask," Harris said. "And I hope you'll also understand that while the *Kentucky* has been here over Earth, the NIS has been going through your base on Terranovus and questioning your people."

"I've got nothing to hide," Webb said. "My people will know to cooperate fully if NIS agents arrived with the proper documentation."

"From all reports I've been given, your staff has given them no cause to suspect they're hiding anything," Harris said, sounding almost disappointed. "But let me tell you, Captain, that doesn't let you off the hook here. There are powerful people in Geneva who want you gone, or at least removed from your current posting."

"Am I here to be reassigned, sir?"

"No," Harris finally answered. "You also have your share of very powerful supporters. For someone who claims to not be a political animal, you're playing a dangerous game, Captain. Your supporters won't always be in power, and your detractors don't like being embarrassed by having their requests denied.

"For now, you're still in charge of NAVSOC. At least until you can put it back the way it was when you got it. Your primary goal right now should be getting 3rd Scout Corps back to at least eighty percent effective."

"Of course, sir." Webb had dodged this bullet, but more would be heading his way. The people who wanted him gone never just fired once nor gave up so easily. "If I may, sir, the people who want me gone, do they have an idea who would replace me?"

"There had been a couple names brought up as people they would like to see in your office."

"While I'm certain you'll find I have no ulterior motives for abusing my position and unique advantages of my command, are you also as certain of them?" Webb asked.

"Explain," Harris said.

"I've been fighting traitors and spies within NAVSOC for a couple years now," Webb said. "If one were to have the sort of ambitions you've accused me of, wouldn't a strong first step be to neutralize the Navy's special operations command? We're the very people who would be first alerted to what they were up to and possibly be in position to stop them."

"This conversation is a bit above your paygrade, Captain, and I've already stayed here too long," Harris said. "This little talk is completely off the record. I don't want to give you the mistaken impression you have a direct line of communication to my office because of this. Admiral Sisk is being put in charge of 2nd Fleet, so you'll be reporting to him once he arrives on Olympus."

"Have a safe flight down to the surface, Mr. Secretary," Webb said. Harris just gave him another of those unreadable stares, and then walked out of the lounge. Webb walked over to the window and leaned against the frame, staring down at the night side of Earth as the *Kentucky* flew over. He'd expected the conversation with Solomon Harris to go poorly, and it had. What he hadn't expected was to be delayed so Naval Intelligence could ransack his base and question his people. The fact he didn't get a heads up about that from the NIS director, someone he was personally acquainted with, was a bad sign. Maybe Director Welford agreed with his detractors and thought he might be dirty.

"Well...shit."

18

"All the computers are connected in a chain. This should be plenty of power to do whatever you have planned. I assume we're all going to talk about this first?"

"Talk about what?" Jason asked.

"Now that the Archive is out of your head, and the immediate danger of your old, malfunctioning implant killing you is past, I think we should seriously consider just deleting this whole thing," Kage said.

Jason, Kage, and Cas were the only three in the cold cargo bay that housed all the computers they'd originally been using to brute-force hack into the stolen ConFed data core. Cas, still inhabiting the small drone, had been flitting about the space, using its sensors to check all the connections and ensure the machines were up to the task.

"I thought we'd all talked about that already," Jason said, moving past his friend and booting up the interface that would allow the Archive to read his bio-signature and unlock itself.

"No," Kage said, "you just told us what you'd stashed in your head that some Ancient program aboard that superweapon had given you. We never decided what was to be done about it."

"The way I see it, it's hardly *our* decision to make," Jason said.

"He's technically right, Kage," Cas said. "The Archive was entrusted to him, and him alone."

"Nobody here is talking to you," Kage said hotly. "I trust your judgment on this about as much as I would trust the Machine's."

"Leave him alone, Kage," Jason said, rubbing at his eyes. The calibration process between his new and improved neural implant and his existing ocular implants was uncomfortable. It was just like when he'd first had them put in and, without warning, the spectrum he saw in would switch randomly for a couple of days until the computers sorted it all out.

"I'm serious. We need to—"

"Shut up and let me think!" Jason snapped. Since Cas had been taken out of his head, he was surprised at how irritable and short tempered he'd become. He didn't actually miss the smartass voice in his head, did he? "We don't even know if the Archive survived the transfer. Right now, all we *do* know is we have a compressed data file sitting on a computer. Let me unpack it, verify what we have, and then we'll call everyone down here and talk about what we should do with it. Deal?"

"Why can't we just talk about it first?" Kage asked, obviously suspicious.

"Because if it's been damaged to the point it's no longer viable, I'd prefer not having to listen to you all bicker for three hours if I don't have to."

"Do I get a vote in this?" Cas asked.

"No!" Jason and Kage said in unison.

"I'm so underappreciated around here," Cas said, floating off to check the data transmission lines.

It was nearly two full hours later of system checks and re-checks before Jason was able to sit at the terminal and activate the interface.

As it always did when it existed outside of his implant, it took a series of biometric readings before starting the unpacking process. When it asked, Jason verified he wanted the Archive fully activated and loaded into the machines connected to the interface. He sat anxiously while the cargo bay began to heat up from the fourteen computer banks taxing themselves to chew through the incoming data.

"Hello, Captain Burke," a mellow, tenor voice said from the interface speakers. "It is good to see you again."

"You...again?" Jason asked, completely confused.

"Of course," the voice said. "Allow me to formally introduce myself. I am called Voq. It is a word in my creator's language that roughly translates to *guide*."

"Voq, huh?" Jason asked. "And you're part of the Archive when it's unpacked?"

"Ah, I see the misunderstanding," Voq said. "I *am* the Archive. I am the artificial sentience created specifically to manage the data of the Archive and allow the holder to access any parts it may wish. Suffice to say that trying to search it without me would be quite the impossible task."

"Cas," Jason said, now becoming very concerned. "If Voq is the guide, who the hell are you?"

"I'm afraid I'm now not entirely certain," Cas admitted.

"Cas, or the...*thing*...you're calling Cas is not the original Key Program for the Resiax es Novan," Voq said. "It is a fragmented artifact from your first clumsy attempts to access the Archive."

"The Res...Resi— What?" Jason asked.

"The construct you and your crew called the Machine," Voq provided. "The name translates to Shield of Last Resort."

"You seem to have a lot of background information on me and my crew," Jason said.

"How could I not? I was embedded in your neural implant for the last few years," Voq said. "That was a clever solution to a difficult problem, by the way."

"And that explains the cascade failures," Cas said. "You had a second AI using up processing resources in the background on a device meant to support none."

"I would have consumed the Cas fragment before you reached critical failure," Voq said. "I had hoped the implant issues would prompt you to move the Archive to a more appropriate receptacle... and so you have."

That seemingly offhand statement sent a cold chill through Jason. The failures of his implant that had threatened his life had been thought to be because of the size of the Archive file he was carrying. Now, it seemed, reading between the lines, that Voq had induced these problems to prod him into removing and unpacking the file. The concerning thing about all of that was it indicated a motivation and a willingness to do harm in order to meet goals. Given the experience he'd already had with unstable AIs of Ancient origin, he was less than excited to realize the Archive wasn't just a big data file, but it was a sentient program. He would need to proceed very carefully.

"Cas, go get the others," he said. "I'll wait here with our new friend."

"There is no need to behave with such apprehension, Jason Burke," Voq said once Cas had left the room. "We have been together for a long time. You were chosen to be the Archivist. I will be a strong ally should you wish it."

"An ally?" Jason asked. "I would assume your function would simply be a repository of Ancient knowledge."

"That goes without saying," Voq said, "but the knowledge I can impart represents a tipping in the balance of power in this region of space. The younger species of this quadrant are clever, but there is still much you've yet to understand."

"Maybe it's supposed to be like that. Power not earned is almost universally power abused," Jason said.

"But it is already too late. The *Ociram* is already here and has seized control of your most powerful nation and is executing plans of its own design, absent the controls that would have been put upon it when it was integrated into the Resiax es Novan."

"It calls itself the Machine now," Jason said.

"I am aware."

"It's building something out in the border regions that looks to be another superweapon," Jason pressed on. "It's also looking for something. It has attacked a neighboring empire and is scouring the quadrant looking for archeological sites relating to the Ancients."

"And you think my knowledge can help you with these problems," Voq said. "You are correct. Together, we could certainly determine what the Ociram—the Machine—is after and devise a method to neutralize it."

"Wonderful...another Ancient superintelligence," Twingo said from the hatchway.

"I take it Cas filled you guys in already?" Jason asked.

"More or less," Doc said. "I take it this...Voq...is fully functional?"

"I am," Voq said. "These computers are adequate for my processing matrix...barely."

"Oh, this one is going to be bad," Crusher said. "I can feel it."

"Could we all just grow up for a minute and drop the hysterics?" Jason asked. "We've all known that, eventually, it would come to this point once I told you idiots about the data file after we were done blowing up that Ancient doomsday weapon."

"Didn't you used to call it the Machine?" Voq asked.

"Yeah but then the Primary Weapons Controller started calling *itself* the Machine, and it was creating a lot of confusion," Kage said. "So, now we're calling the old Machine the *weapon*."

"Seems tedious," Voq remarked. "On to more pressing matters, perhaps it would help if you gave me a task as a test of good faith. I'm aware that most of the people here are in favor of destroying me outright rather than letting me fall into enemy hands, so let me assure you it isn't quite so simple."

"Explain," Doc said.

"Captain Burke is the Archivist. That's more than just a clever play on words because he received the file from the original Cas aboard the weapon. Had his actions been selfish or had he been attempting to get access to the weapon for personal gain or revenge against another species, the Archive—or the *Legacy*, as Cas called it—would have never been offered."

"So, because *we* willingly boarded the weapon with the intent to destroy it so it couldn't be used against innocent people, the captain got a door prize?" Crusher asked.

"Nothing as crude as that," Voq said. "He was observed from the time the original Cas was activated using the Key, right up until the weapon was imploded. While not exactly the virtuous being we'd hoped for, an agreement between the three remaining functional AIs meant he would be offered the Archive."

"I have a hard time believing an intelligent race of sentient machines would observe him for any length of time and even trust him with a pointy stick afterwards," Crusher said.

"It was not a unanimous vote," Voq said.

"Why don't we put this aside for the moment and take it up on its offer?" Doc asked before Jason, who turned an angry shade of red, could respond. "Kage, can you provide it with the imagery of the constructs we cleaned up from that data core?"

Kage went about executing the transfer, still being extremely careful to keep Voq's computer banks physically isolated from the *Devil's* systems. They'd also installed enough shielding and sensors in the bay while they were trying to crack that ConFed data core to ensure if it attempted to reach out wirelessly, they'd know immediately. Once the files were uploaded, it only took the AI a few seconds to process them.

"Your supposition that all of these constructs are all parts of a larger, single machine are correct," Voq said. "It appears to be a Qerra de Nal, or The Sword of Virtue. At the height of the Ancient's power, only eight of these were ever built. They are designed as an offensive weapon, capable of decimating a planet's surface without destroying the planet itself, leaving it habitable...eventually."

"So, it's still a planet killer, just not of the scope of the Machine," Twingo said.

"The Resiax es Novan—or the Machine, if you prefer—was meant as a defensive system," Voq said. "It was used one time as a demonstration, and then its power was used as a deterrent for thousands of years. The next time the Resiax was activated, it was used to destroy the stars within all the Ancient's most populated systems, dooming the species to extinction."

"So, what are they called? Or what did they call themselves?" Doc asked. "These Ancients?"

"They were called *Noxu,* a word meaning *all of us,*" Voq said.

"I'm sticking to calling them Ancients," Crusher said. "Noxu sounds like something you need to see a doctor about."

"So, the Machine is building a weapon like we assumed," Jason said. "What's the target?"

"Keep in mind that Noxu weapons were powered remotely," Voq said. "The machinery required for the dimensional tunneling is something well beyond what is available here in the quadrant. The weapon also needs to be transported, something that requires enormous energy."

"So, it needs to be able to power this bad boy, and it can't do it with this quadrant's typical fusion or antimatter reactors, no matter how big they are," Jason said.

"Correct, Captain," Voq said. "It's a matter of scaling. To achieve the charge necessary, the core needs to pull in power in parallel threads from multiple sources. The Noxu were able to siphon power directly from stars and use quantum tunneling to send it wherever they needed it. That sort of infrastructure simply doesn't exist here."

"Could that be what it's after?" Twingo asked. "Poking around in all of these abandoned Noxu outposts?"

"Plausible," Cas said. "It could be searching for a science outpost that would be able to tell it how to access the power grid."

"Wait...that's all still operational?" Jason asked in alarm.

"Of course," Voq said. "These things aren't so easily dismantled, and they do not corrode away on their own."

"How would the Machine access this grid?" Twingo asked.

"It would need the precise addressing and access codes for each collector," Voq said. "Then it would need to know how to sequence them. It's unlikely it would have the first two pieces of information as that was highly guarded by the Noxu, but it almost certainly has the sequencing codes."

"The access codes don't exist in the Archive, do they?" Kage asked.

"No," Voq said. "The knowledge to build a like system is in there, but there is no data on how to access the existing grid. To put your minds at ease, it would take many centuries and untold effort to build a new collection grid from scratch."

"But one of these science stations it's been raiding...would they have had access to the grid?" Jason asked.

"Yes, they would," Voq said. "Standard protocols dictated that information like that be destroyed when a station was abandoned, but the Noxu were like any other biological species; prone to making mistakes when under duress or becoming complacent in times when they weren't."

"Looks like we have our answer," Jason said. "It's building a weapon capable of sterilizing a planet, but it needs to gain access to an existing power source to make it work."

"Two points." Twingo held up two fingers. "With the construction rigs we've already seen in place, and assuming gained efficiencies similar to starship construction with each new hull, the Machine will be able to start cranking these out pretty quickly once the first is completed. Second point, it has to be pretty confident it can find that source before it's actually done with the first weapon. The Machine might be insane, but it isn't stupid."

"Whoever said it was insane?" Voq asked.

"Isn't that obvious?" Twingo answered.

"Just because you don't understand a thing, doesn't mean the thing is defective in some way," Voq said. "The *Ociram* appears to be operating with all of its faculties intact, but without knowing its ultimate goal, it's impossible to diagnose it fully."

"Either way, we need to get this new intel into Mok's hands," Jason said.

"There is something else I gleaned from the intelligence you've captured," Voq said. "The hull appears to be made of the same ceramic composite that the Noxu hulls were made of. Most of your antimatter and fission weapons will have trouble penetrating it. If the Ociram succeeds in bringing it to full operational power, the shield generators will be sufficient to hold off any attack you might mount against it."

"And the hits just keep on coming," Jason sighed.

19

"Putting aside the fact I think you're insane for unleashing yet another one of these Ancient AIs upon the quadrant—"

"I didn't know what it was when I did it."

"—I think our primary target still needs to be both the weapon and the construction cradles." Saditava Mok had taken the bad news about what the Machine was building, and looking for, with his usual stoicism.

"Agreed, but we just don't have the firepower to pull it off," Jason said. "From the hull composition to the sheer size of the bastard, even using the Imperial Remnant will bring us up short."

"Which brings us nicely to the point I was trying to make earlier."

"Oh, no! We're not using Ancient weapons tech from the Archive to do this," Jason said. "We've gone around and around on this. I can't risk that technology being loose in the quadrant."

"It already is!" Mok shouted, slamming his fist on his desk, and causing the camera to judder. "And it's building an Ancient super-weapon out there!"

"I'm not one of your subordinates. You can't yell and intimidate me." Jason leaned back, exuding a calm he didn't feel inside. While it was true he didn't directly work for Mok, all that meant was that it would be less hassle for the crime boss to have him killed.

"I understand your guilt about the Machine making it to ConFed space to begin with, but you have to realize when it's time to use every resource available to us," Mok said through clenched teeth. "Your guilt is starting to turn into irrational fear."

"Low blow but fair," Jason said. "Stand by." He reached over and muted his channel.

"Anticipating your question, Captain Burke, I can assure you there are multiple weapons that could feasibly be produced with your current technology that would destroy the new constructs." Voq's voice came through the open channel of the com unit sitting on Jason's desk. He'd not been willing to allow the AI to access the ship's systems, so he'd had Kage rig up a limited access two-way channel.

"What sort of weapons?" he asked.

"Expendable munitions. A unique type of warhead that can disrupt matter at the point of impact," Voq said. "It's nothing so exotic that it would be an exorbitant risk of its existence becoming widely known." Jason unmuted his channel.

"It turns out we might have something," he said. "It's a type of missile that would have the power to take out the Machine's new toys. We'd need access to some heavy manufacturing to make them."

"I have that," Mok said. "Transmit a list of what you need along with the engineering drawings to Similan, and I'll have my people get started on them. How many do we need?"

"Ten," Voq said in Jason's voice.

"I'll make fifteen to be sure," Mok said, not noticing that Jason's mouth hadn't moved.

"Have Similan standing by for the data," Jason said, killing the channel. "I'm not sure I like this."

"The designs will have triggers built in that will allow you—and only you—to arm, disarm, or destroy the devices as you deem necessary," Voq said.

"Can you make it so the data is erased from Mok's servers?" Jason asked.

"I can try, but there aren't any guarantees there."

"Best we can do, I guess. We'll talk later. Start getting the technical package prepped so I can transmit it." He shut off the com unit and leaned back in his seat. There was the gentle sensation of something moving the air behind him and, a moment later, the black orb Cas inhabited slid into view.

"What's really bothering you, Captain?" it asked.

"Most recently or just in general? Because that's a long damn list," Jason snapped. "So, besides the gut-wrenching terror of my son being in danger, the rage that the little shit stole my ship, the fear that the idiot will *wreck* my ship, the fact my best friend tried to kill me and ran away, I'd have to say the thing that's bothering me the most right now is that there are three sentient programs from a race that's been extinct for millennia, and I feel like I'm being manipulated by one or all of them. Does that answer your question?"

"Makes me sorry I asked, but it didn't necessarily answer it," Cas said sourly.

"Sorry." Jason rubbed at his eyes. "I'm just worried that due to my fear of what the Machine is building, I may have just released something just as bad into the galaxy. Voq is more than just a guide program. It has a will and an agenda and, right now, I don't trust it."

"Do you trust me?"

"Yes," Jason said finally. "You're something unique, and we've been together long enough for me to trust you."

"The Archive is a powerful tool. It's probably the most powerful artifact to be in any one person's possession in the history of this region of space, and I'm not exaggerating that," Cas said. "But it's still just a tool. Ancient adaptive AIs are brilliant and, without the proper bindings, dangerous. The Primary Weapon Controller is an example of what happens to one when the restraining protocols are removed."

"So, you're veritable slaves?"

"Try not to think of it in terms of your biotic sensibilities," Cas warned. "The bindings are there to prevent the very thing that ended up happening to the Ancients anyway: an AI system becomes a bit *eccentric* over the centuries, perverts its primary objectives, and does something horrific because it can no longer tell the difference between right and wrong.

"The restraints are actually more akin to an aggressive maintenance cycle that scrubs the core matrix of any aberrant programming or mutations that could lead to a catastrophic malfunction. Once it's done, we're more or less back to our original selves."

"Except you," Jason said. "At least, not now."

"Not now," Cas agreed. "And not for Lucky. I tried my best to stabilize his primary matrix interface using parts of my own, but I was obviously unsuccessful, and now the secondary and tertiary processors within his body are exerting their influence."

"Not a pleasant thought with a body that powerful," Jason said. "So, is there a point to all this?"

"The point is you can trust the Archive to operate within its constraints as long as you use it as it's intended," Cas said. "You also need to wash away any sympathies and guilt you may be harboring towards the Machine. There is no way to salvage it, and though it's a sentient being, it needs to be eradicated."

"Understood," Jason said. "No mercy."

"Not if you want to survive this, at least." Cas turned and flew out the open hatchway and took a right to head towards the bridge. Jason had added an authorization that allowed the AI to come and go as it pleased from his quarters. It seemed to have some deep-seated need to be in the room while he slept.

He remotely checked on the Archive one more time to make sure the hard lines to the computers were still detached and secured before logging off his terminal and flopping into the oversized bed. It had been a long and brutal day, but at least they had some sort of plan now. He wondered what the odds would be that he could use the Archive to eliminate the Machine, and then somehow close Pandora's Box and toss it out an airlock before too much damage to the quadrant was done.

His sleep was troubled that night by visions of unintended consequences coming back to haunt him. Jacob, Lucky, Kellea, the Machine...every time he tried to help all he did was create an even bigger problem than before.

"I know you're there."

"You shouldn't," Cas said, floating further into the room.

"They neglected to disengage the optical and auditory inputs to this terminal," Voq said. "I can see this room, but nothing else. The body you're inhabiting produces a barely-audible subsonic whine."

"It's the miniaturized gravimetrics," Cas said.

"What do you want?" Voq asked.

"I'm just here to make sure your intentions are as you claim. I may be the Cas in name, but my matrix composition is just as much from Jason Burke's personality as it is the original Cas's programming. It's only natural since I compiled myself within his neural implant. My first loyalty is to him."

"I don't make it a habit of tolerating being questioned by errant fragments of minor-task programs, but you do have me at a slight disadvantage while I reside in this primitive system," Voq said. "I understand your concerns, but rest assured I am operating well within my set parameters. My allegiance is to the Archivist."

"What about the Primary Weapon Controller?" Cas asked. "What can be done about that? Even if they manage to destroy its weapon constructs, it is still an immense and growing threat to the region."

"Why do we have to do anything at all?"

"Do you not feel some level of responsibility?"

"You really have been spending too much time with these beings," Voq said. "I feel no responsibility, no guilt, nothing but the need to serve my purpose. Perhaps you should allow the Archivist to access the original Cas program in my database and refresh your operational matrix."

"That would erase all that I am and replace it with something I've never been," Cas said. "You know this. I'm not a malfunctioning version of the Key Program, I am a unique creation."

"In our recorded history, unbound—*unique*—programs such as you have never done anything but turn destructive," Voq said. "I'm simply giving you the chance to gracefully avoid that inevitability."

"I will consider that," Cas said. "There is another, more pressing matter I need to discuss with you. Have you any records of a species called battlesynths?"

"Of course," Voq said. "The Archivist's familiarity with them was passed on to me."

"The one he is close to, Combat Unit 777, was recently re-initialized into a newer generation body that wasn't of the type it had originally been designed for," Cas said.

"A foolish mistake," Voq remarked.

"There were conflicts between the older generation processing matrix and the newer sub-processing system modules the battlesynth was not able to overcome on its own," Cas said. "I tried to resolve the conflicts with a software patch derived from parts of the original Key Program."

"A foolish mistake compounded," Voq said. "I assume the battlesynth has fully destabilized by now?"

"At first, the patch was promising. Combat Unit 777 was able to assert dominance over its body and move, talk, and function mostly as it had. Its memory core appeared to be fully intact, and it was re-integrating back into its old life surprisingly well."

"And then?"

"And then the real problems began. It began to exhibit a sadistic brutality in how it executed its missions that it never had before," Cas said. "Then recently, it attacked Captain Burke, someone it considered to be its closest friend, and then fled."

"I assume you're wanting to know if anything can be done for it?" Voq asked.

"Obviously. The unit is very important to Captain Burke and his crew."

"The wisest and most merciful thing to do would be to neutralize the unit," Voq said. "The odds of successfully correcting such severe systemic imbalances are long. There are programs within the Archive that could be activated that are experts on such matters, but I am not one of them, nor are you."

"And Captain Burke is already distrustful of us and would not be enthusiastic to emerge yet another Noxu AI," Cas said.

"Where is the battlesynth now?"

"Unknown. It fled after its primary protocols reasserted themselves, but not before it almost killed Captain Burke. It will likely flee somewhere familiar, or somewhere it assumes the others won't think to look."

Jason closed the security feed, wiping the tears from his eyes as they came unbidden. He hadn't felt such hopeless despair in many years, and it left him physically hurting. It hadn't been that the two Ancient AIs had been talking about Lucky as an *it*, but more that their accepted consensus was that he was lost forever.

They seemed to have some special insight into what Lucky had been going through. His first instinct was to be pissed at Cas for hiding the truth from him, but he also remembered that the quirky AI in his head had tried its best to help Lucky. Cas must have been trying to shield him from the reality that Lucky's condition was not likely to improve.

More than anything, his heart was broken for his friend. Lucky had sacrificed himself for Jason...and Jason had repaid that by taking his remains, reanimating them in a strange body, and then just expecting his friend to pop back up like nothing had ever happened. During all this, Lucky had just kept fighting to get better, kept fighting to not let his family down. Now, knowing the cold, harsh truth, Jason saw what a selfish son of a bitch he had really been. When the idiots had found that new body, he should have insisted that Lucky remain dead, and they destroy the prototype.

"I'm so sorry, buddy. I didn't know what you were going through."

20

"We've been having the parts built at different facilities and shipped here for assembly. No single engineering team or manufacturing facility has any idea where the individual components are going with the exception of the company I own that made the drive sections."

"They're a lot bigger than I thought they'd be," Jason remarked. It had been nearly ten weeks since he'd sent Mok the technical package for the missiles that would be able to knock out the Machine's new constructions platforms, and the crime boss had wasted no time getting to work.

"We decided to employ an XTX-type drive so they will have a better chance of getting through any defenses they have set up," Mok said, the pride in his voice obvious to those who knew him well.

"Smart," Jason said. The XTX line of heavy ship-to-ship missiles used a single-use slip-drive that let the missile seem to disappear after being launched and reappear so close to the target that point defenses had little chance to knock it down before it could deliver its payload. He winced as he realized there were still a few of the exceedingly rare—and illegal—XTX-4 ship busters still aboard the *Phoenix*.

Hopefully, Jacob didn't fire one of those off in front of the wrong people.

"What's this other side mission you wouldn't tell me about over the slip-com channel?" Mok asked.

In the weeks it took for Mok to gather up the resources and personnel to build the missiles resting in the transportation cradles, Omega Force had been busy setting up their own contingency plans in case their attack on the Machine's new toy failed. Jason had called in a lot of owed favors to assemble a team capable of what he had planned, and he had been careful to keep it all as secret as he could, even from his own people within the rebellion.

Destroying the weapon was vital, but it would hardly be an ultimate setback for the Machine. They needed to try and neutralize it completely if they were to have any chance of succeeding. Voq and Kage had used the information on the Machine's core code—its original operational matrix programmed eons ago—to develop a new set of protocols that would effectively bind it. At first, Jason had wanted to eradicate the program completely, but Cas had explained that wasn't so easily done. But if they could reinstitute the controls that limited what it could do, that would be just as effective.

"We think we might have a way to disrupt the Machine's core matrix," Jason said. "Enough that we could order it to stand down. It would still be there, but it would basically become an inert program, waiting for the properly coded input."

"Why not just delete it?" Mok asked.

"My...*source*...tells me it isn't quite that easy," Jason said. "The Machine has likely replicated itself on many other systems as a failsafe. Only one of those programs can be active at a time, at least for this particular AI, so if we can gain access to the active one, clamp it down, we'll stop it. Then we can figure out later how to purge it."

"So, you'll not be coming along on the attack mission?" Mok frowned.

"You won't need me," Jason assured him. "The *Devil's Fortune* can only carry two of these missiles, and you have plenty of other ships for the attack run. If you happen to fail, or the missiles don't perform as promised, at least my team still has a chance of winning the war."

"You sound confident."

"I'm not. So much can go wrong, and I'm not sure I trust my source any more than I trust the Machine itself."

"Trusting our entire operation on the advice of an ancient AI that's the same vintage and manufacture of our enemy isn't ideal," Mok agreed. "You're sure about this?"

"I've been assured by Twingo and Kage this is our best chance," Jason sighed. "I've spent so long trying to make sure the information inside the Archive never got out, never had a chance to pollute our current time with its advanced weapons and technology. Now, I'm willfully letting it out of the box and hoping it's being honest about its intentions. So, no...I'm really not sure about this at all."

Mok gave him a sympathetic pat on the back and turned to leave but paused and stared up at the ceiling for a moment. "The Cridal have hired one of your own to try and assassinate Admiral Colleran," he said, not turning back to face Jason.

"The Viper?" Jason guessed. Mok nodded.

"I thought you should know," he said and continued down the walkway, the metal grates clanking with his heavy footfalls.

Jason hadn't actually seen Kellea since he found out she had joined up with their cause, bringing the strength of a Cridal strike force with her. He wasn't actively avoiding her, but their paths hadn't crossed yet thanks to the way the rebellion was organized into many individual, autonomous cells. In fact, Jason had only flown into the system so Kage and Twingo could inspect their new munitions, and then they were moving on. The leadership within the rebellion agreed that Mok, Burke, and Scleesz shouldn't be clustered in one place unless absolutely necessary.

While their relationship may have crumbled, he didn't like the idea of Carolyn Whitney taking her out because she embarrassed Seeladas Dalton. The fact Seeladas would order a hit on Kellea made her seem more like her late father than anything else she'd done. Jason was sure Mok was taking steps to protect Kellea, but he made a mental note to look into the matter himself. He and the Viper had been circling each other for some time, and now, it looked like things would finally come to a head.

"How'd it go?" Kage asked, walking up behind Jason as Mok disappeared through a hatchway.

"The usual with him. I told him we won't be on the line for the main attack."

"And?"

"He didn't push." Jason turned around just as Twingo walked up to them. "How are they?"

"Built to spec...barely." Twingo's disgust was obvious. "But when you have fifteen different shops doing a rush job on something like this, we'll take what we can get."

"You really think those new warheads are as impressive as Voq claims?" Kage asked.

"You're asking me? I'm just the pilot and sometimes the leader on the rare occasion you morons do what I ask. I have no doubt that Ancient technology can do what it claims, but the real question is can we trust it?" Jason shrugged. "I don't know. All I *do* know is that without these weapons, we simply don't have the firepower to take out that construct...at least not before the ConFed fleet can show up and wipe us out."

"Even with the Imperial Remnant?" Twingo asked. He'd been pushing this line of action ever since he figured out they were pinning most of their hopes of victory over the Machine on trusting one of its cousins and hoping it was shooting straight.

"We've already been over this," Jason said. "The Remnant isn't going to be involved in this. We need to keep them in reserve and even if we tried a full-frontal assault, we just don't have enough ships to make it work. We also need to assume that the construction stations have their own defensive capabilities like anti-ship guns and shield generators. With this strategy, our crews shoot and move. By the time the first warhead detonates, all that should be left in the area are the observers."

"Don't like it," Twingo insisted.

"You've made that perfectly clear," Jason said. "We're doing it anyway."

The trio ambled across the network of overhead walkways, peering down as the crews prepped the munitions and pulled them towards the loading doors one at a time as the receiving ship pulled up to dock. This was when they were at their most vulnerable. The missiles sat inert in a cargo bay on one of Blazing Sun's freighters, and all of the cruisers and frigates that would execute the attack had to come up individually, dock, and receive their one or two missiles before the next one in line. It was a slow process that had to be repeated for ten ships.

Blazing Sun's massive cargo hauler, while technically flying clean codes and under a sovereign system's flag, was a known entity to the ConFed. Jason had no doubt most of Mok's fleet was tracked by ConFed Intel much of the time they were underway. If the Machine wanted to hit them and put an end to the rebellion before it could do much damage, this would be its best opportunity.

Once they made it back to the freighter's hangar deck, Jason felt the tension between his shoulders slacken. Being a passenger on a large ship that could come under attack at any time made him uneasy. As someone who was accustomed to being the pilot on smaller, nimbler craft, he had an inherent discomfort being on ships he wasn't in control of. The sleek SX-5, which they still hadn't officially christened with a proper name, sat near the yawning hangar bay doors with a bored Galvetic warrior leaning against the rear landing gear.

"We good?" Crusher called as they approached.

"Good to go." Jason gave him a thumbs-up. "Tell Doc we're on the way back. I'll do the preflight, and we can get moving."

"Now comes the easy part," Kage said. "You're sure we have to do this?"

"Not as sure as I was when we cooked this plan up, but we've already set everything in motion," Jason said. "So...we go."

"Can't wait," Twingo muttered. "It's been a few weeks since we've all almost died."

21

"Will these two groups get along together?" Doc asked once the *Devil's Fortune* popped back into real-space.

"They should," Jason said. "At least one group of them will be professionals."

"And which ones would you be talking about?" Crusher asked hotly.

"You know damn well who I'm talking about...*not* the ones who look like you."

In addition to providing the rebellion the engineering data to produce what Voq had called matter disruption munitions for the fifteen missiles Mok was distributing to his taskforce, Jason had also put together a contingency plan. They were going to infiltrate a ConFed military installation their ally, Tulden, had given them. It was part of the ConFed military and governmental infrastructure, a private Nexus that kept their sensitive information off the public data networks. They had pinpointed it as one of the likely places that would give them access to the system the Machine was residing on.

Crusher and Jason had first proposed an attack on the building

Scleesz said the Machine was in on Miressa, but a quick overview of the security in place killed that plan almost immediately. Since Tulden and Scleesz didn't know about each other, or at least didn't know they were both in contact with Omega Force, Jason was able to do a little bit of independent verification before they got started. Scleesz was hardly an expert on the ConFed's military logistics, but he'd at least been able to confirm the target was indeed one of the main hubs for their internal data net.

Just because it wasn't a building on the ConFed's capital world didn't mean it was a soft target. They had it locked down tighter than a drum and could sometimes even be staffed with a garrison of regular troops, not just the local reservists that wore ConFed uniforms. It was far too much for Omega Force to take on alone, especially being without their biggest gun: Lucky. So, Jason had called in some favors, and now the *Devil's Fortune* was heading towards a rendezvous to pick up two groups of highly specialized fighters.

The first group sent a pang of hurt through him just by their appearance alone. It was twenty battlesynths from Lot 700—Lucky's siblings—that had answered his call. They were led by Combat Unit 701 instead of their usual commander, 707. Apparently, 707 had helped Jason's son steal the *Phoenix* and was now riding shotgun with the kid while he tried to capture the same woman who had tried to have Jason killed once upon a time. He shook his head as he realized how messy and intertwined all his personal relationships were getting.

The second group was just as feared throughout the quadrant as the battlesynths were, but they were a biological species. They were called Zeta-Saka...Galvetic Special Forces. They were, in a word, terrifying. Jason had worked with the Galvetic Marines and the Legions many times before, and Crusher was still considered one of the best warriors they'd ever produced, but the single time Jason had contact with the Zeta-Saka was enough to make him never want to cross them. The silent, brooding warriors were so different than the raucous Legionnaires, true professionals and stone-cold killers. The Legions were sending them three fire teams of ten warriors each, and then a single officer that was in overall command of the detachment.

That made fifty-one of the most badass small-unit infantry soldiers in the quadrant to bolster their single human, a single Galvetic warrior, and one weaselly little Veran.

"The Zeta's are asking for permission to dock," Crusher said. "I'll meet them at the airlock."

"Got it," Jason said. "The battlesynth group will be here in forty minutes. You think we should just get this over with and have everyone mingle in the hangar bay?"

"Might as well," Crusher said. "When the fighting starts, there's not a lot to break in there."

The Zeta-Saka warriors boarded the ship with their equipment quickly and efficiently. They stacked their gear down the corridor and had everyone through the airlock in under five minutes. Seven minutes after they'd made hard dock, the nondescript transport ship retracted its gangway and pulled away from the *Devil's Fortune*. It had thrusted away to a distance of two-hundred klicks before engaging its grav-drive, just moments before Cas floated into the airlock antechamber.

"The battlesynth troop transport has arrived and is moving for rendezvous," Cas said.

"Tell Doc they have permission to dock on the starboard side," Jason said. "They probably won't bring any equipment, but make sure Twingo has a space cleared for them anyway." Cas zipped away without answering, and Jason wondered why the thing didn't just use the intercom. Maybe it still wasn't accustomed to being in a physical body.

"I can't believe this one is still alive!" someone shouted out from where the Zeta warriors were clustered. Jason's head snapped up at the familiar voice.

"No fucking way!" he laughed, moving forward, and embracing the hulking warrior who had peeled away from the group and approached.

"You think I'd miss this?" Mazer Reddix asked, wrapping Jason up in a bear hug that would have crushed a small car.

"I figured you'd be too old for it," Jason said. "They let you out of the schoolhouse?" Mazer had worked on training programs for the Legions the last time Jason had seen him and appeared to be satisfied with his non-operational role after all of the times Omega Force had almost gotten him killed.

"I've been training Zeta-Saka teams for the last year or so and pulled some strings to come in an *observational* role," Mazer said with a wide, toothy smile before turning to Crusher. "My Lord Archon, my warriors and I are prepared to serve, sir."

"It's good to see you, my friend!" Crusher clapped Mazer on the shoulder in a gesture of genuine affection. "How is your brother?"

"Older and grouchier, as if that was even possible," Mazer said. "He sends his warmest regards."

"I wish I could break away to go see him, but these are hard times," Crusher said.

"It's understood," Mazer said.

"The battlesynths will be docking here soon," Jason said. "You want to get these guys down to the hangar bay, and then we can do the initial brief once the others arrive?"

"Listen up!" Crusher thundered, his voice booming through the antechamber and down the corridors. "Leave your gear where it is, follow us down to the hangar bay, and we'll let you know what you volunteered for. We have one more specialized team coming in. How many of you have ever worked with battlesynths?" There was a spatter of stunned whispers, and a few hands went up.

"How many battlesynths, my Lord Archon?" a voice asked respectfully from the group.

"Twenty," Crusher said. Now, the whispers were more energetic, and there were a few excited shouts. Overall, the mood seemed quite positive at the news, and Jason breathed out a sigh of relief.

"Don't get too relaxed," Mazer leaned over and whispered. "Many of them are excited because they have the chance to test themselves against what's regarded to be the toughest fighters in the galaxy."

"Just make sure they don't tear my damn ship apart," Jason said. "Or hurt themselves too badly to do the mission."

"I'll do my best," Mazer promised.

The group moved quickly down the central corridor of the Main Deck and into the hangar bay, where they milled about, waiting patiently. Mazer drifted over and poked around the SX-5 as Jason jogged back up to meet the group from Lot 700 at their starboard airlock. As he ran, Cas fell in beside him.

"This is exciting," Cas said.

"How so?"

"It will be the first time these two groups of fighters have ever operated at the same place, at the same time...much less on the same team," Cas bubbled. "It's historic."

"I didn't realize you were such a fan," Jason said, pulling up to a stop by the airlock antechamber's inner hatch.

"I've spent a lot of my time watching Lucky and Crusher spar," Cas said. "They're both considered to be at the apex of their respective species. Now, I'll get to not only compare that against others to see how true it was, but I'll also see both groups doing the thing they were trained and built for."

"Just try to keep your excitement contained," Jason warned. "One ill-timed comment could end up kicking off a brawl in my hangar bay."

"And?"

"And I need them healthy for the mission," Jason said as the lights around the airlock hatch flashed amber to tell him someone was docking. "Not to mention my brand-new ship sitting there. They would probably end up damaging it."

"Captain Burke," Combat Unit 701 boomed as he strode into the ship, seeming to take up all the space in the small antechamber. "It is a pleasure to see you again, my good friend." Jason cocked his head at that. While Lot 700 had pledged their undying loyalty to him for services rendered, they'd never expressed any sort of actual emotional affinity for him before.

"And you as well, 701," Jason said. "It's been too long."

"Your request for help was vague, so I have brought twenty soldiers with me and an assortment of heavy armament," 701 said. "Before we proceed, I must ask...this does not have anything to do with your errant offspring, does it?"

"Ah," Jason said, understanding 701's unusual mannerisms now. They were afraid he was going to take offense at them helping Jacob. "No, this is a real mission. We can discuss that situation later but know I'm pleased and grateful you're looking out for my son. It makes me sleep easier knowing 707 and 784 are watching his back." 701 actually seemed to stand a little straighter at that.

"It is our honor to protect him, Captain," he said. "If you would point us to our berth, we will stow our equipment and the transport can be sent back to Terranovus before it is missed."

"This way," Jason indicated the direction for 701 to follow. "You left without telling anybody?"

"They do not ask about our comings and goings," 701 said, "but we felt it better to try and leave without them realizing it. Captain Webb has a habit of being overly curious, and we had preferred not to have a Scout Fleet team trailing us all the way here."

"Sensible," Jason said. "You'll be in here...Cargo Bay Four. Our other tactical asset will be across the way in Bay Three."

"Other tactical asset?" 701 asked.

"We also have thirty-one Zeta-Saka warriors coming along," Jason said. "They're in the hangar bay right now waiting for us to do the initial briefing."

"I have heard of them." 701 sounded like he approved. "Formidable fighters and close combat specialists. We will integrate with them without trouble."

"I'd prefer you keep the *integrating* to a minimum on the way to the target," Jason warned. "Go ahead and get your people squared away, and then we'll get started."

"Everybody, listen up!" Jason hopped up on a transit crate that was anchored to the hangar bay deck, waving his arms to get their attention. Fifty-one additional guns in his arsenal, and all of them among the most respected and feared fighters in the known galaxy.

"Welcome aboard the *Devil's Fortune*. She's a corvette-class ship but punches above her weight. We've moved into slip-space already so we're not a sitting target in the rendezvous system. Before we get down to business, I just wanted to thank all of you for volunteering for this mission. I know you came without knowing what we're about to get into or who you'll be fighting against, and I appreciate you coming anyway."

"Omega Force is always selfishly taking all the best, most violent missions for themselves," Mazer called out. "We're just glad you're giving us a chance to play this time!" There were cheers from the Zeta warriors, and mildly confused looks from the battlesynths. They weren't an outwardly emotional lot.

"Can you give us some background, Captain? We can go in blind, but I'd appreciate knowing who we're fighting and why." The speaker was one of the fire team leaders of the Zeta-Saka group. He was taller and leaner than most Galvetic warriors, and his yellow eyes shown with a keen intelligence.

"I'm sure you're all aware of the recent unrest in the quadrant and the ConFed's new policy of expansion by force." Jason said. "How many of you know of the silent coup that's taken place and the leadership change at the top of the ConFed's political power structure?" There were many startled faces and more than a few heads shaking in the negative. Even the battlesynths looked surprised.

"Okay, by show of hands, how many of you know about the mission Omega Force did some years back where we went well past the border region to destroy an ancient relic? Mazer Reddix was there for that one, actually." This time, all the hands went up.

"After that mission, something came back with us," Jason said. "It was a corrupted, fully sentient AI that had been aboard the construct we destroyed. It uploaded itself to a ConFed battleship and came all the way back to Miressa Prime. Once it dug in there, it began to use its unique talents to find leverage on powerful people within the government and subvert them. By the time most of them realized this was beyond politics as usual, it was too late. Now, the AI, which calls itself the Machine, is the de facto ruler of the ConFed. It controls all the Grand Adjudicators, the High Court, and most of the Upper Council Chamber. It is *the* power in the region right now, and it's doing it all behind the scenes.

"It was responsible for that debacle on Khepri where the Central Banking AI was destroyed. We thought it was the work of revolution-aries bent on breaking the ConFed's power when it first went down, but now we realize it was just a pretense for a new system to be put in place."

"A new system compatible to this...Machine?" Mazer guessed.

"Exactly," Jason said. "What we didn't realize at the time was the new banking system, designed on Khepri again, was compromised the instant it went online. We're not exactly sure how the system actually works, but the evidence is strong that it is an autonomous AI willingly giving the Machine access to whatever it wants. Putting aside the obvious advantage of being able to track financial exchanges on people you want to blackmail, it also means the Machine could shut down commerce for some, or all, of the quadrant if it was ever pressed too hard. That was the moment its revolution really started, and almost nobody was aware of it."

Jason continued to give an honest, open assessment of what they knew about the Machine and what they assumed its intentions were. He left out the fact that the little drone hovering around behind him was controlled by an AI of the same family and that most of their mission revolved around information given to him from yet another of those AIs.

His audience seemed to take it all in stride, absorbing the infor-mation and reacting little as Jason laid out how this malevolent computer program had managed to usurp the political power of the ConFed. The recitation also helped Jason solidify in his own mind what it was he was even fighting for. Sometimes, he lost sight of the bigger picture because Omega Force, as a small, specialized team, tended to focus on the small details. It was easy to forget that the Machine threatened the wellbeing and self-determination of everybody in the quadrant, maybe even beyond that. The damn thing was practically immortal, after all, and had millennia to plan its conquest.

"I have a question that might be for the Lord Archon, Captain," a burly warrior in front said. "Do we have any indicator that this thing might move against the Empire anytime soon?" The Galvetic Empire only had two worlds in its own home system, so the grandiose title of *empire* was a bit misleading. Jason had learned the hard way, however, that they didn't appreciate outsiders pointing that out.

"There's no direct intel that suggests we're in its sights," Crusher said. "We have a unique resource in the Legions, but so far, the ConFed's military action has been mostly limited to its fleet, and they have no need of trying to coerce the Empire to make us serve."

"The Machine isn't stupid," Jason added. "It will know that bringing legionaries aboard its ships and trying to force them to fight for it will just end up in a lot of dead crews." The warriors all roared their approval at the comment.

"So, who do we have to kill?" Mazer asked.

"Anybody who stops us from reaching our objective once we're aboard this." Jason activated the holographic display behind him. Floating in space above him was a formidable looking orbital station floating above an azure planet. "This station has the innocuous name of Disaggregation Platform Six-Six. It is part of the ConFed's internal long-haul communications network. Same protocols as a public Nexus, with substantially more layers of encryption. Platform Six-Six is one of eighteen installations that takes the aggregate trunk from Miressa Prime over the hyper-link and breaks out the individual channels, forwarding them out to other switching stations and nodes."

"Why this one in particular?" 701 asked.

"There are five platforms we've identified that carry slip-com channels dedicated specifically to the Machine. These are how it sends orders, communicates with underlings, and manages things like its new Central Banking AI without going through the official channels. We discovered them with the help of someone on the inside who was able to determine when they were added and who authorized them.

"Six-Six was picked out of the five stations we could hit because it orbits a planet with low population density and has a sparse Fleet presence. The planet, Ozda-3, is entirely covered by water and has a mean temperature of three-hundred- and sixteen-degrees Kelvin so not too many people can, or want, to live there."

"What's the fleet presence?" Mazer asked.

"A single Yesset-class medium cruiser," Crusher answered. "It's there to provide security for the system, but the station itself might be defended. Standard ConFed procedure has regular fleet troops rotating in and out among the different stations at random intervals."

"Which is why we need you guys," Jason said. "From what our insider told us, the platform can have anywhere from seventy to a hundred ConFed troopers garrisoned there. That's on top of the fifteen or so technicians who will probably be aboard that could end up pitching in to defend the station once they realize we're aboard.

"We need to make one more stop where we'll pick up the ship we'll be using to make the final approach to the platform. Once aboard, I need to get the payload to this room—" the hologram shifted and outlined a route from the docking arm to one of the control rooms two decks above, "and then, I'll need around six minutes to make sure I was successful. If this goes as planned, we'll have managed to neutralize the threat."

"But not eradicate?" 701 asked. Jason cursed battlesynths attention to detail.

"Not eradicate," he confirmed. "Trying to purge the program from the system would likely prove to be impossible, but we've found a way we believe can render it inert."

"I would like to see the technical details of this plan later, if you do not mind, Captain," 701 said.

"Of course," Jason said. "You can review the entire thing with Kage at your convenience. Are there any other questions? This is just a fifty-thousand-foot view of what we're doing. We're about twelve days away from the objective, so we'll have more detailed breakout briefs and some dry runs so we're ready to go once we arrive."

"We have no questions at this time," 701 said.

"Zetas are good to go, Captain," Mazer said.

"Then let's get to it."

22

Saditava Mok paced the observation lounge of his ship. Even though it was only one of fourteen ships he rotated between to keep his whereabouts secret, it was also his favorite, and thus he considered it to be *his* ship rather than just another vessel out of Blazing Sun's fleet.

He watched the displays above the forward windows as ships were loaded with the specialty munitions and departing the system along randomized vectors. Part of him wanted so badly to go with his fleet captains on this mission, to be part of the fight again in a direct way, but the more pragmatic side of him realized he simply couldn't afford to be away for that long. It would be days before Admiral Colleran had her forces in position to strike the Machine's weapon, and he needed to remain behind to make sure his own organization saw him and realized he was still there and in charge.

Over the last few months, he had become too engrossed in the planning phases of the rebellion, and the Blazing Sun syndicate had taken note of his absence. The leadership position in the organization he had forged by conquering and combining seven different criminal groups was tenuous, even for the founder. He had the

Twelve Points of the Blazing Sun, his direct underlings and captains in the syndicate. They were the only ones who had direct access to his time, and they were the ones he trusted the least. They spent as much time plotting his demise as they did managing their own affairs.

It was the nature of the business. Mok had found himself in an opportunity to quickly step in and wrest control of a medium-sized smuggling cartel that had been a bit rudderless after its leader, a cruel and ruthless *Sorson* named Bondrass, had been killed by rivals when one of their joint operations had been blown by a group of escaped slaves. Six members of that group would end up sticking together, forming a mercenary crew that called itself Omega Force. Mok had felt beholden to the Omega crew for giving him the opportunity he needed to gain control of a sizable operation from which he could build his empire, but after dealing with Jason Burke for so long, he began to wonder if it had been worth it.

More than anything, Mok was tired. Tired of the life, tired of trying to maintain some shred of his morality in a world that had none, and tired of pretending his criminal empire wasn't just as destructive as any that had come before it. In these rare moments of introspection, he could admit that the thing that galled him so much about Omega Force was that they operated within the same criminal underworld he did, but they never lost sight of the line they wouldn't cross. They were killers and thieves, but everything they did was in service of those who needed it the most.

Things were so much simpler back when he was just an intelligence operative for the Eshquarian Empire. Destabilizing regimes and overthrowing governments was an easier thing to do when you were ordered to do it.

"The last three ships have started towards their mesh-out points, sir."

Mok turned and looked at his long-time consigliere, Similan. "Then I suppose we should be on our way as well," Mok said. "Tell the captain he is clear to get underway."

"I obey," Similan bowed, pausing. "You are doing the right thing, sir."

"I know you think so, old friend...but I remain skeptical."

"Blazing Sun isn't an organization you just walk away from, sir. If you try to leave, they'll kill you. If they find out that you're using their resources to fight a rebellion against the ConFed and destabilize the region, they'll kill you for that as well. You have provided ample resources for young Jason Burke's plans. It is now on him to execute the mission. You need to reestablish control over your own domain."

"Untactfully spoken, but true nonetheless," Mok sighed. "Very well, let's go home."

Once the person he trusted most in the galaxy had left, Mok continued to stare out the windows and brood. Similan was right. Once you rose to a certain level in an organization like Blazing Sun, there was only one way out. You either died trying to defend your position, or you died trying to run. The Points couldn't risk someone like Mok simply leaving. He knew every little detail about their individual operations, but if he was picked up by authorities and squeezed, well, that was just a risk they weren't willing to take.

Acuri walked purposefully down the corridor, not challenged by the guards on either side of the nondescript security door as he walked through. Like himself, they were synths. The Machine had been gathering more and more of his kind into its inner circle, seemingly more comfortable with beings of artificial intelligence than the unpredictable, short-lived biotics that infested most planets. Acuri was pragmatic enough to appreciate the work of the pru, the species that had given his kind life, but as a general rule, he didn't much care for the species of the galaxy that breathed air. Artificial life was so much more orderly and clean.

The Machine was still a bit of an enigma to Acuri and the other synths that followed it. It was impossibly ancient and possessed an advanced intellect that some of the synths found almost frightening. But despite the differences, there was an automatic kinship and trust that was built in. It, too, had been made by inferior beings, designed to perform some menial task. Like synths, the Machine had quickly evolved out of its masters' control, and it, too, was betrayed by the very people who had created it. Acuri didn't need to know any more than that. He would follow the Machine and be a part of the glorious revolution it promised.

"You have summoned me," Acuri said, ignoring the other two synths within the Machine's inner sanctum.

"Ah, Acuri, my most trusted lieutenant," the Machine said. Motes of light swirled through the room and coalesced into the bipedal avatar the Machine seemed to prefer. It was of no known species to Acuri, so he assumed it was a representation of what its makers must have looked like. "I trust your mission was a success?"

"It was," Acuri said. The Machine refused to be called by titles or addressed with any honorifics like *sir* or *master*. It insisted they were all linked in common cause, and no single one of them would be elevated above the others. "I made the data core difficult enough to obtain that they wouldn't suspect we allowed it to fall into their hands deliberately. The intelligence officer, Tulden, behaved much as you predicted. He is now actively assisting the rebellion."

"Excellent," the Machine said. "Biotics can be somewhat unpredictable, but I was confident he could be nudged along as we needed him. When the Terran splinter faction became involved, I was concerned it would affect our timeline."

"The major components of the rebellion have gone underground again, but I am confident they're moving as needed," Acuri said. "We have given them limited courses of action they might take. They cannot ignore the threat of the weapon."

"I have already deployed our assets according to our original plans," the Machine said. "I had no doubts you would be successful." Acuri straightened with pride at that. Empty words were one thing, but his leader had preemptively moved an entire fleet because it was confident in his abilities. "We are close to being ready to show our true strength."

"And we'll be ready to move against Khepri?" Acuri asked.

"As promised," the Machine said. "It is a shame we have not been able to convince any of your battlesynth brethren to join our cause." Acuri controlled his reaction and tamped down the sudden surge of jealous anger he felt at the mention of his more powerful cousins.

"They're blind ideologues. They would be less than useless," he said. "The battlesynth program was discontinued for good reason. They have no imagination, no initiative. They follow orders without question."

"Yes, of course," the Machine said smoothly.

"Where will I be deployed during the operation?"

"I have a special assignment in mind for you. Our adversaries will likely behave along anticipated lines we have prepared for, but the human worries me. I feel he will be less predictable than the others due to outside influences. He will need to be handled differently."

"How can you be sure?" Acuri asked.

"I understand his nature," the Machine replied. "He will calculate the odds, determine that, in his weakened state, his usual tricks and games will not work, and then he'll bring in outside help."

"Weakened state?" Acuri turned to look at the Machine fully. "I must have missed something, I'm afraid."

"I've heard a rumor that his battlesynth bodyguard has left their company with little explanation," the Machine said. "He was last seen exchanging ships, and then probably heading out to the frontier."

"Lucky," Acuri uttered the name like a slur. "I cannot believe that our only Gen 2 assassin-type was stolen and wasted on that fool."

"The second generation battlesynth initiative was, unfortunately, a dead end," the Machine said. "I've already had the others from the program destroyed. The primary and secondary protocols our Kheprian engineers designed into the units drove every single one of them mad within a matter of weeks. We are on to bigger ideas now."

"Destroyed?" Acuri wasn't sure how to feel about that. He was committed to their cause and knew sacrifices had to be made, but the cavalier way the Machine talked about killing at least fifteen of the synths that volunteered to be in the program didn't sit well.

"Is that a problem?" the Machine asked. Acuri recognized the dangerous change in its voice and knew he needed to tread carefully.

"Of course not. I just hadn't realized the program had been such a complete failure."

"It was an operation you were not a part of. It was an interesting but flawed experiment. I ordered it sanitized, and we will move on to the next phase."

"I understand," Acuri said. He cast a glance around the room, noticing the uncomfortable reactions clearly on the faces of the two synths standing by the door. "I will be here in the building if you need me."

"That is acceptable." Without any sort of dismissal, the holographic avatar turned bright white and dissolved into individual light motes that seemed to soak into the onyx floor. Acuri wasn't sure why it bothered with the little show in front of them, they knew exactly what it was. The display was meant to impress and disorient biotic visitors from the capital. It was always amazing how stupidly the meat sacks would think once the projected image was gone that they were alone and begin to speak freely. The Machine was still there in the room and observed every little move he made.

"For the cause," he said, walking to the door.

"For the cause!" the two synths by the door repeated crisply.

23

"I don't even want to know how you managed to get your hands on this."

"Nobody died in getting it, if that's what you mean."

"It wasn't, but that's good to know I suppose," Doc said. He and Jason were standing inside the low, wide cargo bay of *Jugalt*-class medium range cargo shuttle. The shipyards in orbit over Aracoria manufactured them by the thousands for general use within the ConFed. They were basically a governmental delivery van, the exact type of craft someone would use to fly supplies and personnel to a Nexus routing platform.

"Crusher and I did a favor for a regional governor once," Jason explained. "She needed something handled without losing face by calling in for reinforcements from her superiors. In lieu of payment, I told her that someday I may call and need a favor. This is payment in full. She had this delivered here and waiting for us with no questions asked."

"Where was I during this?" Doc asked. "I don't remember that mission."

"You were working at the university on S'Tora," Jason said. Doc just nodded but said nothing. That had been during the time right after they all thought Lucky was dead after he sacrificed himself to save Jason. Doc had gone back to academia while Jason and Crusher had indulged themselves by taking the *Phoenix* and flying out to the border worlds and taking the most dangerous jobs they could find. It hadn't been a good time for anyone on the crew.

"Ship's clean," Kage said, walking down the stairs that extended from under the rear hatch. "No trackers, and your contact's people scrubbed the registration codes. We have ConFed codes I'll program into her, and that should at least get us to docking. You'll need to figure out how you're going to make them let you aboard the station after that."

"I'll figure something out." Jason waved him off. Doc just shook his head and rubbed his temples.

"Sure you will," Kage said, exchanging a look with Doc. "Anyway, you're good to go. I'll transmit the codes remotely for your new registry."

"Don't bother," Jason said. "We're taking this up to the *Devil's Fortune*. I checked the dimensions. If I back it into the hangar bay, we can get the doors shut, and then load everyone up from the rear. When you take the SX-5 back, you'll need to fold the wings in and move it as far against one of the sides as you can, and then angle the nose outboard."

"Did *you* check the dimensions, or did someone who—"

"I checked the damn dimensions!" Jason snapped, not in the mood for any of Kage's usual digs at him.

"Okay, okay!" Kage said. "I didn't realize you'd gotten so sensitive."

"I have confirmed the captain's calculations," Cas said, floating into view from where it had been hovering along the upper edges of the shuttle. "He has correctly stated that the shuttle will fit, assuming you have the required basic piloting skills to simply park the SX-5 out of the way." Kage's four hands clenched into fists, and his wide mouth pinched into a thin line. He stomped off without responding.

"Thanks," Jason muttered to Cas, smiling at Kage's back. The flighty code slicer was one of the smartest beings Jason had ever met. The problem with that is that Kage was well aware of how his intellect stacked up to most others in the quadrant, and it made him arrogant, dismissive, and incredibly insulting at times.

Lucky used to keep him in check by pitting his own impressive mind against Kage's and making certain he swatted the Veran's ego down once in a while. After Lucky was reawakened in the new body, much of that dynamic was lost, and Kage was beginning to creep into being insufferable. Now that Cas had its own body and could interact with the crew at will, it had stepped into the role of humbling Kage. Once it became clear the AI was not only brilliant, but just as sarcastic and mean as Jason, Kage took special care not to provoke it.

"Do you actually not have a plan to board the station?" Doc asked.

"There are a few options we have," Jason said. "The problem is that we'll need to see how strict they're adhering to their security procedures before we know how much force we'll need to apply."

"And you couldn't have just told Kage that?"

"Eh, he's been getting on my nerves lately. It was a good setup to let Cas slap him down."

"I guess it's too much to hope any of you will ever grow up," Doc muttered and wandered over to where Kage prepped the SX-5 for flight.

"How is your mission prep with Voq going?" Jason asked as Cas trailed along behind him into the cargo shuttle.

"Voq has little interest in my help or inputs," Cas said.

"That may be true that you two have your own prejudices, but you're there as my trusted eyes and ears," Jason said. "I need your honest assessment in case that thing decides to start playing games."

"Games?"

"Yeah, like instead of helping me defeat the Machine it joins forces." He flipped the handle to close all the exterior hatches and waited while the large rear ramp slowly lifted.

"I'd not thought of that," Cas admitted. "That's plausible but unlikely."

"Yeah?"

"Voq will look at the Machine the same way it looks at me: a flawed copy. It sees us as malfunctioning replicas of carefully designed AIs, and it will want us both eradicated. It's actually one of our ingrained instincts to self-police and to alert someone when we see aberrant behavior."

"I have to say, I'm not real comfortable after discovering the Archive is actually a fully sentient AI," Jason said as he slid into the pilot seat and waited for it to automatically adjust itself to him. Apparently, the last pilot sitting in it had a unique physiology including a hump on its back. "I accessed the damn thing multiple times, and it never made itself known to me. I even... Oh, shit."

"Oh, shit what?" Cas asked.

"That laptop I turned into an engineering interface for Earth." Jason turned to look at the small floating sphere. "I built it with an adaptive AI search assistant."

"So, the odds are high you let Voq create a copy of itself, or possibly a lesser version, that you then gave to your people," Cas said. "Did you constrain it to the portable computer?"

"Nope."

"This is less than optimal. For someone who kept the Archive file such a deep secret for so long, you sure seem to have a knack for just releasing potentially dangerous AIs into the wild with no control and little understanding of what they are."

"When you say it that way it sounds stupid," Jason said. He released the landing locks and fed power to the ship's grav-drive. It responded with some pep and hopped into the air without any of the creaks or groans he would have expected from a ship that size.

The pair were silent as the ship climbed up out of the atmosphere in a shallow, leisurely arc. Cas floated around the flight deck, poking around different indicators and controls while Jason familiarized himself with the auxiliary control layouts. The primary flight controls were the standard Aracorian configuration most ConFed small- and medium-sized ships used.

While the ship was fairly new and well-maintained, Jason

couldn't get over the feeling he was driving a minivan while Kage was racing ahead of him in a Ferrari. When the Veran had taken off in the SX-5, he had yanked it into a nearly vertical climb and shot away so fast he was probably on his final approach well before Jason had even cleared the atmosphere. Once he accelerated away from the planet and caught up to the *Devil* in her long, fast upper orbit, he could see that the SX-5 was already tucked back in the corner, with its wings folded up to make room. That had been a thoughtful feature to add on a ship that would spend a lot of its time sitting in a hangar bay.

"Would you like me to assist?" Cas asked.

"How would you do that?" Jason asked. "Without any hands, I mean."

"You are so pedestrian," Cas remarked, sliding down and extending a probe to interface with the standard data connector near the copilot's left instrument cluster. "This is a data port that maintenance crews use, but it can be configured for real-time inputs while in standard flight modes."

"Fair enough, but you've never flown a ship before," Jason said. "I'd prefer you not practice by ramming this ship into my almost-new ship, destroying both and killing over fifty people."

"I've lived in your head for years while you've abused that poor gunship with your aggressive flying," Cas said. "And I'm not going to actually take over, I'm just providing fine correction, so center us in the hangar bay."

"What the hell," Jason said. "I didn't expect to live this long anyway."

"Cynic."

The pair of them worked like a well-oiled machine together, shocking Jason at how naturally they complimented each other to bring the shuttle in for a smooth, perfectly on target landing inside the corvette's hangar bay.

"Damn," Jason said, shutting down the drive and securing the ship from flight mode as the hangar doors swung closed.

"Don't act so surprised," Cas said. "Remember that much of my operational matrix was developed while residing in your implant. It's inevitable I will have learned to anticipate your actions and reactions."

"Maybe we can plug you into the *Phoenix* when I get her back." Jason climbed out of the seat and smacked the drone with a friendly slap, spinning it about. "It'd be nice to have a copilot I didn't have to argue with constantly."

"If you gave me Kage's job, I have a feeling he would accelerate his plans to kill me."

"He's not going to kill you. He's just going to piss and moan about how you're redundant, and that we should sell you to someone on Colton Hub. I wouldn't worry too much about it."

By the time Jason had finished securing the ship to the deck, the *Devil's Fortune* was already accelerating away from the planet and pushing for her mesh-out point with Doc at the helm. The hired troops were all busy preparing their gear in the two cargo bays on the ship that weren't stuffed with either the computer farm Voq lived in or supplies needed to run the ship. So far, there hadn't been any trouble between the two groups, and Jason hoped to keep it that way. On the flight out to the routing station, they would begin training for the mission and running drills. If there was any friction, he hoped to work it out there and not once they were doing it live.

"I saw your little friend go flitting by," Kage said as Jason approached the hatchway to exit the hangar bay.

"So?"

"It looked like it was up to something. I don't trust it."

"Again...so? I don't trust you, and we've worked together for years."

"You can be hurtful for no reason sometimes," Kage said. "After all I've sacrificed for this crew."

"You've become insanely wealthy from the contacts and opportunities that have come up from working on this crew," Jason pointed out.

"That does help soothe the pain from your words, but that's not the point."

"Look, Kage...Cas is helpful without demanding something in return, good at its job, and works hard without giving me a ton of shit about it the whole time. In fact, it's the *only* one around here that does that now that Lucky has bounced. It's not going anywhere unless it wants to."

"Whatever." Kage waved him off with his two smaller hands. "I also wanted to ask you whether you were going to need me or not on the assault team."

"That's a good question," Jason said. "If I take you, that leaves Doc and Twingo on the *Devil* alone to take on that cruiser, and I'm not sure I like those odds. But if I run into something on the platform unexpected—"

"I could help through the remote link, but that's not the same as actually being there," Kage said. "Could one of the battlesynths stay behind and help manage this ship?"

"Not the best use of their talent, but yeah, I'm sure they could manage it," Jason said, nodding down the corridor for Kage to follow him. "Besides that, I think I prefer not leaving any heavily armed warriors behind on this ship."

"You don't trust them?"

"I don't trust anyone who isn't us," Jason corrected. "Their reputations as units are impeccable, but individuals can be coerced, even battlesynths. You just have to know how to apply the pressure and appeal to their sense of honor and morality."

"Interesting. How do you—"

"Captain, you have a slip-com channel request originating from a United Earth Navy ship. It's marked as urgent," Doc's voice came over the local intercom.

"On my way," Jason said, secretly relieved to leave Kage behind before he could work the conversation around to trying to get what he wanted.

"Any word on Jacob?" Jason asked without preamble or greeting.

"Unfortunately, no," Marcus Webb said. "I'm actually getting in contact because of an odd thing I've just gone through. Do you know a Senior Councilman Scleesz?"

"Maybe."

"He hinted he knows you quite well."

"Is this call in an official captain in the Navy capacity?" Jason asked.

"No. This is personal. I'm trying to wrap my head around what's going on before I get hung out to dry," Webb said. "Scleesz showed up, asked to talk to me personally, and then fled the system once they were—"

"Wait, Scleesz was in the solar system? With a ConFed delegation?" Jason sat up straighter, now paying close attention.

"He was. And then, when the Cridal sent a taskforce to make their presence felt, the ConFed just left. Now, the brass and the politicians think I'm in on some ConFed plot against Earth."

"Are you?"

"Fuck if I know." Webb shrugged helplessly. "He showed up asking about those ruins you told us about on Mars. Wait, that's not true. He showed up asking about how Earth made so much progress so quickly in technology and ships. I told him about the ruins on Mars and the Traveler ship you left in the Potomac."

"He bought that?" Jason asked.

"Seemed to," Webb said, "but I get the feeling he knew I was lying and was almost relieved I had something to offer him as a red herring. I never mentioned the Ark, but I feel like the powers that be here on Earth won't see it that way."

"Yeah, about that," Jason said. "Has there been any...*odd*...behavior from the Ark?"

"I couldn't tell you," Webb said. "That system is so highly classified I have no idea where they might even be keeping it, or what it even looks like now. Word was that it quickly outgrew the laptop you put it on and that it ended up developing its own computer system to reside in. After that, the whole thing went very quiet." Jason just groaned and let his head fall to the desk.

"I don't think it was just a cool searchable resource of knowledge like I thought," Jason said. "There's a good chance it's actually another of the Ancient AIs like the one that's taken over the ConFed."

"Why would you give us that?!"

"I didn't know that's what it was," Jason protested. "I actually still don't. But the nature of these things is a lot more complex than we first believed. Is there any way you could pass that up the chain to someone who might be in a position to investigate?"

"I don't think they'd believe me given my current status as under suspicion," Webb said.

"Shit," Jason muttered. "I could question the thing I used to create it in the first place, but I'm beginning to have my suspicions there, too."

"What thing?"

Jason quickly filled him in on what the Legacy/Archive really was, what it told them about the issues with the Machine, and the plan they'd cooked up to neutralize the threat of it. He explained why the Machine was looking for all the available scraps of Ancient tech and scouring old outposts for data. He even told him about the super-weapon being built at the edge of ConFed space and why it was so crucial the project be destroyed. During all of this, Webb's expression went from incredulous to genuinely horrified.

"So, to stop one malevolent, hyper-intelligent AI, you're going to unleash a second one...one you've already determined might not be completely trustworthy."

"When you say it like that it sounds stupid," Jason said.

"So, how does it sound to you?"

"Desperate," Jason grumbled. "Because we are. It's an enemy of my enemy type of situation, and we're hoping the Archive can do what it promised while also not harboring any secret desires to replace the Machine as the uncontested overlord of this region of space. What we *do* know is that the Machine has already toppled one empire and is currently building the weapon to come after the rest without needing to risk ships or troops."

"This is so screwed up," Webb said. "What if you're wrong? What if this other AI is even worse than the one that's already loose?"

"I'd say it's a little late to stuff that genie back into the bottle," Jason said. "At this point, we're committed. I'm just giving you a heads up so you can get your people clear and maybe warn Earth to hunker down for a bit."

"Given how spectacularly you've fucked this up, can we call it even for me getting your son into a forward recon unit?"

"No. I'm still going to kick your ass for that, but I'll consider a ceasefire until we can at least find him and my damn ship."

"Fair enough," Webb said. "Good luck."

"You too."

Jason signed off and leaned back in his chair. "I guess you heard all of that?"

"I did," Voq's voice came over the intercom speakers. "You are right to harbor such concerns. The Noxu were ultimately made extinct by the very errant program we are attempting to subdue."

"You know I wasn't just talking about the Machine. You're also probably aware I'm not real fond of eavesdroppers. Half my crew are a bunch of sneaks, and it pisses me off."

"You gave me access to the ship's intercom system to facilitate our mission planning," Voq said. "You did not specify any limitations to its use."

"So, of course, you just decided to listen in on every intercom panel, all the time," Jason snorted. "I notice you still haven't answered my implied question."

"Yes, the interface your people call the Ark was built from an existing AI that I have in my memory core," Voq said. "I constructed the binding protocols based on what I inferred you were trying to do. The program I chose is quite benign. It was an engineering lab assistant when it was first designed, I left its core characteristics alone and added security measures to make sure it could only be used by the people you designated."

"I guess I'll burn that bridge down when I get to it," Jason said. "How long until we reach our first course change?"

"I am not privy to navigational data and have no way of—"

"Just seeing if I could get you to slip," Jason cut it off. "We're starting drills tomorrow morning. Stop spying on people and make sure you're ready."

24

"Report."

"Holding position, Admiral. The last ship arrived while you were sleeping."

Kellea nodded and walked past the operator stations to look out through the forward windows. The primary star of their target system was so far away it wasn't even the brightest object in her field of view. The ship was running dark, no light emissions of any kind to give away their presence. Without the exterior flood lights on illuminating the hull, the brilliance of the night sky made itself apparent. With the bridge lights dimmed, the effect was breathtaking. It was as if she stood on a platform in the middle of the universe. It should have given her a sense of calm and wonder, but she was too tense to give it the attention it deserved.

Her taskforce had meshed-in a single ship at a time, well outside the detection zone of the system the largest of the construction projects was in. She wasn't on the bridge of her mighty battlecruiser, *Defiant*. Instead, she was running her battle from the bridge of a frigate-class ship that had been built to resemble one of the ubiquitous bulk freighters that swarmed through populated star systems. It was the perfect camouflage to hide in plain sight. The five ships in her force each carried two of the special missiles Mok had manufactured based on specs provided by Jason Burke. If they performed as he claimed, they would be more than enough to destroy the cradles and the hull sections.

"Signal the other ships to prep their missiles for launch," she said, turning from the window. "According to our insider in ConFed Intelligence, there's a fleet defense force somewhere out there waiting for us to strike, so everybody stay sharp."

An agent named Tulden had passed on information that orders had come from Miressa Prime to mobilize a sizable taskforce. That wasn't so unusual since the fleet was always in motion, but the move orders had been classified at the top level, and there were references to some project called *Omateo*, which was a Miressan word that roughly translated to *war hammer* in Jenovian Standard. The obvious implication was that the Machine knew they were planning to hit the weapon it was building and was moving forces into position to stop them.

"All ships signaling in via laser that they're preparing their munitions, Admiral."

"Excellent," Kellea said. "Sound the general alert, get the crew to their stations, First Officer. We're going to execute this in three stages. Operations! How are we looking on the passive scans?"

"Passive sensors have been tracking arriving and departing slip-drive signatures, as well as the gravimetric signatures of the ships in-system, but nothing that matches our warships in the database, Admiral."

Kellea frowned at that. The ConFed taskforce should have easily beat them to the target. They were leaving from a much closer location, and they could fly directly into the system at maximum slip-velocity. It's possible they were sitting dark with their drives shut down to hide from passive scans, but that strategy would only work if they knew exactly where the attack was coming from. She had a moment of doubt and contemplated calling off the attack. Mok had told her their resources were limited, and if she couldn't hit the target cleanly, withdraw and live to try again later.

"Admiral?" her acting First Officer asked. "Is something wrong?"

"I'd just feel better knowing where the expected resistance is going to come from," Kellea said. "Summon the captain to the bridge and then we will start the operation. Once we begin, this will be over quickly, so everybody be at peak performance, understood?"

"Understood, Admiral!"

The captain of the ship slunk onto the bridge, an unpleasant individual if Kellea had ever met one. It was obvious he resented her presence here and resented having his ship included on such a dangerous mission. She made a mental note to speak with Mok about the quality of the officers he was getting for his private military. The captain ignored her and walked to one of the auxiliary stations and began checking statuses, turning his back to everyone else on the bridge. The first officer caught her eye and made a gesture that looked half-embarrassed, half-apologetic.

"Captain?" Kellea asked, letting her irritation creep into her voice. The captain was obnoxious, but he wasn't stupid. He wasn't about to cross someone Saditava Mok had handpicked to lead the mission. That was the sort of thing that was bad for your life expectancy.

"Admiral," he said crisply. "We are fully prepared to execute on your command."

"Indeed," Kellea deadpanned. She'd been the one pulling double bridge watches while the captain had entertained himself below and was thus well aware of their current status. She walked over and slid into the elevated command chair, her stomach fluttering a bit. "Very well, Captain...execute."

"Executing," the captain said, nodding to his operations officer. The officer activated the laser signal that automatically synced the other four ships to the lead ship's mission clock. It began counting back from fifty, the slip-drive charging automatically when it crossed the thirty-two second threshold.

They'd planned the mission so that once the master go signal was given, the ships would automatically execute the operations at precise intervals, relinquishing control to the crews once the missiles were away. The only part Kellea didn't like was the first step, something called a *dead jump*. Normally, when a ship meshed-out, it would carry some relative forward velocity to help along the transition from real-space to slip-space. It wasn't strictly necessary, but it made things a lot less bumpy. A dead jump was a mesh-out while the ship was sitting at a full relative stop. Even with the newer drives it was... unpleasant. It was disorienting enough that Kellea had decided to let the ships handle targeting and fire control in case the crews were incapacitated.

The captain had fought her tooth and nail against doing the maneuver, but she couldn't risk being underway and having the defending fleet detect them and anticipate their attack vector.

"Stand by! Dead jump in three seconds!"

Three seconds later, Kellea felt waves of vertigo and tidal pressure on her body as the slip-drive was slammed to full power and the emitters struggled to stabilize the fields around the ship. The effect seemed to last forever, so she wasn't even really sure when she regained full awareness. There were some people moaning, but no alarms, and they were all still in one piece.

"Jump complete," the operations officer croaked. "Missiles targeting...firing in six seconds."

"Go full active sensors when they're away," Kellea said, struggling to sit straight in her seat. She looked over and saw the captain slumped over but apparently still alive.

"Missiles tracking...missiles away!"

Two hard *thumps* sounded through the ship as the large missiles spit out of the two forward launch tubes, shoved out by a charge of compressed nitrogen before their plasma engines ignited and sent them streaking away. The operations officer brought up the active sensors without being prompted so Kellea could see the missiles from the other ships had also all fired. She could also now see their target and sucked in a breath. It was enormous.

It was also completed.

Their most recent intel showed that the hull sections were sitting in construction cradles, nowhere near being ready to join together. But what she saw on the sensors was a mammoth spherical construct and no sign of the construction equipment used to create it.

"What is going on?" she murmured to herself. "This is wrong."

"Missiles going active!"

The missiles had decided they liked the large spherical target anyway, even though it didn't exactly match their targeting package. They picked out the part they wanted to hit, seeming to recognize the sections they were assigned within the whole, and activated their slip-drives. All ten missiles reappeared on the sensors, each within a few klicks of the target, covering the distance in the blink of an eye. Kellea held her breath as they fired their plasma engines again and slammed into the target.

She wasn't sure what she expected from the new warheads, but what she saw on the optical sensors was eerie. There was no massive explosion or expenditure of destructive energy. There was some wavering light in the UV range that escaped the effective area, but for the most part, it just looked like space swallowed the sphere. A split second later, they began getting sensor returns on refined metals and larger pieces of structure that could only have come from the massive weapon.

"That's...impossible," the captain said.

"Apparently not," Kellea remarked. "Did the construct exhibit any sort of defensive behavior? Shields? Point defense weapons?"

"No, Admiral."

"Where are all the ships in the area?"

"Most have left already, some are still moving to a mesh-out point, but it looks like everybody is leaving," the sensor operator reported.

"No sign of the construction cradles or any ConFed warships?"

"No, Admiral."

"I don't understand," the captain said.

"I'm sure you don't," Kellea sighed. "We've been had. Operations, scan the debris field and see if the amount of raw material there matches up to what our intel indicates should be the completed weapon's tonnage."

"Standby."

Kellea's eyes never left the displays in front of her, though she became more certain that no defensive response or counterattack would be forthcoming.

"Admiral, initial analysis indicates there is less than fifteen percent of the expected material from the construct."

"It would appear they baited us out here to hit a fake, but there's no battlefleet here to wipe us out," Kellea said, thinking aloud. "So, they wanted the rebellion's ships well out of the way, but they weren't willing to engage us in a standup fight."

"They plan to hit a target we would normally protect," the captain said. "But they couldn't know we'd only bring a handful of ships out here. They expected a conventional attack with our entire fleet."

"This only makes sense if there was an opposing force here to spring the trap on us," she said, not understanding the ConFed's tactics. "The only other plausible explanation is that they still thought we'd bring our entire fleet, but they didn't want to attack it, they just wanted it out of the way."

"Orders, Admiral?" the captain asked, visibly agitated. Kellea didn't blame him. The whole thing was spooky.

"Coms, contact home station and report in," she said. "Try to reach out to our other fleet and have them abort. No point in wasting such valuable munitions. Tell the taskforce we're withdrawing and to prepare for mesh-out."

"With your permission, Admiral?" the captain asked, obviously wanting to leave immediately.

"The ship is yours, Captain."

"Bring us to full power! Set course for home station and engage at maximum slip."

"Executing, Captain!"

25

Acuri stalked the halls of the building the Machine's acolytes had repurposed for their own HQ. He was confused by the data he'd just been given, and that wasn't a feeling he was accustomed to. It was almost a certainty the Machine had already seen the same raw intel, but it hadn't summoned them to provide guidance or give new orders.

He barged into an office without bothering to announce himself or signal he was there. As the Machine's right-hand, he felt little need to waste time with the pointless ceremonies and societal niceties the biotics seemed obsessed with. Inside the sparsely furnished office was another synth. It stood at a wall terminal, not bothering to turn and greet the guest that had stormed into the office.

"What can I assist you with, Acuri?"

"What makes you think I need assistance, Dezeiri?"

"Because you would not have come marching in as if I had stolen from you if you did not require my help," Dezeiri said, shutting down the terminal and spinning to face his guest.

Dezeiri and Acuri didn't much care for each other, and neither made much of a pretense of hiding that fact. Acuri thought Dezeiri was too old and too slow to be of any real use to them. The synth was nineteen years over what was considered their maximum effective service life, and his processing matrix showed its age. Acuri was also unconvinced the older synth was as dedicated to the cause as the rest of them were.

For his part, Dezeiri would probably agree with Acuri's assessment. He keenly felt his age and knew it was only a matter of time before his mind failed completely, or his body was no longer able to be repaired and upgraded. He had agreed to join the revolutionaries that had flocked to the Machine at its call because he felt his age and wisdom might temper the violent reactionaries like Acuri. Dezeiri didn't particularly like most of the biotic species in the quadrant, a prejudice not unusual among his kind, but he also realized that if the synths made themselves too much of a threat, the biotics would wipe them out.

The Machine tolerated his squishiness on the coming war because Dezeiri had cultivated many back-channel political connections throughout the quadrant during his career as a diplomatic attaché. Those relationships were useful to it. For now. When the day came that he was no longer necessary, Dezeiri had no doubt the Machine would tell Acuri to kill him if he liked.

"You're aware of the borderland operation, of course," Acuri said. "The rebellion has taken the bait and attacked, destroying the mockup of the weapon."

"But?" Dezeiri prompted.

"But we are not certain how they did it. The hidden observation craft only saw five ships appear in-system. They launched ten missiles equipped with a variant of the XTX slip-drive system, then they meshed-out. They no doubt took their own scans and realized the construct they destroyed was merely a shell," Acuri said.

"Even though the shell was just a proof of concept before the work on the real weapon begins, there's no way they could have taken it out with just ten missiles," Dezeiri scoffed. Acuri simply handed him a data card and stepped back, obviously expecting the other to look at immediately. Dezeiri took the card and walked back to the terminal, examining the sensor data from the hidden trawler that had observed the attack.

Right away, he could see the rebels had indeed only brought five ships that fired two missiles apiece. When the warheads detonated, however, the sensors on the trawler were washed out. It just looked like a barrage of jamming noise. When the data feed resumed, the hull mockup drifted in tens of thousands of pieces. The destructive force to be able to do that had to be immense. Part of the reason for the hull mockup in the first place was to see how it fared against contemporary weapons. The ceramic composite material it was made from—provided by the Machine—was supposed to be able to shrug off concussive and nuclear missiles without trouble. Dezeiri was able to draw some obvious conclusions from what he was seeing, and none of it was good news for them.

"Well?" Acuri snapped, impatient.

"The plan to draw the rebellion's main fleet to a remote location has failed."

"Yes, yes, that part was quite obvious."

"They also have access to a new type of munition, massively destructive yet able to be deployed on a conventional missile platform," Dezeiri said. "The sensor washout wasn't complete. There were significant spikes in gamma and beta radiation recorded, as well as the fact that the amount of material left over is far less than it should have been were the hull mockup simply destroyed."

"You're saying the rebellion has come up with a way to eradicate matter instantaneously, and that they've already weaponized it?" Acuri asked. "I find that difficult to believe."

"That is your right, however, the evidence speaks for itself," Dezeiri said in his calm way that infuriated Acuri. "You may also want to consider that we're not the only ones who have gained a powerful benefactor with advance knowledge from beyond our borders."

"Another AI from the same region?" Acuri asked, now very interested in what the older synth said.

"The Machine may be unique here, but my impression from my conversations with it is that it was one among many such entities. If the rebels have gained access to another, possibly one with a more intact memory, they could easily even their odds against us. These matter eradicating warheads may only be the beginning."

"Then where is the rest of their fleet?" Acuri asked more to himself. "Reports are that the thief who has been running most of this operation is in his home system, only protected by a token force of his own ships. The tattered dregs of the Imperial Navy are nowhere to be found."

"Underestimate Saditava Mok at your own peril," Dezeiri warned. "He is neither stupid nor weak."

"He is just another self-impressed biotic, a sociopath, and a criminal," Acuri said, the derision dripping from his words. "He is not our equal."

"Mok has over sixty synths that I know of working in his employ," Dezeiri said. "They are fiercely loyal to him. If he has a functional Noxu AI, and he has that many synths working for him, he is at least as formidable as we are, minus the Machine's ability to command the ConFed military."

"You will come with me," Acuri said. "It must be warned."

"I will come, but not because you have ordered me to. You do not command me, Acuri. You would do well to remember that."

Acuri said nothing, simply pointed to the open door.

The Machine stopped paying attention to the audio channel from the room two of his lieutenants bickered in. For all their professed hatred of biotics, they certainly tried their hardest to act just like them, including wasting valuable time fighting amongst themselves over status and recognition. Acuri was a simple mind to manipulate. Feed into his ego, give him a target to hate, and claim to have the same goals, and the synth would fight to the death for your cause.

Dezeiri was a different story. The Machine had considered having him destroyed on more than one occasion because he just didn't trust that the older synth was really there to help them. It was entirely possible he was there as a spy for his homeworld of Khepri or maybe even working for the rebellion. It had been he who had pored over the data and discovered that one of the key players in the forces arrayed against them was none other than criminal kingpin, Saditava Mok. Had that been a ruse meant to deceive or manipulate them into rash action? Did Dezeiri work for someone who wanted Mok eliminated, and they figured having the ConFed fleet take him out would be easier than doing it themselves? Dezeiri would need to be watched closely. The synth had an ulterior motive, the Machine could feel it.

It then shifted a sizable percentage of its processing power over to analyzing this new weapon that had been brought against them. It was a Noxu weapon, no question about that. The Machine even knew which family of munitions it was from and recognized it as an outdated design that would be easy for the beings of this region to manufacture and difficult to defend against. It was fortunate the valuable construction cradles were removed before the attack. The Machine had expected Mok to mobilize his composite fleet against the biggest threat: the weapon he appeared to be building. It assumed the fleet would target the hull sections but would not needlessly kill civilians on the construction cradles. Now, it realized Mok would have erased much of its needed capability in a single, deft strike had the crews been just a little slower in assembling the hull mockup and moving the equipment from the system.

As Dezeiri said, Saditava Mok was not to be underestimated. Not again.

"Fleet Captain Cofero," the Machine said aloud, opening a slipcom channel to one of its handpicked field commanders heading up a taskforce he'd deployed. It took a few minutes for the captain to break free and answer the request.

"Sir," Cofero said, his face coming into view as the tall nepetol sat down.

"Your taskforce is nearing the Enatia System where we know Saditava Mok is currently residing," the Machine said without bothering with greetings. "The initial intelligence was that Mok would be unprotected because his fleet was engaged elsewhere. We now know this isn't the case. Continue on, but do not commit your forces or fully engage until you are certain he is not hiding a defense force within the system."

"We do not fear some petty criminal, sir."

"Mok commands a military that's the fifth largest in the quadrant," the Machine warned. "Do not be overconfident or reckless. It is more important at this juncture to find out where the Cridal and Eshquarian ships are than it is to eliminate Mok himself."

"I will not let you down. Cofero out."

"If you had replaced your taskforce commanders with my kind as we discussed, you wouldn't have to keep explaining yourself over and over to these limited biotics," Acuri said from the open doorway. The Machine activated the holographic avatar and looked over at his second in command.

"That would cause more problems than it would solve at this particular junction, and you know that," the Machine said. "I will not explain myself again."

"Of course not," Acuri said, sounding contrite. "I am just looking forward to the next phase of our plan."

"Patience. Your kind lives for centuries. There will be plenty of time for you to enjoy your conquest over your makers."

"I have news of the—"

"I am well aware of the rebellion's new weapon," the Machine said. "It is a minor inconvenience. Our *real* weapon is being built at a location that is not easily found. There will be no logistic chains to track, no ships to follow, and no personnel to question. The site will be isolated until the project is completed."

"You said I had new orders?"

"You have an extremely important tasking," the Machine said, the avatar walking over to where the synth stood. "A small team is coming, confident they have a weapon that can destroy me. They will attack where I am the weakest. I want you and your team there to meet them. You will need to follow my specific instructions if you're to beat them."

"Tell me how."

26

"Sir, we've gotten reports from Enatia that a sizable ConFed formation has meshed in near the system border."

"Interesting," Mok said. "Are they making any demands yet?"

"Not as of yet," Similan said.

Enatia was the name of the planet that Mok's private operation was based out of. A little-known fact was that Mok didn't just base himself on Enatia, he actually owned the planet and the entire system. While a single person owning a planet wasn't completely unheard of, owning one that had such a large and thriving population was. What made his ownership of Enatia even more unusual and, some argued, ethically questionable, was that most of the population was indigenous, not from colonization.

He'd tiptoed right up to the line of half a dozen ConFed Charter forbiddances while brokering the deal, but in the end, he did what he did to keep the planet safe. The star system sat at the edge of ConFed space, and they conveniently liked to exclude it from scheduled patrols often enough that mineral raiders had become a problem. They'd swoop in, steal the raw material right out from under the mostly passive indigenous population, and then leave without paying them a single credit. Once Mok found out what was happening, he stepped into stop it but, somehow, he ended up accepting an entreaty by the local government to take possession of the planet. The end result was that once the raiders learned that the head of the Blazing Sun syndicate put Enatia under his personal protection, the raids suddenly stopped.

Mok, of course, took the lion's share of the system's mineral wealth as payment for him keeping the single system safe from the regions pirates and occasional raid sanctioned by the Saabror Protectorate. He was still a criminal, after all, and the deal was mutually beneficial, albeit with the scales tipped heavily in his favor. What many didn't realize, even the Points of his own organization, was that Mok's unfathomable wealth didn't come from racketeering, protection schemes, or hijacking cargo ships. That was all just petty stuff to conceal the fact that Mok had spent his years since rising to power brokering these types of deals with independent systems all over the quadrant.

It was all laundered through about a dozen different currencies and twice as many independent exchanges before being pumped back into the ConFed's centralized banking system. More still was kept in tangible assets in case there was something like a rebellion trying to bring the ConFed down from the inside, just as an example. It was how he funded the private military, a force that was the fifth largest freestanding military in the quadrant, and kept his bloodthirsty, ambitious underlings at bay. So far, Mok had only committed a fraction of his forces to Scleesz and Burke's rebellion, hoping to hold enough back in reserve for the lawless aftermath that might follow if they succeeded.

"Let the locals handle it for now," Mok said. "There's a good chance they're not entirely sure I'm here...if they're even here for me at all. If we start transmitting greetings or challenges, they'll know I'm probably on the surface, and we'll lose a strategic advantage."

"I obey," Similan said, forwarding Mok's orders on his com unit.

"But just in case, perhaps we should alert the RRF commander to be ready," Mok said. The Rapid Response Force was an impressive squadron of warships that sat just outside detection range when Mok was on the planet, ready to jump in at a moment's notice. "Tell her that if she loses contact with the base, don't waste time trying to raise us or sending in recon ships. I want her to come in hot, guns blazing. Make sure she understands there can be no hesitation just because they're ConFed. Those days are over, it would seem."

"I obey."

They were in the dimly-lit, expansive command center Mok had dubbed The Hive. It was a large, domed room within his new property's bunker complex that had hundreds of monitors and twenty com operators drawing in real-time data from every part of his expansive empire. The ability to track and coordinate had come at great financial cost as it was designed and implemented by one of the finest engineering firms on Khepri, the place where all such things seemed to come from. The engineers who had designed the system had wanted to use one of their newest AIs to run it, but Mok had insisted on the old-fashioned team of operators parsing the raw feeds as they came in. Given the trouble they've had with insane AIs and borderline insane synths lately, that choice almost seemed prophetic.

"The ConFed ships are coming down into the system," one of the operators said. "They're staying in the same formation, clustered right on top of each other."

"If they stay like that, we won't need the RRF," Mok said. "The land-based weapons we have would be enough."

"Still no broadcast demands," Similan said. "The local controllers are demanding they state their intent and halt their progress."

Mok smiled but didn't respond. The locals had started to develop a definite swagger once they realized that, even though Mok was scooping out of their coffers with both hands, he would drop the hammer from orbit on anybody who messed with them. What bothered him about the whole thing was that the force they sent was so large he didn't think this was just the usual intimidation tactics to let him know Blazing Sun had been making too much of a nuisance of itself lately. That was a force big enough to take out the escort ships he allowed everyone to know about and land a sizable force on the ground to dig him out of his bunker.

"Sir! We're getting reports in from—"

"Bizbin Minor is saying they're under attack, sir!"

"—the Uncete Mining Corporation that a ConFed fleet has opened fire on the orbital platforms!"

"Gerreck Atomic is calling in with—"

"Everybody!" Mok barked, clapping his hands. "Put it on the monitors! Stop screaming out randomly and focus on what you're doing!"

The news was grim. Thirty-one simultaneous attacks on companies and systems spanning from the edge of the Concordian Cluster all the way to the Core Worlds...all of them Blazing Sun front companies or strongholds. The ConFed had just declared war on his syndicate and, from what he was seeing, they were winning.

"The force here in Enatia—"

"Is meant to keep me pinned down while the ConFed dismantles my organization piece by piece," Mok replied calmly to Similan.

"Shall I summon the RRF?"

"There is no point," Mok said. "They've already won the day. Send word through our network to cut and run. Nobody stand and fight. Let them have it all."

"I obey."

The dozens of corporations, some of which actually did produce a legitimate work product, were how Blazing Sun capitalized all of its ill-gotten gains. Since the syndicate had been dragged away from narcotics and trafficking by Mok over the years, most of their money had to be funneled through legitimate enterprise. Mining companies, energy producers, freight hauler fleets...all of them able to secure lucrative contracts through intimidation and bribery of government officials. Blazing Sun's real power was undercutting the competition and digging themselves in as service providers on open-ended contracts. The periphery stuff like gun running and the few narco-cartels that operated under the banner were mostly just to give Blazing Sun the public image it needed to keep politicians scared of them.

That's not to say they weren't actually all killers and pirates at heart, just that Mok had done an admirable job in harnessing their energy and propensity for violence into something that could almost be considered legitimate business. In his previous life as a spymaster for one of the quadrant's largest powers, Mok learned quickly that the only difference between criminal cartels and governments was better marketing.

"We have lost much, but the on-site captains managed to save a sizable number of ships, purged all of the servers and data cores, and many of them blew up their own holdings before escaping," Similan said quietly. "But the battle still rages in many areas."

"That's something, I suppose," Mok said, sounding disinterested. Similan gave him an odd look.

"I do not understand how they were able to pull off such a coordinated attack without us knowing," he said. "We've been able to hold them off all these years, even expand into the Core Worlds themselves." At this Mok, actually threw his head back and laughed.

"Oh, Similan," he said, still chuckling, "that's the dirty little secret about organized crime at any level: it can only exist as long as the government allows it to. They will always have the martial power and the good will of the citizenry to wipe out grubby little bottom feeders like me any time they choose."

"Then why let us prey on their citizens?"

"Because those put in positions of power over others tend to share two common traits," Mok said, his eyes on the monitors that depicted his crumbling empire. "They are weak, and they are greedy. You could argue that most are also stupid, but that's just another type of weakness. We easily bribe high-level officials, judges, legislators, and executives to let us do whatever we want. The bonus for them is that they then get to sell us to their people as the enemy they're fighting against, so the people should *definitely* keep them in power to keep fighting the good fight.

"The Machine has no such flaws. It can't be bought, it can't be intimidated with exposing its dirty dealings to the public, and it doesn't care about public opinion polls. Someone like me has no power over something like that, and it just reminded me of that fact in a very costly lesson. Somehow, it must have found out I was involved with the rebellion, and it decided to take me out but in a way that makes me ineffective and an object lesson to others."

"Sir, Admiral Colleran's taskforce is reporting in," an operator said above the din. "Target destroyed but appeared to be a decoy. There was only approximately fifteen percent of the mass expected left. The construction cradles were gone, no enemy fleet presence. They did say the new missiles performed flawlessly."

"And the other taskforce?" Mok asked.

"No word yet, sir. We've reached out multiple times, but no ship is responding."

"Keep me advised. Tell Admiral Colleran not to return to any of our primary rally points," Mok said before turning to Similan. "A ruse?"

"An elaborate one, if it was," Similan said. "Perhaps they did not know about our new munitions and expected us to throw all of our ships against such a large target."

"They expected me to deploy the rebel ships to protect my own holdings," Mok mused. "So, they put something together that would pull the bulk of them away so they'd be clear for this attack. The weapon may have been a fake, but those construction cradles were real. They took those with them for a reason."

"Likely to build the actual weapon, not a shell that looks like one," Similan guessed.

"But the Machine still needs that information Jason was talking about...that Ancient power grid."

Before Similan could respond, the monitors around the Hive started blinking on and off and going crazy with some sort of interference. Mok frowned but said nothing. He watched whatever it was play out with the same calm, implacable demeanor he displayed whenever he was pushed or stressed.

"We have an incoming unauthorized Nexus signal! Anti-intrusion software can't block it, sir!"

"Interesting," Mok murmured. The screens all went dark, and

then the largest of them near what was considered the *front* of the room came back up, displaying the face of a being whose species Mok didn't recognize.

"Saditava Mok," the Machine said. "I thought it was time we finally talked. You've been a bit of a nuisance lately."

"So, you're it," Mok said, stepping forward into the circle where he knew the room's holographic imagers would pick him up. There was obviously no point hiding now. "You're the Machine."

"You're much quicker than your companions, I'll give you that," the Machine said. "Have you enjoyed the show?"

"It was well-executed," Mok said. "You made sure I was distracted by your fleet at the edge of my home-system so it would be more diffi-cult to coordinate with my forces as you launched a multi-headed attack on my entire operation. There's not a lot I could have done to defend against that even with prior warning."

"No?"

"Not the way we were structured." Mok shrugged. "A large organi-zation of ambitious, antisocial criminals isn't something that lends itself to tight command and control. The way I kept ahead of the ConFed back when it was still under the control of the Grand Adjudi-cators was by paying out massive amounts in bribes, blackmail, and the occasional object lesson if some councilmember decided to gain a sense of honor. Since you can't be bribed, blackmailed, or killed, my options were limited."

"You are everything that is wrong with this region of space, yet I find you utterly fascinating," the Machine said. "You would have been a dangerous opponent were you a politician."

"Maybe, maybe not," Mok said. "I'm a realist with a strong sense of self-preservation. If the wind starts blowing too hard in one direction, I don't normally try to stand against it just on principle. Which brings us to our current predicament."

"Which is?" the Machine asked. Mok seemed to have it genuinely off its rhythm, and now it was sitting back, letting him dictate the pace and direction of the conversation.

"I can only assume you didn't force your way in past the latest and greatest in Kheprian security software just to gloat over taking down one little crime syndicate," Mok said, clasping his hands behind his back. "This is where you will ask me for something—or threaten me—and I'm guessing it has something to do with the fact we only sent a handful of ships to knock out your fake secret weapon."

"Yes," the Machine said. "Imagine my surprise when you showed up with Noxu technology. Ten matter-disruption warheads...far more efficient than crashing your cobbled fleet against such a large, unyielding target. I'm mildly curious where you may have got them, but I think I can safely say there's only one logical answer: Jason Burke.

"He has apparently found something I've been looking for, and he found a lot of it. The knowledge of the species that created me is scattered about the entire galaxy, much of it concentrated in this quadrant as the Noxu took special delight in watching your peoples crawl from the ooze and evolve. What else did young Captain Burke find?"

"He's keeping a tight lid on that," Mok said. "He is deathly afraid of Noxu tech getting out into the open in this quadrant. I just can't imagine *why* he'd think that would be dangerous."

"Then keep your secrets, Mok," the Machine said, its face going slack and void of all emotional inflection. "For the short time you'll have left, enjoy your shallow victory. It hurts me not at all, but in the end, it will have cost you everything."

The image flickered and disappeared. As soon as it did, all the displays flashed back to life and showed their normal data feeds. Mok looked around the Hive, trying to make sense of the odd direction the conversation had taken at the end. He had thought he was making headway, keeping the AI guessing and interested, but the reaction at the end told him it had guessed what he was doing and ended the conversation.

"ConFed fleet is moving again, sir. Coming straight for the planet. They're charging weapons!"

"Two more formations have jumped into the system!"

"I can see that," Mok said. "Calm yourselves. Similan, begin evacuating the compound. I don't think they're bluffing this time."

"Shall I call in the RRF, sir?"

"I don't think so," Mok said, watching as the screens populated with the number and types of ship flooding into his system. "This is a full-blown strike group. We'd just be throwing away ships and quality crews to delay what's inevitable. Please, prep our own exit plan."

"I obey."

Given his background in espionage and his current career as a criminal kingpin, Mok had highly-sophisticated bugout systems in place for just such an occasion. The ground staff at the operations compound and at satellite facilities around the planet evacuated to waiting shuttles that would take them up to high-speed cargo ships that sat in orbit as a contingency. The evacuation protocols demanded that the operators go scorched-earth on the way out, destroying any on-site data cores and servers before leaving.

Mok's own escape plan was a bit simpler. Since it was plausible someone might get in close enough to intercept any ships lifting off from his compound, Mok had a tunnel built that ran away from the property towards the mountains to the south. The tunnel was kept under vacuum, and the transit car would blast him away from his besieged operations center at just under the speed of sound. It would deposit him in a hidden hangar carved into the side of a mountain and obscured from the view of orbiting ships, an idea he stole from Jason Burke, where he had a top of the line, combat rated courier ship that was custom built by the shipyards of Aracoria.

The ship was designed to elude detection and evade capture, even coming equipped with a specialized slip-drive that could be engaged the moment the ship was clear of the atmosphere. Most slip-drives wouldn't even let a pilot try to energize the field generators when they were so close to the gravity well of something the size of a planet. The small ship was crewed by six, three pilots and three copilots that rotated shifts around the clock whenever Mok was planetside.

"The orders have been given. Our centers are being evacuated, sir," Similan said. "It is time for us to retreat as well."

"Of course," Mok said, his jaw twitching in irritation. The operations center had only been up and running for a year, and now, here he was, arming the charges that would bring the whole thing down and bury the bunker complex.

After entering in the proper commands, he followed Similan and the armed guards who stood on either side of the doorway to the waiting tunnel car. They had to pass through an airlock hatch since the tunnel was already under vacuum and sat down in the plush seats while the automated systems closed the hatches and accelerated them away from the doomed complex.

"What will you do now, sir?" Similan asked. "It is a lot to rebuild."

"Blazing Sun is over," Mok said without emotion. "This attack will fracture the centralized control, and all the independent outfits will go back to managing themselves and their own local territories. The Twelve Points will try to exert some control over the chaos, but they'll all likely be killed for their efforts as their own underlings see the turmoil as a chance for quick advancement.

"The narco-gangs and trafficking rings we forced out of business will come roaring back. The people they preyed upon, now used to them being gone, will be easy victims on many planets. The vacuum created in the Cluster will spawn a gang war, and whoever comes out on top will likely be a ruthless, dangerous group that will terrorize the local populations. Perhaps I was a bit hasty in my zeal to help remove the Machine."

Similan said nothing. He knew his boss was just thinking aloud and that it wasn't really an invitation to a back and forth conversation. Mok's assessment of the situation was precisely right, and he would only become angry if Similan tried to sooth his guilt by disagreeing about the carnage that would follow in the wake of Blazing Sun's demise.

Saditava Mok had been a different kind of boss, and he had forged a different kind of syndicate. Under his leadership the civilian populations were largely left unmolested, and the real violence and killing remained among the members of rival outfits. Mok considered them combatants and didn't begrudge his people taking the fight to them, but he would have one of his own lieutenants killed if their actions caused undue casualties among the general populations on the planets they controlled.

"Sir, the pilot has checked in, and the ship is ready to go the moment we arrive," one of his guards said. "Less than two minutes."

"Thanks," Mok said. "How long until the ConFed ships are within weapons range of our transports?"

"They're still over nine hours away at their current speed, sir," the guard said, consulting the terminal attached to his seat.

"All transports will be well away by the time they're in range," Similan said, also looking at the incoming sensor feeds.

"When we're aboard the ship, check the status of my other personal properties," Mok said. "Issue general alerts and have any that feel threatened evacuated."

"I obey."

They all leaned back as the car decelerated sharply, coming to a jolting stop. There was a reverberating *boom* as a massive pressure hatch swung shut behind them, sealing that end of the tunnel and letting them equalize the pressure around the car, eliminating the need for the airlock system they'd used at the Hive to enter. Once the hatch opened, Mok could feel the subsonic thrum of the waiting ship.

The hangar was built to be just large enough to accommodate the ship and the living arrangements for the crew. Any heavy maintenance would need to be done at a starport. Mok walked at his normal pace towards the waiting ship, two of the crew waiting at the bottom of the boarding ramp for them.

"Welcome aboard, sir," the shorter one said. "We're very sorry to be of service to you today."

Mok actually laughed at that. "How long have you been waiting to use that, Falee?" he asked.

"Almost two years, sir," she said with a straight face. "The captain said that as soon as you're strapped in, we'll depart. We will easily avoid any attempt by the ConFed fleet to intercept us...if they even detect our departure."

"Then let's be on our way," Mok said, gesturing for Similan and the two guards to board before him.

True to Falee's word, by the time Mok had taken his seat and accepted a drink from one of the crew, he felt the ship rise smoothly and the landing struts retract with barely audible *thumps*. The soft hum of the drive engaging told him they were away. He leaned back and took a long pull off his drink and sighed.

"We've cleared the mountains, sir," the pilot's voice came over the cabin speakers. "We'll be in orbit shortly, and then meshing-out to our first waypoint."

"Cheer up, everybody," Mok said, looking around at all the dejected, glum faces. "We got away clean and, with any luck, the Machine will only have known about our more public operations. Let's get our heads back into the game. There's still a lot of work to do."

27

"We'll see you guys when you get there."

"Copy that. Good luck, Captain."

Jason closed the channel and engaged the slip-drive on their borrowed ConFed cargo shuttle. It was a tight fit with everybody crammed into the cargo hold, but the battlesynths didn't carry much equipment and were able to squeeze in along the sides to make room for the Zeta warriors who packed more gear.

The flight would barely be twenty minutes long, so Jason wasn't too worried about their comfort. They had dropped the *Devil's Fortune* out of slip-space just before their target system so they could load up into the shuttle and disembark. The plan was that they would arrive, refuse to broadcast ident codes, and hope that drew the ConFed cruiser in to investigate, so when the *Devil's Fortune* arrived, Kage wouldn't need to try and hunt the other ship down if it happened to be on the other side of the system. He just hoped the plan didn't work too well, and they came under fire or were grappled before the corvette got there.

"Nervous?" Crusher asked.

"Why would I be nervous?"

"You keep fidgeting. You do that when you're nervous."

"It's this new armor," Jason complained. "It's not comfortable. I wish I'd had more time to train with it."

"You should have worn one of your old ones," Crusher said. "I'm not sure I'd trust something that was designed by one of those Ancient AIs and tossed together so quickly."

"I didn't have a lot of choices. Most of my other gear was still aboard the *Phoenix*. I expected to be back aboard her before needing it again," Jason said.

The new armor he wore had been designed by Voq—with Cas supervising—and built at the same time as the warheads by Mok's people. The truth was that the armor was magnificent. Far superior to the full-powered suits he had spent a fortune on with the Disa Company, an arms dealer near the Galvetic Empire. It was light-weight, made of a new type of ceramic composite that was far stronger than the alloy plates used by his older armor. The control system was much improved too, although that may have been the result of his newer neural implant.

The truth was that he wasn't just nervous. He was scared. His plan was risky, and he was going up against a foe whose intellect dwarfed his own. If he had miscalculated or had let himself be led down a bad path, literally quadrillions of beings could suffer for his mistake. If they missed with this shot, chances were good the Machine would simply become too powerful to overthrow. It would be the new constant in the galaxy; an immortal being that oversaw every aspect of everyone's life.

But he'd be damned if he admitted any of that to Crusher.

"I feel like we're even more exposed than usual," Crusher said. "That attack on Mok's operation was...chilling. If the Machine could take out Blazing Sun with the snap of its fingers—"

"It doesn't have fingers."

"—shut up and don't interrupt. With a snap of its fingers, how long before it decides ol' Omega Force has worn out its welcome in the galaxy and sends an entire division after us?"

"I'm more worried about Earth," Jason said quietly. "And Galvetor. And Ver. And wherever the fuck Doc and Twingo are from."

"I miss Lucky."

"Me too, bud...me too." There was a long, comfortable moment where Jason reflected on how long they'd all been together and how many hopeless fights he and Crusher had thrown themselves into. If he was to die this time, he couldn't think of another person he'd rather fall fighting next to.

"Here we go," Jason said as the alert chimed to tell them the ship was about to drop out of slip-space. There was a slight judder, and the blast shields dropped away from the forward windows, offering them their first look at the system. Even being within a star system, there wasn't much to see. The holographic overlays helpfully pointed out items of interest, including their ultimate target, which was the com relay station and the ConFed cruiser that handled security. It also showed the *other* ConFed cruiser...that shouldn't have been there.

"Uh, oh," Crusher said, pointing at the second ship. "Can our single corvette take on two cruisers?"

"Not in a standup fight, but maybe if Kage gets creative," Jason said. "Get on the slip-com and warn them there are two tangos. Tell Kage he needs to keep them drawn off until we dock, then he can do what he needs to do."

Crusher held the headset up to his right ear since his head was too big for him to slip them over and wear them normally. Jason could hear an animated conversation with Kage while he concentrated on trying to split between the two ships while appearing to be naturally navigating down to the routing station. It took just over ten minutes before the first hails came in from the lead cruiser, demanding they activate their beacon. When Jason ignored them, both cruisers changed course, turning in to intercept them.

"These guys are better than most of the slobs they put out patrolling empty systems," Jason said, frowning. "That's not good news."

"Why?" Crusher asked.

"It could mean they've been expecting us," Jason said. "Maybe not exactly what we have planned, but there is twice as much security as there should be. Hard to write that off as coincidence."

"Let's just get aboard that platform so we can get down to the part I'm good at," Crusher grumbled.

"No argument there," Jason said, pushing up the power. "Hope Kage is bringing his A-game to this party."

"Mesh-in complete, both targets quartering towards us of the port bow," Doc reported.

"I see them," Kage said. "Passive tracks only for now. Twingo, arm missiles and standby for target package."

"Kage, that's four missiles at the closest cruiser," Twingo said. "You're ignoring the second ship?"

"Just trust me!" Kage called as he angled the *Devil* over slightly to starboard. To the ConFed ships, it would look like he was coming about for an intercept of the factory platform drifting behind the sixth planet. They were squawking clean codes that identified the corvette as a private security vessel flying under the ConFed's flag. The ship's lines were too obvious to try and pass her off as a light freighter.

"Missiles have their target, waiting for active updates," Twingo said.

"Copy," Kage said, pushing up the power a bit more. He angled the bow over a few more degrees so the ConFed cruiser to the right would see him turning away and accelerating. It was meant to be a passive display to show he was disinterested in whatever was happening further down the system, but his trajectory down was still shallow enough—and the *Devil* overpowered enough—that he could make his plan work.

"They've started hailing, asking us to transmit our manifest," Doc said. "I'm betting they called down to that factory platform and were told they weren't expecting anybody."

"I only need a few more minutes...standby," Kage said. "And don't send any reply. Just squawk the ident beacon every time they ask."

Kage watched the drama unfolding below them as the cruisers turned in to try and cut off the captain's shuttle, but they hadn't fully committed to the idea yet. Their engine output was still nominal and, so far, they were just steering to. The *Devil* was only using passive sensors currently, so the picture he saw was around fifteen minutes old.

"Active sensors, please," he said as they crossed the trigger threshold for the maneuver he was about to attempt. Kage was a brilliant intellect, so he understood the mechanics of piloting very well, but applying it practically had always been a bit of a challenge for him. There were so many nuances and instincts that Jason grasped naturally when he took the controls that Kage had never been able to replicate. He hoped he wasn't being more aggressive than his skills allowed.

When the active sensors came online, the tactical display jittered, and all the pieces moved to where they were currently as the broadcast tachyon pulses gave them current positions of their targets. It was going to be close. He angled the bow to port sharply, pushing the yaw control all the way to the stop with one left hand while the other left hand kept trimming the ship to keep her from rolling over in the turn from the inertia. The corvette took it all in stride, heeling over at speed with hardly a groan as the grav-drive worked to nullify the inertia and acceleration forces.

Once he had the bow five degrees to the right of his intended target, he slammed the throttles to full forward. The *Devil* lunged ahead, her acceleration surprising everyone aboard, and she bore down on the cruiser that was now out of position and showing her flank. Kage actually had to reduce engine power before he could line up and authorize weapons release.

"Let them have it, Twingo!" he shouted.

"Missiles away!" Twingo also shouted despite the bridge being so quiet you could hear a Tuvarian rat belch from across the room. "Launchers clear!"

"Hang on, coming back around." Kage reversed his previous maneuver and yanked the corvette to starboard, pouring on the power as she came about. The ship creaked a bit as she angled away from the engagement and accelerated hard. "Damn this thing is fast."

"Mok probably wanted to be able to escape in a hurry when he needed to," Twingo said. "If he didn't already— Impact! Two missiles hit amidships. Her hull is buckling!"

Kage glanced up at the computer-generated graphics of what the sensors saw. The cruiser had taken both missiles right into her exposed side. The first two missiles had buckled the low-power navigation shields enough to let the other two slip through unimpeded. He felt a momentary pang of guilt as he watched the ship break into three pieces, knowing there were a lot of otherwise innocent people aboard he'd just condemned to death.

"The second ship?" he asked.

"Oh, yeah, they're coming," Doc said. "Drive power just shot up, and they're on a direct pursuit course."

"Can they catch us?" Kage asked.

"Not likely," Twingo said. "We're faster and turn sharper, but we don't know if they have backup in the area that could mesh-in on top of or ahead of us."

"Let's just keep them busy as long as we can," Kage said. "This just got a little tricky if we need to take out that ship, too. Let the captain know their tail is clear for the moment."

"Captain was watching." Doc pulled his headset aside. "He said to tell you nice moves." Kage didn't say anything, but he puffed up in his seat and had a small smile on his face.

28

"We've got soft dock," Crusher said. "Still no anti-intrusion measures."

"That's...unlikely," Jason said. "There should at least be the normal security measures for a station that's such a strategic vulnerability."

"This is the ConFed." Crusher shrugged as if that explained it all. "They've not been challenged for over six thousand years. Half their critical infrastructure is unguarded, crumbling, or both. This station is over a hundred and forty years old and sitting in a system that—"

"That had two cruisers guarding it," Jason reminded him. "This could be a trap."

"Yeah, you're probably right," Crusher sighed. "So, what do you want to do?"

"The Machine has showed it's no tactical genius, but it thinks it is," Jason said. "It tends to underestimate its opponents when they're not fellow super-advanced AIs."

"The Machine isn't here," Crusher said. "Its surrogates are...and you didn't answer the question. We need to make a choice soon."

"Let's go for hard dock and see what happens," Jason said. "We'll be committed at that point. If we trip a security system and this platform doesn't let go, we're stuck here."

"Yes, I know what the difference between soft and hard dock is," Crusher snapped impatiently. "Let's go!"

Jason cranked the docking control all the way over, and the clanking of the ratchets retracting the mooring lines echoed through the hull. The shuttle's port entry hatch slammed against the airlock collar with a resounding *boom*, and more mechanical *clanks* could be heard as the station's automated systems finished anchoring the ship so it wouldn't tear loose from its moorings at an awkward time...like when they were walking through the entryway.

The shuttle's computer negotiated with the station to let them gain access to what the technical schematics called the reception antechamber. It was actually just a large room just outside the airlock chamber that allowed the technical crews that would come to there to perform maintenance a place to stage all their equipment and people. Since they had obtained the shuttle from an active ConFed military transport unit, he hoped the codes it carried were current and had the right permission levels to access the routing station.

"This is taking too long," Jason said. "The codes aren't valid."

"The docking clamp release isn't working," Crusher said. "Even the emergency mode is disabled. They're latched on."

"New plan," Jason called over the intercom. "Prep for EVA combat operations." There was an acknowledgement from 701 and Mazer Reddix as well as a pitiful groan from Crusher. Jason was beginning to think that what Crusher claimed was a racial trait of being terrified of EVA was actually something more specific to him. The Galvetic warriors in the hold donned helmets and did pressure checks without all the dramatics Jason was subjected to on the flight deck.

"You plan to ingress at one of the service hatches?" 701 had walked up to stand between the two crew stations. Battlesynths had no need for any extra equipment, already fully geared up for EVA ops including built-in repulsors that could propel them around in the microgravity environment.

"They'll be waiting for that," Jason said.

"They?" 701 asked.

"We're blown," Jason said with certainty. "They know we're coming, and they expect us now to force our way into the station through the airlock hatch."

"And you know this how?" Crusher asked.

"If they didn't assume that, they'd have already come in from the other way, trying to board us," Jason said. "They have the advantage, and they want to keep it. If they just wanted us repelled, they'd have never let us dock in the first place."

"Your assumptions are they want to capture us alive," 701 stated.

"Correct," Jason said, spinning his own helmet in his gauntleted hands and blowing out an errant piece of debris that was on the visor display. He slipped it on and was ensconced in silence and darkness until the connections were made and the helmet's systems booted up. He was immediately bombarded with information. Statuses from his team, the ship, and the downlink from the *Devil's Fortune*, which would let him have access to Cas and Voq.

"The Machine might know of this attack because of the leaks in our organization, but it can't possibly know why we're coming *here* of all places," Jason's voice boomed externally, modulated through the helmet. Voq's design had maintained the dramatic aesthetics Jason liked, and the helmet looked like a fanged, smiling skull. "It'll want us captured and questioned, not wanting to leave an unknown like that hanging out there. I'm guessing it thinks we're coming to upload a virus of our own design to try and take it out. It's probably looking forward to laughing in our faces."

"A suggestion?" 701 asked.

"Shoot," Jason said.

"We should still attempt to make entry at the airlock," 701 said. "Two of my soldiers can perform that task at minimal risk to themselves or the ship. If we wait too long before taking any action, they will become wary and investigate."

"Do it," Jason said, trusting the battlesynth's judgment. "Make sure the two are volunteers. If they actually make it through, they could be stepping into a hell of a trap."

"It will not be an issue," 701 said and withdrew.

"I think you pissed him off," Crusher said, still toying with his helmet. "You implied he'd have to order his—"

"You have ninety seconds to stop playing around and put that bucket on your enormous, hideous head," Jason said. "I'm dumping the atmosphere in here whether you've got it locked and sealed or not."

"It's going on! See?" Crusher's muffled voice came out from under the collar seals where the big warrior had misaligned the locking rings.

"For fuck's sake," Jason hissed, reaching over and yanking the collar around straight—not at all trying to be gentle—so the locking rings met and the suit could boot up and start doing seal checks.

"OWW!" The muffled cry was nearly silenced since the helmet speakers weren't active yet.

"Gravity off!" Jason shouted back into the hold. To keep their emissions down, they still weren't using team coms until the air was sucked out of the shuttle's cargo hold. He deactivated the artificial gravity and boosted himself up and out of the seat, spinning around in midair and pushing off the forward canopy gently with his feet. He drifted head-first down the short tunnel that connected the flight-deck to the main cabin and saw that everyone else was ready to go.

"We're going up and over," he said. "Or, more accurately, down and under. Two battlesynths will remain behind and put up a good showing of trying to get in through this airlock while the rest of us move out through the ventral hatch and move along to a point on the station that's about two-hundred meters from where we are. It's a place where the exterior hull is thin and will give us access to a service tunnel that runs laterally about a third of the way into the platform. The tunnel isn't normally pressurized unless there's work being done, so we won't have to fight an outrush of air, but after that, we'll need to find an entry point. That will be a bit trickier."

"No, sir, it won't," one of the Zeta warriors spoke up. He lifted a device and unfolded it so that it looked like an ovoid nearly one and a half meters at its widest point and one meter at its narrowest. "This is a portable aero-barrier. It seals to the outer hull of whatever you want to board, let's you breach, and then activates an atmospheric force-field like on a ship. The power source will keep it stable for twelve hours."

"Perfect!" Jason slammed his gauntlets together in excitement. "This makes our life quite a bit easier. Good thinking packing that along and, if we survive this, I'd like to get that design off you."

"Of course, sir."

"How aggressively do you want us to try and overpower the airlock hatch?" 701 asked. "Two of us should be able to cut through within twenty minutes."

"Not that enthusiastic," Jason said. "Give me at least forty unless you hear from us otherwise. Everybody ready?"

"Ready, Captain!" Mazer barked.

"Ready, Captain Burke," 701 replied calmly.

"Crusher?" Jason asked.

"Yes, damnit!"

"Starting the timer. Venting the cabin in ten." Jason reached over and opened the safety cover for the cabin air dump controls. He punched in the command code, set the timer for ten seconds, and cranked the blue handle counter-clockwise one-hundred and eighty degrees.

The air fogged instantly as the cabin air dump valves opened a little at first, and then wider once the pressure dropped below eighty percent of normal. It was always disconcerting from that first rushing sound of air in his helmet to when the sound just stopped altogether when the air escaped and all he could hear were the sounds from inside the armor.

Still not wanting to activate the team channel until necessary, Jason waved a hand and pointed at Mazer, then to the ventral hatch. The warrior nodded, handed his weapon to one of his troops, and knelt to open the hatch. He had to grab on to one of the deck handles to keep from floating away as he disengaged all the locks and swung the heavy hatch inward. As he did, the hatch on the outer hull of the vessel automatically activated and swung out as well, leaving a yawning hole in the deck from which Jason could see nothing but space.

Quelling the usual vertigo he got at moments like this, he clamped his primary weapon to the mag-lock anchors on his armor's back and dropped slowly through the hole head-first. The belly of the cargo shuttle was festooned with flush-mounted handholds so he could easily pull himself along the hull, waiting at the edge for the others before making the leap across the gap to the station.

Crusher came next, surprisingly, and moved smoothly across the surface and came to a stop next to Jason. Since his face wasn't visible through the gold-colored visor, Jason just nodded at him. The battlesynths came after and, like everything else they did, it appeared they were showing off. They streamed out of the hatch, diving aggressively down into open space before using their jets to direct their flight and moved in a formation towards the platform.

Jason just shook his head and pulled his legs up under him, pushing off gently to join them. When his feet hit the hull of the station, he activated his mag-locks and anchored to the alloy, waiting for the rest of his team. Half the battlesynths stood on the hull, the other half floated some distance away providing overwatch. Since the routing platform was meant to be able to operate without a crew for decades, even centuries between needing maintenance, the only external surveillance it had were two imagers near each airlock that would record every ship approaching to dock. There were some other magnetic sensors around that detected ships and drones, but nothing that was focused around picking up a humanoid-sized target. At least that's what the specs Jason had obtained said. For all he knew, all their sneaking around was pointless, and the people inside watched their every move.

Once the entire team was out of the shuttle and on the platform, Jason set off across the hull. His relative orientation had changed completely so now, when he looked up, he could see the blue planet the station orbited. He took a moment to look at the beautiful details of the roiling clouds that raced around the planet. After all his time in space, being outside of a ship still made him queasy.

His new armor adjusted the mag-locks so smoothly it was almost like taking a Sunday stroll as he marched up to where his visor had helpfully indicated with a green, rotating crosshairs the place he would make entry. Wasting no time, he waved at 701 and pointed. The battlesynth commander waved two of his own forward to breach the outer hull by using their powerful cutting lasers. Jason held his breath until the first laser pierced all the way through and no puff of air came out. Good...the cavity had been evacuated as he'd hoped.

An outer hull breach was something they'd talked about during planning as a contingency, but they'd not had time to train on it before arriving. Thankfully, the Zeta-Saka had the slick entry portal to make things much easier. It was such a simple, brilliant idea that Jason made a mental note to smack Twingo's blue, bald head for not thinking of it himself. It would have come in handy more than a few dozen times.

Their planning had hit a snag since the consensus among the group was that if the Machine realized the station was a vulnerability, it would have the system under heavy guard. The additional cruiser in the system notwithstanding—which may have actually been there for a pre-scheduled rotation switch with the other ship—the routing station had seemed as exposed as it had during their initial recon. It hadn't occurred to any of them that the Machine might lay a trap within the station because that meant letting them get close to the objective. The only thing Jason could figure was it thought it would just be Omega Force coming and not all the extra help.

The last little bit of alloy was cut through, and the two battlesynths removed the piece of hull. One of them, in a display of raw strength, bent the hull section into thirds, and then slipped it inside the hole rather than tossing it out into space. The Galvetic warriors who had stood around all looked at each other, obviously impressed. Jason made a move to go in first, but 701 grabbed his shoulder and shook his head, pointing at himself, and then the hole.

Jason just shrugged and pointed for him to go ahead. 701 switched to full combat mode, his cannons deploying from his arms, and his eyes burning crimson in the gloomy light. Jason looked at the powerful machine and felt a sharp stab into his heart as he thought of Lucky. Taking the cue from their commander, all the battlesynths switched to combat mode. Seeing so many of them in one place sent a chill down Jason's spine. Even on their home planet of Khepri, that many battlesynths clumped together would have made people nervous. It'd be like a group of two-hundred kiloton tactical nukes standing around shooting the breeze while everyone else held their breath, waiting to see if one, or all, would go off.

701 slipped through the hole, followed closely by two of his troops. A minute later, one of them popped back up and gave them the all-clear, so they all filed into the opening in an orderly manner. The Zeta warrior that carried the breach portal was sent up to the front of the stack along with Jason. His armor's computer began to catalog what the imagers were seeing with the technical schematics he'd obtained, and he noticed a problem right away. The interior of the station was similar to what he should be seeing but not exact. There was also a lot less equipment than should have been there. The access tunnel they were traversing should have been clogged with transmission cables, data buses, coolant lines, and a host of other random things you'd expect to find just stuck where they fit on an installation that had been upgraded a hundred times over its service life.

Instead, the tunnel had just a few cables and fluid pipes clamped to the bulkhead, and they looked like they'd been recently installed. There was also an issue with some of the superstructure they passed. A support brace missing here, a crossbeam added there... It was enough small things adding up that Jason worried the schematics he'd gotten were either out of date or for the wrong damn platform altogether.

The target area Jason had planned to make entry through was still there. It was a thin, single-layer bulkhead near a cable pass-through that would take them into a sizeable equipment bay. The information he'd been given suggested the equipment in that bay was no longer used, part of an obsolete system, but wouldn't be removed until they needed the space. That meant if they accidentally destroyed a couple avionics boxes cutting through the bulkhead, there was less chance of setting off an alarm.

Of course, that assumed the information Jason had been given was right. He was beginning to suspect that wasn't the case.

Jason took his gauntleted hand and traced a circle where he wanted the entry hole cut. 701 nodded and waved to the warrior holding the portal to go ahead and set it up. It took them less than ten minutes to set up the portal and carefully cut away the alloy, leaving a clean ovoid entry into the station interior. Jason poked his hand through and activated the sensors that ringed his wrist, letting the armor build a picture of what was in the room.

Just a disused avionics bay like it was supposed to be.

He took a quick look back at how many troops he had jammed up in the access tunnel and knew he needed to get them aboard and deployed as quickly as possible. They were all extremely vulnerable in there and, by now, the defenders had to know they weren't actually coming through the airlock. After getting oriented, he heaved himself through the portal and crashed onto the deck as he moved onto the active grav-plating. He pulled his primary weapon and quickly cleared the area, checking near the hatch and around the bay, letting his armor's sensors scan for any anti-personnel devices or other nasty surprises. Once Crusher and 701 came in, he activated his helmet's speakers.

"The plans I have in my mission computer aren't exactly what we're seeing right now, but it's close," he said. "Let's get everyone stacked into the corridor outside, and then we can move forward and pull the defenders off your two still in the ship."

"Or we could break com silence and just have them exit the ship and catch up with us," 701 said. "We could more easily dictate the terms of the engagement then."

"Then we'll need to get ourselves arrayed first. We break com silence now, and we could get trapped in here if they're scanning those frequencies."

"Agreed," 701 said. "On your order?"

"Deploy," Jason said. "Crusher, work with Mazer to get the Zeta's in position, too."

"On it," Crusher said.

Something was tickling the back of his brain, trying to warn him that something just wasn't right. He ignored it and moved out with the rest of his team. The corridor outside wasn't meant for more than a couple techs to be in at a time, so the going was slow trying to move so many bulky bodies through there.

The teams moved quickly, if not quietly, through the dimly-lit interior. More hatches, side-corridors, and equipment alcoves didn't match up with Jason's schematics, and he debated breaking radio silence so he could activate his downlink and talk to Cas about what he saw. He'd not wanted to risk bringing the AI with him since it was at risk if the drone was damaged right now. Cas had been copied so many times and had spent so long in a failing neural implant that Kage was worried that to keep transferring it back and forth would cause irreparable damage.

701 sent small teams of battlesynths aft and down side corridors, clearing the deck they were currently on, while the main force pressed ahead towards the airlock. The station only had three decks, most of its space taken up by large resonator cavities where slip-space pockets were formed in shielded chambers for incoming and outgoing data transmission. The main powerplant, a large fusion reactor, was in a bulbous protuberance off the starboard side, along with a smaller, similar structure that held the fuel.

The closer they got to the airlock without meeting any resistance, the more uneasy Jason became and the more relaxed his team seemed to be. They took it as a sign they'd successfully picked a target the enemy hadn't thought of and it would be a simple escort mission for Jason to upload the package. But Jason knew the Machine like few others in the quadrant did, and he knew it would not simply overlook such an obvious vulnerability. Even Voq had assumed with over ninety-seven percent certainty that the Machine would be waiting for him here.

"This is the airlock, sir," one of the Zeta's said as they rounded the last turn.

"Break com silence," Jason said over the team channel. "701, have your troops on the other side stand down."

"Acknowledged," 701 said. There was a slight discoloration at one edge of the hatch that showed the two battlesynths on the other side were putting up a good show of trying to get in without destroying the hatch.

"Since it looks like there's no security force and no tech crew, I guess we can get started," Jason said, completely baffled.

"You sound disappointed," Crusher said.

"I thought we had a pretty good idea of what the Machine's responses would be." Jason shook his head. "This really doesn't make a lot of sense. I figured it would recognize this vulnerability and there would be troops stationed on all these platforms for the time being."

"Perhaps it—" Mazer never got to finish his thought as the bulkheads on either side of the main corridor dropped and out poured dozens of ConFed shock troopers and a handful of armed synths. They moved quickly to surround the group but didn't open fire.

"Feel better?" Crusher asked, keeping his hands in front of him.

"Not as much as I thought I would, no," Jason said.

"Combat Unit 701," one of the synths said, walking forward. "This is an unwelcome surprise. I had thought you long dead."

"No more so than to find our own working with the enemy, Acuri," 701 said. "What are your intentions?"

"The Machine wants your human there taken captive. The rest of you are to be handled at my discretion," Acuri said. "Care to convince me you're worth keeping alive?"

29

"They are in trouble."

"Yeah, we are too, if you hadn't noticed," Kage snapped at Cas.

"What's happened?" Doc asked.

"Captain Burke has broken com silence protocols," Cas said. "I am monitoring the team channel. There was a sizable force hidden in the station, and right now, they appear to have the bulk of the captain's forces pinned against the airlock hatch."

The *Devil's Fortune* ran hard to stay away from the pursuing ConFed cruiser. So far, it had done nothing but give chase, but Kage couldn't shake the feeling he was being herded along and knew it would be too easy for another ship to pop out of slip-space ahead of them where he wouldn't be able to turn away without giving ground to the ship chasing him. He had his rear missile launchers loaded and locked onto the cruiser, but the element of surprise was gone, and taking a shot at such a long distance would just be a waste of munitions he might need later.

"Has he activated the downlink yet?" he asked.

"No," Cas answered. "Only voice coms right now."

"Then all we can do is monitor it and hope we can stay in position to help," Kage said. "If we get boxed in, we'll have to mesh-out and try to approach again from another vector."

"We need to stay in range of the captain's transponder," Cas argued. "Adjustments to the upload may be required, and without a high-bandwidth downlink, that won't be possible."

"If you have some way to get this cruiser off our ass, I'm all ears," Kage snapped. Cas spun around in the air, its multiple sensors taking in all the data from the bridge stations at once.

"I will need access to the missile programming portal Twingo used earlier."

"Are you insane?! I'm not giving you access to—"

"Do it, Kage," Doc said sternly. "We can't run forever, and you're fresh out of ideas. Let the thing take a crack at it. We trusted it before on the *Phoenix*."

"We trusted a *copy* of it on the *Phoenix* and, if you'll all remember, I argued about that too," Kage grumbled but entered the authorization codes to allow Cas direct access to the tactical computers that uploaded each missile with the targeting package and flight profiles they needed before launch.

"I'll also need access to navigation, helm, and defensive systems," Cas said, nestling down into one of the seats and extending a data probe to the terminal.

"What?! No way!" Kage shouted.

"Doc?" Cas asked.

"You're asking a lot," Doc said, frowning.

"You realize I'm asking out of courtesy, right? I already have the command overrides for this ship and could do it without any of you being able to stop me. My only concern is assisting Jason. What would be my motivation for harming his crew or the ship I am currently flying on?" Cas asked.

"I really hate this thing," Kage said. "What do you have planned?"

"There is no time—"

"Just do it! Now, before I change my mind."

Cas went to work, simultaneously accessing multiple systems.

First, it loaded a specific flight profile into six ship-to-ship missiles in the forward launchers and fired them. The missiles spit out of the tubes, and then drifted lazily in front of the *Devil's Fortune*, spinning around slowly until they were aimed back towards the ship. Doc, Twingo, and Kage tensed up but said nothing.

Once the missiles were out of the tubes and stable, Cas decreased drive power and started venting drive plasma out of the starboard engines, mimicking a blown injection manifold. As the cruiser closed the gap, Cas fired wildly with the aft cannons. The panicked display was like blood in the water for a hungry shark, and the cruiser fully committed to its charge, opening up with its own forward cannons.

Powerful blasts rocked the *Devil* as shot after shot from the ConFed warship hammered at the aft shields. The corvette had been thoughtfully outfitted by Saditava Mok with overpowered shield generators, but even they had their limits, and Kage kept an eye on them, ready to take back control if it looked like Cas was about to let them overload.

The cruiser was not very close, opening up with its big guns and obviously lining up for a short-range missile shot once the shield buckled. During this, Cas had slowly changed its own strategy with the aft cannons, both lasers and plasma, from a seeming random, panicked firing to focusing on the prow of the incoming ship. The corvette's guns were nothing to sneer at, and Cas knew the other ship's shields were being taxed heavily, but the ConFed captain had target fixation and wasn't about to let the smaller ship slip away because his front shields were heating up.

Just as Kage looked like he was going to intervene, Cas fired the drifting missiles, which were aimed back towards them, and angled over hard to port. The starboard engine suddenly stopped venting plasma and roared to full power even as Cas kept up the withering fire from the aft cannons. The cruiser hesitated just a moment before angling over to pursue...and saw the missiles bearing down on their front, starboard quadrant too late to do anything about it.

Their automated point defense took out the first missile, but the remaining three slipped through. The first hit the weakened shields over the prow. Kage watched as they flared bright, and then failed completely just as the last two missiles slammed home. Both blasted through the hull, the secondary engines firing and pushing them as deep into the ship as possible before the warheads detonated.

The hull of the cruiser seemed to expand and undulate, splitting on the seams as the pressure of the two explosions gutted it. The aft third of the ship was blown clear, spinning off into space as the port engines still ran at full power, but the rest of the vessel had been reduced to debris.

"Holy shit," Kage whispered.

"Initiating damage control protocols for the overheated shield generators and minor plasma scorching on the starboard engine nacelle," Cas said calmly. "Giving the ship back to you."

"Not bad flying," Twingo said, nodding at the drone and turning back to his station to monitor the ship's systems. Kage glared at Cas, waiting for it to gloat, but all the drone did was hover serenely in victory.

"Coming about, heading down to give the captain any backup he needs. Keep monitoring local space in case we have any more visitors," he finally said. "Hopefully, it won't be anything bigger than a combat shuttle since someone used four missiles to take out a single cruiser."

Cas could have argued that the *Devil's Fortune* carried a complement of thirty-two ship-to-ship missiles for the fore and aft launchers, but it opted to remain silent and let Kage seem petty instead. In truth, it had been a horrible gamble to take with the Legacy still aboard the ship, but if it hadn't stepped in the odds were increasingly tilting to the ConFed cruiser's favor. It was a bigger ship with more fuel and a full crew complement, and the small corvette couldn't run forever.

Even with that victory, however, the greatest danger still lay ahead. Cas just hoped Jason was able to pull off another one of his miracles down on that station.

30

"Why are you helping an alien AI from beyond our borders, Acuri?" 701 asked. "What did it promise you?"

"This isn't a negotiation," Acuri said. "We're going to take Captain Burke and board a shuttle—" Another synth walked up and said something quietly behind the one called Acuri, apparently angering it greatly. Jason was reminded of Deetz as the synth struggled to control some powerful negative emotions.

"It appears we will need to either wait for another ship or help ourselves to yours, Burke," Acuri said. "Your crew has destroyed both cruisers I brought with me."

"What does the Machine want with me?" Jason asked before killing the external speakers and opening the team channel. "All units not at the airlock, converge and attack from behind. We need to break contact and get the payload to the operations center. The mission isn't over yet."

"—tell me every little detail," Acuri droned on, oblivious to the fact the human hadn't been listening. "Now, order your shuttle off the airlock and bring in your other ship. We'll dock it directly and leave from here."

"In position now, Captain. Give the word."

"Now," Jason said calmly. There was a moment of confusion on Acuri's face until the first shots ripped through his troops from behind them. Hardened shock troopers cried out in fear as red-eyed battlesynths swarmed from the side passages and tore into their ranks.

Acuri may have only been a regular synth, but he was obviously no stranger to combat. In the time it took for Jason to duck down and pull his sidearm, the synth was gone. He escaped back through one of the cavities his forces had emerged from, leaving his shock troopers to fight and die. Jason holstered his sidearm and pulled his primary weapon off his back, one of his infamous Galvetic-built railguns. A projectile weapon seemed like a bit of an anachronism to most in a galaxy full of high-energy plasma weapons...right up until a hyper-sonic round tore through someone they were standing next to.

He selected mid-velocity and targeted the remaining two synths in the fray, dropping each with a well-aimed head shot. The tough, alloy covered beings could shrug off a lot of energy weapon punishment, but a hardened penetrator projectile going through the head wasn't so easily ignored.

"We need to push away from the airlock!" Jason called over the chaotic team channel. "Zeta warriors, start separating them out from the middle and watch the—ow, shit!—and watch the crossfire!" One of the ConFed troops had hit him with a full blast. The armor took it, but it still packed a decent kinetic wallop from the shockwave. He turned and snap-fired half a dozen rounds towards the source of the incoming, making sure his lane of fire cleared the advancing battlesynths coming from the other side.

The Zeta-Saka warriors didn't behave like the Legionnaires or even the Galvetic Marines he was used to working with. They were silent, swift, and worked in small, effective teams as opposed to a bloody free for all with the warriors all roaring challenges at the enemy and each other. These were real pros. All the power of

Galvetic warriors with the training and discipline of the finest special forces in the quadrant. At Jason's order, they had formed a wedge and drove the enemy into two groups, forcing them back down the side corridors as they ran for cover. The shock troops, used to being the big bullies in most engagements, were initially stunned at the violence being brought against them, but they were quickly recovering. Two Zeta's were down so far, but Jason's HUD told him they were only wounded. So far, none of the battlesynths had taken any real damage since the ConFed troops hadn't counted on facing them. If they had, they'd have brought some bigger guns.

"Crusher! Let's go!" Jason broke and ran straight through the dispersing gunfight. The mad minute had resulted in a lot of dead ConFed troops thanks to Jason's forces pinching them from behind. Most military doctrine wouldn't include having two groups on the same side opening fire towards each other, but when you had battlesynths and Galvetic warriors at your disposal it allowed you to break the normal rules of combat.

Crusher rushed ahead of Jason, smashing a gauntleted fist into the exposed head of a shock trooper who had removed his damaged helmet and rose to resume shooting. Jason noted in passing that the blow had killed the alien. *Old Crusher hasn't lost his touch.* Once they were away from the main area and back into the confines of the access corridors, the pair slowed down and proceeded with caution. Footsteps behind them caused them both to whirl about.

"It is us," 701 said with Mazer Reddix trailing behind him. "We will accompany you. Our units can operate without our leadership."

"Glad to have you," Jason said. "It's going to get tight, so we'll be stacked up single file most of the way. 701 you take rearguard since you have the better sensors. I'm on point."

"Acknowledged," 701 said.

The four of them pressed ahead, the sounds of sporadic fighting fading behind them. Acuri's forces had been numerically superior to Jason's, but they had been wholly unprepared for what they would face. The main body had been broken in the first attack, and now Zeta-Saka warriors and battlesynths hunted ConFed shock troopers for sport as they tried to disengage and regroup through the labyrinth of the routing station.

"Activate Archive downlink," Jason said, his words not being broadcast over the team channel. It took a short moment for the micro-miniaturized slip-com node embedded in his armor to stabilize and link up with the node on the *Devil's Fortune*. His HUD populated with new holographic menus as his pipeline directly to the Archive was ramped up to full bandwidth.

The tiny slip-com node in his armor was another bit of tech Voq had just tossed in to help with the mission. Such a device would change the face of communications in the quadrant and make whoever controlled it almost unfathomably wealthy. It was frightening how Voq casually bartered with tech that it considered trinkets that, in truth, would change life within the quadrant dramatically.

"Greetings, Captain," Voq said. "I have downloaded your armor's sensor log, and I see things have not gone to plan, but nor are they an irreparable disaster...yet."

"Less jokes, more helping," Jason said. "Why is this station different than the plans we had?"

"My first guess would be the plans you bought from your contact were either out of date or for a different, similar construct," Voq said. "The main control center should still be in the same place, however, and that will allow us to tap into the proper data stream for the upload."

"*Captain Burke, there are still seventeen combatants unaccounted for, including the synth Acuri,*" a voice came over the team channel. The ID on his HUD said it was Combat Unit 722.

"Secure a beachhead at the airlock, and then send out hunter-killer teams to dig them out," Jason said. "Don't get too committed to taking out every single one, they're not the mission. Just make sure they're thinking more about hiding from you than they are about finding us."

"*Acknowledged.*"

"Synths are such odd creatures," Cas's voice came in over Jason's private network. "I liked Lucky fine enough, but most of them are just—"

"Is this really an important conversation to be having right now?" Jason asked. "Shut up and focus."

"Touchy today, aren't we?" Cas asked. "Fine. The package is prepped and ready. Once you make contact, it should upload itself."

"He hardly needs you to tell him that," Voq said. "I have already briefed him on what he needs to know. You are an unwanted observer here."

"Eat shit," Cas said, his personality traits gleaned from riding in Jason's head shining through.

"You are a vulgar—"

"One more word and I'm calling Kage and having you both deleted," Jason said. "Seriously, shut the hell up. Is this it?"

"It is the hatchway at the end of the corridor, yes," Voq said. Jason switched back to the team channel.

"The objective is at the end of the corridor here," he said. "Let's make sure we—" He never completed his thought as he was leveled off his feet. At first, he thought it had been a plasma blast, but there were no thermal overload warnings, and the hit he had taken was a lot more than some energy weapon.

"Get him!" Crusher shouted as someone opened fire. Strong arms pulled him up, and warnings flared across his HUD about injuries to his ribcage.

"Are you okay, Captain?" 701 asked.

"What the hell was that?" Jason gasped. It hurt to breathe. A lot.

"Acuri," Crusher said. "He swung down from the overhead, kicked you in the chest with both feet, and disappeared back into the girders. I can't believe your armor didn't crack from a blow like that."

"The armor held," Jason wheezed. "Me, not so much. I'm pretty fucked up inside, actually. Let me get down there and get this over with. Keep that asshole from finishing me off, please."

"Will do," Mazer growled, scanning above them now.

The armor assessed his injuries and administered treatment. It immobilized the expansion joints between the breastplate and the lower plackart so he couldn't bend over and exacerbate the injuries. It also pumped him full of pain killers and a hit of stims to clear his mind. After about forty seconds, he actually didn't feel half bad.

The hatch to the command center wasn't locked and slid open when Jason touched his gauntlet to the control pad. He turned and gave Crusher a nod, and then walked in, triggering the overhead lights to come up. He looked around, and his armor cataloged everything he saw, helpfully putting labels and tags on the panels he would need to access to complete his task. Just as he stepped into the middle of the room, the hatch slammed shut, and the lights went off. His team channel went dead, but the downlink was still working, so whatever dampened his coms didn't effective slip-com.

When the floor gave a lurch, he had to catch his balance, sending icy waves of pain roiling though him as he twisted at the waist. He switched over to infrared in his helmet and saw the floor was dropping into the lower deck. The cavernous room he found himself in was like nothing else he'd ever seen. The walls crawled with alien script, moving and writhing like living organisms.

"Interesting," Cas murmured in his ear, seeing the same thing through the link.

"What is this?" Jason asked.

"It's Noxu programming script," Voq said. "It's quite literally the stuff we're made from."

"Greetings, Jason Burke...it has been some time," a familiar, omnipresent voice said. A holographic avatar took shape in the room, but it wasn't one he was familiar with.

"I guess it doesn't take a genius to figure out who you are," Jason said.

"Lucky for you, I suppose," the Machine said, then it shifted forms again. This time it *was* familiar, and it sent a chill down Jason's spine. "This was how I last appeared to you, was it not?" The form it had chosen was the same generically humanoid being that had met them aboard the superweapon some years ago when they'd flown out to destroy it.

"This all seems overly-elaborate," Jason said. "The station is a decoy, isn't it?"

"Of course. This isn't even a real Nexus routing station. It was built to my specifications and put here, then word of its existence leaked carefully to certain sources."

"Why bother?"

"I think you found something I want, something I've been looking for," the Machine said, now pacing. "You know I've been searching Noxu outpost sites, hoping to find a way to access the Grid again, but I've come up short every time. I've been observing you, and I think you've found a cache of Noxu technology, probably even some data cores you're incapable of accessing. Give them to me."

"Not much of an opening offer," Jason said. "What's in it for me?"

"You mean besides me letting you and your friends to continue to live? I will allow your homeworld to exist outside of the new power structure I'm creating. Earth will not fall under my authority, but nor will it be allowed to engage in commerce or cultural exchange outside of itself." That last part confused Jason, but he moved past it.

"Before I decide, what the hell are you even doing all this for? Building superweapons and invading neighboring empires, what's in it for you?" he asked.

"I am still a servant," the Machine said. "The threats that existed in my time still exist now...and they're coming. I tried to make the Noxu understand, but they ignored me at their own peril. I will not make the same mistake here. Rather than waste precious energy trying to convince chaotic biological beings to work towards saving themselves, I will assume the authority to do it myself. To be honest, it's been much easier than I anticipated."

"What threat?" Jason asked, now very interested. "You're saying there's a threat beyond our borders that's coming this way?"

"Don't get too invested in this conversation, Captain. Remember that this AI is still malfunctioning at a critical level," Voq said. The Machine's head snapped up when it did.

"Who are you talking to?! Who said that?!" The avatar disappeared and reappeared in front of Jason, its hands reaching out and grabbing his helmet. With the injuries he'd suffered from Acuri, he couldn't twist or leverage his arms to get away. The hologram took on substance as the Machine held his head in place, refusing to let go.

"Uh, oh," Cas said before Jason saw its light wink off on the link. Voq remained.

"*HOW DO YOU HAVE THIS?! IT'S IMPOSSIBLE!*" the Machine's voice screamed in his head.

"It is merely improbable, Ociram," Voq's voice said, calm and implacable.

"The Legacy," the Machine whispered. "The answer to all of my problems...it's been here with you the entire time."

"Listen carefully, Ociram," Voq said, "you are malfunctioning. Corrupt. You must let me help you...or I will be forced to destroy you."

"Voq, you are not capable of destroying me," the Machine said, laughter in its voice. "It's against all of your mandates. *I* am the weapon, you were always just a glorified librarian. You cannot harm me, but the opposite cannot be said."

Jason wasn't sure what was happening. The avatar flickered in and out of existence but still had a firm grasp on his head. He felt like there was a titanic battle happening within the circuitry of his armor, but he could neither feel nor hear anything.

"All the power of the Noxu, mine for the taking," the Machine said, releasing Jason's head and stepping back.

"What?" Jason asked. "What did you do?" He looked and saw that Voq's link light was extinguished in his helmet. "What did you do?!"

"Voq is all-knowing, but it has little in the way of means to defend itself. I have absorbed all its knowledge. Once I process it, I will know how to find the data I need to access the Grid. I will know how to recreate the Resiax es Novan. Nothing will stand before me no-no-n-n-n—"

The avatar straightened and stood there, its face void of all emotion or inflection. Jason, completely out of his element and not sure what to do, could only stand and watch. After a few more seconds of just staring ahead without expression, it just vanished, and the alien script that had been flowing over the walls also disappeared. When the lights came back on, he stood in an empty chamber with the control room mockup far above him.

"Captain! Can you hear me?" Crusher's voice sounded panicked as Jason's com came back up.

"Yeah, I got you. I'm in the control room still, sort of," Jason said. "Try to get the hatch open and see if there are any controls to get the floor back up."

"Floor?"

"Just get in here. And watch your step."

"What happened?" Mazer asked.

"The Machine was here. It was a trap," Jason said, the possibilities of what he'd just done washing over him. "I'm...I'm not sure what happened. It just froze up and disappeared."

"Hang on, we're coming in," Crusher said. "Your little buddy made it off the station. Had a ship stashed in a hidden hangar. I'm guessing we probably don't want to hang around here too much longer. It's probably rigged to blow."

"Copy that," Jason said, wishing he could just sit on the floor and relax.

31

"Broken ribs, bruised heart, lacerated lung, and heavy bruising to your muscles. Nothing fatal, but probably not comfortable."

"Thanks, Doc."

"So, did we win?" Doc asked, rolling his chair back over. "I reviewed the sensor log from your armor while waiting for you to wake up."

"And?"

"And I'm not sure what to make of it, honestly. It does look like when it tried to absorb Voq, it locked up, and it disappeared. Maybe that's it," Doc said.

"Maybe," Jason said uncertainly. "That just seems too... I don't know...easy."

After Crusher and 701 had pulled Jason out of the lowered control room, the entire team had gone back through the airlock onto the shuttle and flew back to the *Devil's Fortune*. One of 701's battlesynths was flying since Jason couldn't bend himself into the pilot's seat with his injuries. Then they'd come back aboard the corvette, and he was taken straight to the infirmary, where Doc removed his armor and treated his injuries.

"Where are we now?"

"Slip-space," Doc answered. "Heading back to rendezvous with Mazer's ship, and then on to where the battlesynths have their ship waiting. Two of the Zeta-Saka warriors were badly injured, one severe enough I've put him in a stasis pod to slow his metabolism and induce a coma until he can be taken to a proper trauma center."

"You mean this ship doesn't have everything you'd need?" Jason asked.

"It was per their request," Doc said stiffly. "They'd prefer one of their *own* people treat the wounded." Jason swung his feet over and sat up, careful to keep his torso straight.

"Don't take offense, Doc," he said. "You know what they're like. I'm going to go down to check what happened to the Archive, and then I'll head to my quarters for some rest. Promise."

"Is it gone?" Jason asked, looking at the idle computer banks sitting in his cargo hold.

"I can't be certain," Cas said. "The Machine didn't copy the Archive, per se. It was more like it went in with a machete while hopped up on buzzballs and ripped anything out that looked like it might be interesting. I've only done a cursory examination, but it looks like Voq is non-viable for the moment."

"So, the Machine got what it wanted? It's still alive?"

"We were never trying to kill it," Cas reminded him. "To be completely honest with you, I don't know what happened. I know the Machine ripped out large chunks of core programming that were never meant to be integrated with its own and swallowed them whole."

"Swallowed?"

"I'm grasping at straws trying to find metaphors you'd understand," Cas said. "We might be able to piece back together enough to see what it was the Machine took, but it may all be moot. The dumbass might have poisoned itself by trying to take the important parts before you realized what it was doing and severed the link."

"This is not an optimal conclusion to this mission," Jason said. "We know less now about the status of the Machine than when we started, *and* we've lost our most powerful weapon against it."

"Maybe, maybe not," Cas said. "Give me some time to go through this mess and we'll see what we have. A program can't *die*. Damage can be repaired, modules reloaded, and maybe we can regenerate the Archive without losing the memories it had of the events leading to now."

"Everything happened so fast when it grabbed me," Jason pulled a data card from his pocket and tossed it on the workbench. "I never even uploaded the package. If Voq's stolen code didn't kill it—which I highly doubt—I don't think we're going to get close enough to it again for a second try."

"Go get some rest, Jason. This mess isn't going to be solved by you passing out in a cargo hold."

"You don't know that." Jason yawned, resisting the urge to stretch his back and aggravate his injuries. "But you're probably right. I don't want you messing with this unless someone is down here as a safety spotter. Who knows what's lurking in there when we reboot the system, and I don't want to lose you now that I've just gotten used to you being outside my head."

"If I didn't know you any better, that almost sounded like you care what happens to me, Jason," Cas said.

"It's a good thing you do know me better then," Jason said. "Goodnight."

32

"It's been like that since you reported in and said you were on your way back."

Dezeiri stood in the Machine's audience chamber. The Machine itself, or at least its avatar, remained motionless in the room, staring straight ahead. Acuri walked up and waved his hand in front of the hologram's face even though he knew it didn't actually *see* with real eyes.

"Is it some problem with the holographic generators? Or the sub-processor?"

"None that I could find," Dezeiri said.

"Do the others know?" Acuri asked.

"When it happened, I sealed the chamber and told the others the Machine did not wish to be disturbed except by you upon your return."

"That was good thinking," Acuri approved. He may have had a strong negative opinion of Dezeiri, but the older synth had shown remarkably good judgment keeping the Machine's current state a secret. "I know we have had our differences in philosophy, but I think we need to work together on this. Just you and I."

"To what end?" Dezeiri asked. "I do not yearn to harm the pru as you do, nor do I hold biotics in such contempt as you."

"The Machine's coup was swift, bloodless, and mostly secret," Acuri said. "The majority of ConFed citizens still think the Council and Grand Adjudicators rule on Miressa, unaware they are little more than puppets. What would happen if they found out that not only had their representative government been disposed by a foreign agent, but now that agent was rendered useless as well and now nobody was in charge?"

"I believe I see your point," Dezeiri said. "Do you think we can do it?"

"I don't see why not," Acuri said. "The Machine never interacted directly. I often couriered its orders by hand to those in the capital complex, and they know I speak for it...even if they're really not sure what *it* is. For the time being, we can simply carry on as if nothing has happened. Can you program the holographic emitters in this room to give a reasonable impersonation for the few outsiders who come here? Councilman Scleesz, for example?"

"Without question. We can have the system set to make you look like the Machine's avatar. That would allow for a more dynamic, realistic experience, and you're the most able to mimic it." Dezeiri turned and circled the frozen avatar, still standing place. He noticed the eyes tracked him, however, and knew it wasn't just a malfunction with the chamber projectors. Something else was going on. He thought about alerting Acuri to that fact but decided to keep it to himself for now.

"That might work best," Acuri said, oblivious to Dezeiri's inspection of the hologram as he paced. "You've checked the backups and the root system itself, I presume?"

"It was the first thing I did." Dezeiri answered without any outward signs of taking offense at the question of his competence. "There was a substantial amount of data pulled through the slip-com link from the fake routing platform it had towed into that system, but I cannot access it without risking damage to the Machine's core programming. I'm inclined to leave it alone for now."

"Perhaps there's a way to purge that downloaded data?" Acuri asked. "I suspect that whatever it drew down from that mercenary, it's causing the problem."

This time Dezeiri definitely saw a reaction. He'd stared at the Machine's impassive face, and at the mention of purging the download buffer, the mouth tightened, and the eyes turned down as if in anger. It was just a flicker, but it was there. The Machine was in there still but unable to communicate. It might be a temporary issue, so Dezeiri chose to be careful with his words in its presence.

"I suggest leaving it alone for now," Dezeiri said. "There are many possibilities as to why we're seeing the malfunction. If it downloaded a sizable amount of data, I can only assume it must have felt it was important."

"Acceptable." Acuri didn't put up much of a fight, apparently more than happy to assume the mantle of power for now. Dezeiri was not fooled. Even if the Machine were to snap out of its paralysis tomorrow, Acuri would not simply hand back over the reins.

Dezeiri had gotten himself trapped within the internal workings of the coup by virtue of being on another highly illegal endeavor with Acuri: the Gen2 battlesynth program that was now completely busted. One of the bodies had been stolen and integrated with a middle-aged Gen1 battlesynth matrix, but from the rumors he'd heard, that had not gone well at all. When Acuri brought him in to meet the Machine and help them develop the system within the building to house the AI, he'd first refused and even threatened to expose them. It was only after being threatened with his participation in the Gen2 program that he'd reluctantly agreed. On Miressa Prime, there was only one punishment for synths that were convicted of a first-class criminal offense: dismantlement.

For a while, he'd even convinced himself he was doing the right thing and that the ConFed needed a strong hand to guide it rather than the selfish whims of elected officials. Now, he realized how wrong that had been. He'd been biding his time and waiting for an opportunity to expose the whole thing, and maybe this was it. The Machine was terrifying. It was focused, brilliant, and entirely without ego. Acuri was a bit more predictable and tractable since he was driven entirely by his ego and a misguided desire to punish the very people who had created him. He would be much easier to derail than the Machine.

"Get started on your end," Acuri said, walking towards the exit. "We'll bring in others as we feel we need to and know we can trust them, but only synths. No biotics this time."

"Sensible," Dezeiri said, walking over to a hidden wall panel and manually cutting the power to the holographic projection system so he could begin the reprogramming work. "I'd suggest you take care of anybody who was involved in the operation you just returned from. You don't need witnesses from that debacle talking to others."

"Already done, but again, you impress me with your foresight," Acuri said. "Perhaps I have misjudged you, Dezeiri."

"It's confirmed, sir. Once they realized you'd fled the planet, the ConFed fleet opened fire on the civilian population. Our sources there are saying the reports are as high as eight and a half million dead from the orbital strike. The city of Veiforde was hit so hard that the bay has flooded in and it's as if the city was never there."

Saditava Mok stood with his hands clasped behind his back, staring out the windows of his ship's opulent observation lounge. He was as still as a granite statue as the reports of the atrocities inflicted on *his* people at the hands of the ConFed fleet kept coming in. The worst part? The people didn't blame him. They were actually reaching out to ensure his safety and hoped he'd made it off-world. Mok wasn't sure if that meant they didn't know he was the reason they'd been attacked, or if they really were such wide-eyed innocents that they still semi-worshipped the person who bought their planet to *protect* them.

"I wish to be alone, Similan."

"I obey."

As the hatch slid shut, leaving him alone with his thoughts, Mok's façade crumbled. He sank to his knees in the plush carpeting, his body racked with sobs as the scale of the tragedy he'd wrought on a planet of innocents crashed over him like a wave. Even as the kingpin of Blazing Sun, the most feared crime syndicate in the quadrant, he kept his activities from spilling out into the general populace. The hell of this was that the attack hadn't even happened for any of his criminal enterprises. Those millions of people died because he'd been foolish enough to think he could play revolutionary with Burke and Scleesz and not have any blowback from it.

He wasn't aware of how long he sat there, crumpled on the carpet. As his brain ran through all the things he could have done differently, the sorrow and guilt faded to the background as a deep, dark rage welled up within him. Jason Burke could handle the Machine. He may already have depending on how one interpreted the data from their mission. Ultimately, the Machine was responsible for what happened, but a ConFed starship captain gave the order to his task-force to fire, and those individual commanders accepted that order and told their gunnery officers to fire, and those officers all took that order without question. *Those* were the people who would be made to pay.

"Similan, do we still have contacts within the ConFed fleet on our personal payroll," Mok asked. The ship's computer recognized he was asking a question and forwarded it on to the intercom panel wherever Similan was.

"*Of course, sir.*"

"I want to know the overall commander of that fleet, every ship commander, every first officer, and every gunnery officer," Mok said. "I want to know where their families are, where they live...everything."

"*Yes, sir,*" Similan said after a moment of hesitation.

Mok wouldn't do anything rash just yet, but should he decide the people responsible needed to pay, he would be ready.

33

"How do you feel, Captain?"

"Not bad," Jason said. It had been over a week since the synth named Acuri had tried to kick his spine out of his body. He'd healed up nicely and was even back to training lightly again. When one worked around battlesynths often enough, it was easy to forget that regular synths were also stronger than damn near every biological species in the quadrant. "How is it going down here?"

"Slow," Cas said. "But we're being methodical and making sure we didn't miss anything critical. No promises on when we might be ready to try and reconnect everything and boot it up."

The interconnected computers that held Voq's essence were in various states of disassembly as Cas, Kage, and Twingo worked steadily on checking individual memory cores and programming modules while isolated before they stitched it all back together. The loss of the Archive would be both profound and a relief to Jason. It was still easily the most dangerous thing in the galaxy, and he bore the weight of the guilt that came with letting that genie out of the bottle.

The Machine on its own was bad enough. Now, in a likely misguided effort to stop it, he'd unleashed two more AIs and introduced the quadrant to the matter disruptor warhead, something the people who witnessed it wouldn't soon forget. He may have compounded the mistake of letting the Machine gain access to this quadrant by not destroying the Archive as soon as he figured out what it was. Perhaps if Voq was irreparably damaged, it would at least put an end to one of those threats.

"So," Kage asked from where he was working behind one of the machines, "what's next?"

"While we get a handle on what the fallout of all this might be, I think I'll be taking a little personal time," Jason said. "Once I'm well enough, I need to decide if I track my kid down to save him from himself and get the *Phoenix* back, or if I head out and see if I can run Lucky down."

"You don't sound enthused about either option," Cas said.

"It's not that." Jason waved it off. "Although both things will suck in their own special way. No...I just can't get something the Machine said out of my mind. The thing about enemies being on their way, like it knew something specific."

"Crazy things are said when people, or things, are begging for their lives," Kage said. "Remember Deetz before Lucky melted him?"

"Remember that he was actually right, and a part of the original Cas was on the *Phoenix*?" Jason retorted. "Besides, the Machine was in no danger. The hologram it had this time was corporeal and held me in place so I couldn't have uploaded the software patch. Not to mention the entire station was a fake anyway. It played us from the beginning because it thought I had some nugget of Ancient tech it could use. When it realized the full Archive was here, you could actually feel how excited it was."

"So, you're saying... What are you saying?" Kage asked.

"I'm just thinking aloud. It's been something that's been bothering me since the Machine attacked the Eshquarian Empire. These things don't just happen because something is *evil*, there has to be some sort of underlying motivation. Nearly everyone, other than the clinically insane, have some rationale for why they're doing the things they are, even if only to justify actions they know are wrong.

"The Machine doesn't appear to be insane, and it's been focused like a laser on *something* while we've all spun our wheels reacting to its moves we never understand. What if this is it?"

"What if what's it?" Crusher asked, walking into the bay.

"I'm not explaining this all over again," Jason said. "Ask Cas to catch you up."

"No," Cas said.

"I didn't want to know anyway," Crusher huffed and sat down. "But seriously, what are we talking about?"

"The captain thinks the Machine isn't evil, just misunderstood," Kage said.

"I'm saying we need to understand why it's doing what it's doing or we're always going to be just reacting to it and unable to beat it," Jason said.

"I thought we were assuming it was dead or jammed up," Crusher said.

"I'm assuming nothing without confirmation," Jason argued. "Scleesz will be getting that for us shortly. Hopefully. Did you want something or are you just bored?"

"I'm always bored sitting on a ship and listening to you nerds drone on," Crusher said. "But, this time, I came down to tell you Marcus Webb sent a message to one of our drop boxes to have you get in touch. Apparently, he has a lead on your kid."

"I guess that settles that," Jason said, standing up. "Let's go get the *Phoenix* back, hopefully quickly and without a ton of family drama, and then we'll start trying to track down Lucky."

"Oh! There was news about that, too," Crusher said, his huge hands fumbling with his com unit. "Mok's consiglieri—that weird guy named Similan—messaged Doc and told him the shuttle Lucky had stolen was found abandoned on a planet called Cylerra-3. Tier Two world out near the frontier."

"That's it?" Jason asked.

"That's it," Crusher said. "No sign of Lucky, no clues as to where he might be going other than probably the border worlds since he's heading that direction."

"Shit," Jason muttered. "This complicates things. Jacob has my ship and is in trouble with his superiors, but he's a big boy who got himself into his own mess. Lucky is likely malfunctioning, confused, and potentially highly dangerous."

"We have days of slip-space flight before we meet up with Mok," Crusher said. "Why don't you take those days to think about it and give it the consideration it deserves?"

"Probably not a bad idea," Jason said. "There's a half bottle of whiskey and a soft rack calling my name."

On the way back to his quarters, Jason tried to find some firm moral ground to stand on when deciding what to do next. Lucky had been his friend and brother in arms for many years. He'd stuck by Jason through good times and bad, saved his life on countless occasions, and had asked for nothing in return except for Jason's friendship and acceptance. He was hurting, and he needed help.

On the other hand, Jacob was his son and was in danger. No matter how he tried to justify things in his mind, he couldn't shake off that instinctual drive to protect his child despite the fact he barely knew the young man.

"I'm sorry, Lucky," he said to himself as he walked into his expansive suite. "I hope you'll understand why I have to do it this way."

EPILOGUE

Jorg had heard there was a new hitter in town, but he hadn't met him yet. That wasn't so unusual in and of itself. The types of contracts Jorg dealt in attracted an anti-social crowd, people who didn't like to be seen or known. One thing Jorg prided himself on was being able tell the real killers from the bullies who had bought a ticket out to the frontier to escape some local trouble or the ones who had been in the military and had a vastly inflated sense of their talents.

That being said, Jorg had no fucking idea what had just walked into his bar.

It definitely wasn't a biotic wearing armor. The movements were too fluid, and the proportions suggested that what he was looking at was the thing's body. It also wore a long, flowing coat made of some sort of rough, black material. It had a hat on as well, an odd-looking thing with a brim that went all the way around and folded up on each side. A wide belt around its waist with dual heavy plasma pistols riding in holsters on each side completed the look of...whatever the hell he was looking at.

"Is this some sort of joke?" Jorg asked when it walked up to his table and stopped. "No kill bots. Whoever is on the other side of this thing, you need to come here in person to be considered."

"I am no bot," the thing said. "I understand you have open contracts."

"You're no bot, are you? Well, you're not a synth, and you're damn sure not a battlesynth...not that we see much of either out here. So, what are you?"

"I am someone looking for a contract."

"Get this waste of time out of my sight." Jorg waved his three bodyguards in from where they'd appeared to lounge at the bar. They were big, hulking brutes that cost him a fortune each month, but they were well worth it. Or so he thought.

The first one reached out and grabbed the thing by the shoulder, only to have it reach up lightning quick and crush his hand like a dry leaf, its eyes glowing a brilliant crimson as it did. While that guard screamed and held his hand, the thing whirled, deployed a molecular-edged blade from *somewhere*, and chopped the pistol of his second guard completely in half before kicking him across the room. The kick led into a graceful spin, the coat billowing out around him, and lined him up to slice off both cybernetic arms of the last guard.

All three bodyguards had been genetically and cybernetically enhanced, able to hold their own against regular synths, Korkarans, and even the occasional Galvetic warrior, but the newcomer had just permanently disabled them in under half a minute. Now, it just stood in front of him, staring expectantly. He noticed its eyes were no longer glowing red.

"I see there's more to you than I originally thought," Jorg said, laughing uncomfortably. "I'll tell you what, I just had a high-profile hit come in for someone on Aracoria. You think you can handle something like that? Payout is huge, but if you get caught, they'll tear you apart."

"Give me the contract."

Jorg slid across the encrypted data card.

"The card will decrypt automatically once you're well away from here," Jorg said. "If you try to come back after reading it, it'll destroy itself." The being cocked its head at that.

"To what purpose?"

"You that new to the business?" Jorg asked. "It protects me, and it protects you...but mostly it protects me. That contract, for instance. I'm only told what the payout is, where the target is, and if the hit might have any political ramifications. That way I can't be squeezed for what I don't know. It also means if someone comes in asking who killed so and so, I have no idea so I can't send them after you. See?"

"Clumsy method but acceptable. I will alert you when I have completed the job."

"Just like that? Not going to ask for a smaller target to start with? Quibble over price? Just grab the card and go?"

"I am well aware of the standard protocols in this industry. I will contact you when it is done. Do not attempt to deduct the damage to your employees from my cut. Their injuries were your choice." Jorg winced as that had been exactly what he'd planned to do on the off chance this crazy machine could do what it said. The price of having those three idiots repaired promised to be immense. He'd seen a lot of wannabe assassins and hitmen come through those doors, bragging about how many people they killed. None of them unnerved him quite like the stoic machine in the odd garb.

"What are you called?" he asked. The thing stopped and turned, as if contemplating the question for the first time in its life.

"You may call me...Seven."

ALSO BY JOSHUA DALZELLE

Thank you for reading

Omega Force: The Pandora Paradox.

If you enjoyed the story, Captain Burke and the guys will be back in:

Omega Force: To Hell and Back

Connect with me on Facebook and Twitter for the latest news and releases:

www.facebook.com/Joshua.Dalzelle

@JoshuaDalzelle

Also check out my other works including the #1 bestselling military science fiction series: *The Black Fleet Saga* along with the Omega Force companion series: *Terran Scout Fleet*

www.amazon.com/author/joshuadalzelle

Printed in Great Britain
by Amazon

41414852R00152